ABOUT THE AUTHOR

Roger Ede has spent a lifetime working in the criminal justice system. He has trained criminal defence solicitors and is a published author of books on criminal defence practice.

NONFICTION BOOKS BY THE SAME AUTHOR

Criminal Defence
Good Practice in the Criminal Courts
With Anthony Edwards

Active Defence
A Solicitor's Guide to Police and Defence Investigation
With Eric Shepherd

Forensic Practice in Criminal Cases
With Lynn Townley

POISONOUS

A case of transferred malice
murder – with a twist

ROGER EDE

Copyright © 2025 Roger Ede

The moral right of the author has been asserted.

Apart from any fair dealing for the purposes of research or private study,
or criticism or review, as permitted under the Copyright, Designs and Patents
Act 1988, this publication may only be reproduced, stored or transmitted, in
any form or by any means, with the prior permission in writing of the
publishers, or in the case of reprographic reproduction in accordance with
the terms of licences issued by the Copyright Licensing Agency. Enquiries
concerning reproduction outside those terms should be sent to the publishers.

This is a work of fiction. Names, characters, businesses, organisations, places, events
and incidents are either the products of the author's imagination
or used in a fictitious manner. Any resemblance to actual persons,
living or dead, or actual events is purely coincidental.

Troubador Publishing Ltd
Unit E2 Airfield Business Park,
Harrison Road, Market Harborough,
Leicestershire LE16 7UL
Tel: 0116 279 2299
Email: books@troubador.co.uk
Web: www.troubador.co.uk

ISBN 978 1 83628 115 3

British Library Cataloguing in Publication Data.
A catalogue record for this book is available from the British Library.

Printed and bound by CPI Group (UK) Ltd, Croydon, CR0 4YY
Typeset in 11pt Minion Pro by Troubador Publishing Ltd, Leicester, UK

Thanks to the many friends who read and
commented on the drafts of this book.

Author's note

This contemporary story of infidelity, blackmail and murder is a work of fiction, but the centuries old law it is based upon is not.

In 1573 a jury heard how John Saunders gave a poisoned apple to his wife, and then watched his young daughter Eleanor die after his wife had innocently passed the apple to Eleanor to eat. To avoid suspicion, Saunders had not tried to stop Eleanor. His accomplice, Alexander Archer, had supplied the poison as part of the plan to kill Saunder's wife.

The jury found both men guilty of the murder of Eleanor, even though they had not meant to harm her. They applied the legal principle of transferred malice, by which the intent to kill the wife was transferred to Eleanor. The judges agreed with the jury's verdict for Saunders and ordered his execution. But they interpreted the law in a way which allowed Archer to avoid a conviction for murder and buy his freedom.

Set in London in modern times, the lawyer in this murder story defends her client by employing the interpretation of the law which allowed Archer to escape the gallows over four centuries ago.

The Warwick Sessions case *R v Saunders and Archer*

is reported in 75 ER 706 [All England Law reports]. The report was originally written in French by Edmund Plowden of the Middle Temple (1575) 2 Plowden 473.

1

Poisoned Apple

"If he finds out what you're doing, Bryan, he'll kill you. And if he suspects that I've helped you, I'll end up in the river with you, feeding the fish."

"There are thousands of species of fish, Janice, but only two eat people and neither of those have been spotted in the Thames."

"Be serious. I'm scared for you. And I'm scared of him finding out that I'm talking to you."

"I can't stop now, after months of research and risk taking. Finally, a newspaper will publish a report that will bring down that arrogant bastard Shadwell, together with his corrupt police cronies."

"Is it safe to talk here? How do you know that we're not being bugged, or that someone isn't watching us?"

"This is just a back room in a pub by the Thames and, so far, we're on our own."

"Walls have ears," Janice said portentously, looking around.

"Now you're being paranoid. They do, but not the sort that you are referring to. Do you know that an artist attached casts of his ears to walls in London?"

"You're making light of my fears, Bryan. Why are you so determined to uncover him when you were one of them?"

"Big difference: I refused to take the money that he was dishing out."

"But you didn't report him either. Instead, you turned a blind eye and then left the job."

"Who could I trust? We both know Shadwell has friends higher up. Too many rotten apples. Let's eat, I'm starving. The food's good here. I recommend the scampi, Janice, my treat."

"I had a dog named Scamp, which puts me off. No, I'll have the battered cod, thanks, Bryan."

"So, it's not 'you are what you eat', but you eat what you are, eh Janice?"

"No, those days are long over, Bryan. Nobody's going to treat me like that again."

DCI Victor Shadwell stood talking to Frank, the doorman, in Striptease at Scylla, a busy club in London's East End. The building was a pub for one hundred and fifty years until a decade ago, when the regulars opted to drink at home instead, forcing its closure. Listed as a community asset, the brewery was not allowed to convert it into flats and so sold it to a company which was allowed to open a strip club instead. The pub sign was taken down, to be replaced by a white flashing neon *Striptease at Scylla* in a handwriting font, splashed incongruously across the traditional brick facade.

Aged in his early forties, Shadwell was a tall, thin faced man, with a pointed nose and chin. He had walked out of an interview at Southwark's Union Street Police Station in disgust at the suspect's refusal, on his lawyer Ben Bolt's advice, to answer Victor's questions. "You're taking liberties," he told Bolt. "You might think that you know the law and what's best for that piece of shit you represent, but how do you live with yourself?"

"That 'no comment' trick won't wash in court," he told the suspect. "What I'd like to do," he said, turning to face Ben, "is arrest the likes of you for perverting the course of justice as soon as you advise 'no comment' in an interview." Victor's threats were ignored by Ben, who had heard them many times before, and were never going to persuade a suspect to start talking.

There were five scantily dressed women, sitting at tables, chatting with the male customers and waiting for their turn to perform. The DJ turned up the music and lights to introduce Eva. She left her table and paraded through the crowd of customers towards the stage, tottering on a pair of ridiculously high heels. As she wobbled past a blonde-haired man wearing a casual T-shirt with the Chelsea FC badge, he reached out and slapped Eva playfully on her arse, knocking her off balance and laughing at her obvious irritation.

Frank strode over to the blonde man and took hold of his arm. "You, out now," he ordered.

"Relax big guy," the blonde man said, flourishing a police warrant card with his free arm. "I'm PC Watt from Bridge Grove."

Victor walked over to them. "It's cool, Frank, I'll take care of this Chelsea bad boy. I could nick you for being an embarrassment," Victor told Watt, showing his warrant card. "I'm DCI Shadwell from Union Street."

Watt and Victor laughed and shook hands.

"So, you're one of us," Victor said.

"Victor Shadwell, the head honcho of Vice," PC Watt said in awe. "Let me take a selfie with you, to show the boys at Bridge Grove."

"It's just honcho, the word means head. What you said was 'head head'. And I'm homicide now."

"Strange name for a strip joint, Scylla," Watt commented after taking the picture.

"She was a Roman prostitute," Victor explained. "She competed with Empress Messalina, the wife of Emperor Claudius, to see who could have sex with the most people in one night."

"Oh, I didn't know."

"Messalina won, with twenty-five partners."

"Wow, respect, that's impressive."

Moments later, he watched as PC Watt took Eva by the arm as she walked back to her table, having finished her dance.

Watt gave Victor a knowing look as he and a smiling Eva, hand in hand, headed for the stairs to the first floor. A complete role reversal for PC Watt: he was her catch; she was in control; and he was the one who was going to be charged.

Victor walked over to the bar. "You going to watch the Arsenal on Saturday?" he asked Ivan, the club's manager.

"Naah, mother-in-law's visiting for the weekend and the missus wants to go out somewhere. What about you?"

"This year's the first season not playing in the Champions League. Highest number of league defeats for over twenty years. *Arse*nal, managed by *Arse*ne Wenger. It's more than a coincidence, Ivan. They are trying to tell us it's a shithole. I'll be there as usual though, cheering them on. That Watty there, going upstairs bold as brass. He knows that he shouldn't be going with a girl here, and in front of a senior officer. Some of them think they're untouchable."

"Shocking state of affairs: the sense of entitlement," Ivan said, laughing.

"Almost like the good old days in the 60s and early 70s, or bad old days, depending upon your point of view. Before Robert made his mark."

"Robert who, Victor? You've lost me."

"Commander Robert Mark cleaned up the CID. Famous for saying, 'A good police force is one that catches more crooks than it employs.' He put the uniforms in charge of the detectives. My dad was in uniform. A sergeant, he gave his life to the service: fell through a garage roof when chasing a burglar. My mum Margaret never got over it. What a waste."

"I didn't know, Victor. Condolences and all that. So, you followed in his footsteps."

"Not quite. He was polished with steel toe caps. I'm more Hush Puppies, sneak up on you."

Victor placed his folded newspaper on the bar top so that Ivan could slide a brown envelope underneath it. The dancers would take clients to one of the upstairs rooms and Victor knew what took place there. The first floor was run as a brothel and Ivan and the club's owners would be arrested for controlling prostitution if the goings on upstairs were exposed. And the club's sexual entertainment licence, which did not encompass such activities, would be taken away. So, they paid Victor, or gave him a drink, as they used to say, to turn a blind eye.

"How is Margaret?" Ivan asked.

"She's in a home now. Costs a small fortune. I go to see her when I can, but she doesn't recognise me anymore. She smiles at me, and I think that's nice Mum, then I see her smiling in the same way at all the other visitors. She doesn't even speak to me."

"How about your daughter Sharon, how's she getting on, Ivan?"

"She's good. Can't say that about her useless boyfriend Dan."

"Why is that?"

"I gave her a tidy sum for her twenty-first and that idiot Dan went and spent it on a crap car that will cost a fortune to put right. He's too scared to come 'round for Sunday roast now."

"Buying a second-hand motor is always dodgy. Maybe it's not his fault. Best to bury the hatchet if she loves him."

"If I saw him, I'd bury the hatchet, in him."

Victor laughed and turned to leave. "Yuri's unwell, that's why I'm doing the shakedown today."

The book lay on the duvet cover. It was open at the chapter that Kate was reading when she had fallen asleep the night before: 'Bloodstain and Blood Spatter Pattern Analysis'.

She woke when Arthur softly brushed her cheek. "You old rascal, what you been up to? Two-timing me again, out on the tiles? Trying to make it up to me now? I know what you do after dark, leave your favourite place on the shag pile and down the fire escape looking for a mate."

Arthur snuggled sensually up to Kate and closed his eyes in pleasure. Kate stroked his tummy and he started to purr. The warm sun shone on them both through the arched windows of the stylish rounded dormers in the roof of her attic flat. By the meteorological calendar it was still spring, but it felt like the summer of 2018 had arrived.

"Sorry, Arthur, I must love you and leave you."

In her early thirties, Kate was tall with a youthful face. She has bright blonde hair, cut short, and blue eyes. It took time for her to decide what to wear for an appointment at the bank. Smart was not her style. Casual looked like she was not taking the appointment seriously. She picked something in between.

Over breakfast she listened attentively to the morning's news on her kitchen radio. *Serving police officers have committed serious offences, are linked to organised crime and are part of a culture of misogyny and predatory behaviour,* the reporter announced. Kate turned up the volume. *This shocking state of affairs is revealed in a damning review today by the Police Standards Board. Kevin Knott, the PSB Director, told this programme that they have uncovered disturbing failings in counter-corruption and examples of appalling behaviour towards women. One officer was married to a brothel keeper and others engaged in so-called booty patrols where they would stop cars containing attractive women.*

"'You poisoned the wells of criminal justice,' that's what a judge once told some senior police officers when he sentenced them to imprisonment," Kate told an expectant Arthur, who was sitting at her feet hoping for more cuddles.

The 9am train left Victoria station, heading towards Kent. Kate returned to her book.

The origin of blood splatter can be established by drawing straight lines through the long axis of individual bloodstains. The point of convergence of the lines represents the point from which the bloodstain emanated.

"*DNA, Blood and Hair*, I couldn't help reading the title," the young woman sitting opposite Kate observed. "Bit heavy isn't it, so soon after breakfast?"

They both laughed.

"It's revision for an exam: Human Biological Contact Trace Evidence. I'm actually on my way to see my bank manager to ask for a business loan. Do you think I'll need to offer them a bribe?"

"Definitely, just don't insult them by making it too little."

A Victoria-bound train passed, travelling in the other direction. If Kate had looked out of her carriage window, she might have seen Gilbert Osling in conversation with Charles Sumner, a grey-haired man sitting facing him.

"Sex for the over-sixties, Gilbert, look here, the *Daily Splash* says that far from it being too late, there is even speed dating for seniors." Gilbert and Charles were frequent fellow commuters.

"Are you sure that they are not referring to the sixties, the time of libertine sexual attitudes?" Gilbert asked.

"Bedroom adventures for the over-sixties, wait until I tell Janet tonight," Charles said. "I can see the startled look on her face. A mixture of surprise, bewilderment, and alarm."

Gilbert was the Lord Chief Justice in his last year

before retirement and he hoped that his fellow judges, like Charles, would manage to keep it scandal-free.

As Kate and her conversation partner left the train at Bromley, Kate turned, and they waved goodbye to each other. On the way to the bank, she called at The Best Bean for a coffee with her sister Mary, a social worker. Mary had stories about her clients which made Kate catch her breath in horror.

"The mum was only fourteen years old when she had her," Mary reported. "The dad went to prison for underage sex. The daughter's in physical and emotional danger from dad now. Mum promised that she had stopped any contact with him, and that since his release he didn't even know where she lived. I thought she was doing well until a neighbour complained to mum's landlord, claiming that two or three times every week there was loud arguing between mum and a man in her flat, and the young girl would cry until late at night."

"People's messed up lives," Kate remarked.

"The mum was diagnosed with an STI and told the health visitor that she loved the dad and was back with him. Then she denied that she'd said that, told me that she hadn't had sex with the dad, but admitted that she had no other partner. She claimed that the arguments and the sounds of a girl crying were from programmes on her TV. She won't listen to any advice and calls us social workers 'the witches' when we try to monitor her. Now she expects to keep custody of the child."

"It's not love, is it? just dependence," Kate said. "He may treat her and the girl badly, but he's convinced the mum that his bad behaviour is really her fault and that he's the only man who would want to have anything to do with her. I couldn't do your job, and you are not paid enough."

"What about your love life?" Mary asked. "It usually makes my relationship with Derek seem very dull."

"Nothing doing, very boring, I need to go on a booty patrol."

"Is that what you call it?" Mary laughed. "Where's the romance in that?"

"I do have a new assistant though, Chi, she's Japanese, she lives with me and is a lot of fun."

"What sort of fun?" Mary asked, pulling a quizzical face.

"Not that sort. I don't mix business with pleasure, well not often. Anyway, she needed accommodation in Central London and she's as straight as you are."

"Now you make me sound even more boring, I have had my moments."

"Moment more like. When you were a drunk uni-student at that festival camp site doesn't count. If you ever want to give up social work, you could always come and work with me. When I get my business loan, there'll be no stopping me.

"But I could give a job to that mum you were telling me about, who bought a miniature recording device and placed it in her young son's coat pocket when he had contact sessions with the dad. You remember she could hear the dad on it, complaining about her to his new partner, calling the mum mentally unbalanced and a 'fruitcake' and swearing repeatedly at the boy. The dad sounded a bit drunk. It may have been underhand of her and more the sort of trick that I might play, but it convinced the court that she was telling the truth about the dad's bad behaviour around meeting up with their son."

Mary's phone rang, and she went outside the café to answer it. Kate paid for their drinks and joined her.

"Got to dash." Mary hugged Kate. "There's a client in the office asking for me and he's as high as a kite. Lucky that it's just around the corner."

Jane Fleming, the branch manager of Simmons Bank, met Kate at the reception desk. "So good to see you. We've missed you since you moved away. Sorry, I must warn you that I'm a bit distracted. I can't wait until tomorrow, can you?"

"You've lost me, what's tomorrow?"

"Saturday 19th May. Ring any bells? The wedding of course: Prince Harry and Meghan. Do you know that her veil took five hundred hours to make, embroidered by hand with fifty-three individual flowers representing all the countries of the commonwealth."

Before Kate could dampen Jane's exuberance by explaining she was not a royalist, a woman walked over to join them.

"Can I introduce Jacqui Peters? She's our new manager for small-business customers and she'll take you through your application for a business loan."

"We've met already," Kate said, "on the train this morning." *Promising*, Kate thought, *she looks cool for an account manager*.

"Ready for the bloodshed?" Jacqui asked, laughing. "You must be used to it."

"What?" Jane said in surprise. "That's not usually how we greet our customers. The interview's not that bad."

"It's an in-joke," Jacqui replied.

"Maybe I need to see someone else," Kate said, joining in the repartee. "I may be too tall for a small business customer." She put her hand on her head to show.

Jane and Jacqui looked lost for a reply.

"Sorry, that joke fell flat," Kate said.

"I'll leave you in Jacqui's capable hands," Jane said.

"You do that," Kate replied, glancing at Jacqui.

"That bribe suggestion was just a joke," Kate said when Jane had gone, and they were sitting in Jacqui's office.

"That's a pity," Jacqui replied, laughing. "An unsuitable job for a woman? I need to get to know you properly and understand how your business works. Please tell me how you got started."

"My first job after university: quite by chance I was a general dogsbody in a small detective agency. My father was a police officer and he arranged it for me."

"General Dogsbody eh, is that a rank?" Jacqui asked, laughing.

"Watching the guys at work, I was the only girl. I decided that there was money to be made from female clients who, despite my inexperience, preferred to confide in me. I investigated men who were being unfaithful or conning women out of their money and using fake dating profiles. A woman looking for romance won't always have a good nose for a wrong 'un. And the cheats have a large box of tricks to pick from, depending on the nature of the catch."

"Like choosing the right bait to use in fly fishing," Jacqui said, "my dad used to take me."

"This is catfishing," Kate replied, laughing. And it's just as likely to be a woman conning a man nowadays. My career had a boost when our trade journal *Professional Investigators' Review* wrote a feature about me 'New Kid on the Block.'"

"I've read your loan application but tell me in your own words how you see the future."

"There are so many opportunities now that police chiefs are over-stretched because of budget cutbacks. They are short of detectives and areas of police investigation work will soon be privatised, hopefully to be done by someone like me. I'm studying part-time for a postgraduate Diploma in Forensics and Crime Scene Investigation."

"Is your job dangerous?"

"The biggest danger is boredom, on a long surveillance job. I do find myself in embarrassing situations though. Mistaken for an escort, I was unceremoniously marched out of a five-star hotel last week because my obviously flirtatious approach to the fiancé of a new client, assessing how easily he could be seduced by a stranger, was misunderstood by the hotel's staff. The security man looked me up and down and said that he'd have let me stay if I'd paid him 'the usual' when I arrived. He assumed that I pick up men for a living. I wouldn't know how much 'the usual' is."

"Takes a flirt to catch a flirt I suppose," Jacqui said, laughing. "Is it challenging, knowing how far to let him try it on before you say gotcha to yourself and call a halt? Particularly if he's good looking."

"It's not always a 'him,'" Kate replied, "and I don't mix business with pleasure. That's the second time I've said that this morning."

"You don't carry a gun, do you?" Jacqui asked, looking

nervously at Kate's shoulder holster which was sticking up out of her bag.

"If I did, I wouldn't tell you. That's a wallet and mobile phone holder. I use it when I'm jogging."

"Do you spend hours in the gym? You look very trim."

Kate smiled at the compliment. "Running up and down four flights of stairs every day helps. My flat is the top floor of a building in Berwick Street, Soho. My grandmother left it to me. I need more space and a proper office now if I'm going to impress potential clients."

"I can picture it," Jacqui said whimsically. "A glass door with the blind pulled down. The sign *Kate Sullivan, Private Investigator* painted on the glass. Inside, you sit with your feet up, at a desk lit only by an Anglepoise lamp, whilst you draw contemplatively on a cigarette. Soho sounds edgy. I looked up your address on Streetview. Those windows are pretty."

"They are called bonneted dormers, as if the windows are wearing hats. Sweet isn't it. They are quite unusual in London. And it's professional investigator, if you don't mind, like on my card."

"Let's go through the figures," Jacqui said, and she opened Kate's file.

It was lunchtime when Jacqui declared, "I think we've covered all the bases."

"So, that's it? Do I need to see you again?"

"Well, sometimes I like to visit the business premises," Jacqui said teasingly, "to see for myself what goes on. You'll have to invite me over."

"With pleasure, assuming you say yes to my loan. You

can hunt for the noses of Soho. An artist glued plaster casts of his own nose on buildings around London."

"Sniff them out you mean. Are there any which are close to you? I'd like to see them."

"Meard Street and Great Windmill Street are the nearest. Why did a fun person like you decide to work for a bank Jacqui?"

"I like to please people and make their day."

2

Poison

It was late July when Gilbert looked up from his desk in the Royal Courts of Justice. He put down the law report that he was reading as his assistant Sally walked into the room. She placed some papers in front of him.

"Today's case list, Chief."

"Thank you, Sally. In case you wonder, I'm reading the report of a 16th century murder trial, in preparation for the Edmund Plowden Memorial Lecture. It's my turn to give it next year, but no time like the present to start work on it."

Gilbert returned to the dusty leather-bound book lying open on his desk.

In 1572 in the reign of Queen Elizabeth, John Saunders had a wife. In love with another woman, he planned to murder his wife so that he could re-marry. Saunders told his friend Alexander Archer about his intention and asked him for advice and help. Archer advised him to poison the wife, bought the poison and took it to Saunders.

The deadly concoction was a mixture of white arsenic and roseacre. So as not to cast suspicion on Saunders, Archer had brought him a slow poison, which would not kill the wife straight away, but would remain in her body, weakening her little by little.

But the wife had already fallen sick, so when Saunders gave her two pieces of a roasted apple, mixed with the poison, she ate only a small part of it. She gave the rest of the apple to their three-year-old daughter Eleanor. Seeing what she was doing, Saunders scolded her and said that apples were not good for young children. She replied that they were better for Eleanor than they were for her as she was ill. Eleanor ate the poisoned apple and Saunders, afraid of being found out, watched her eat it and did not try to take it from her. The wife recovered from her illness. Eleanor, being an infant, died only two days later. Saunders had been very fond of Eleanor, yet he had chosen not to save her life.

Suspicion quickly fell on the trio and when the truth came out it was agreed that the wife had not committed a crime. But Saunders and Archer were tried for murder. Saunders was convicted of Eleanor's murder and hanged. The panel of two judges agreed that Archer was not an accessory to the murder but chose not to ratify their decision. Instead, they kept him locked up and eventually allowed him to buy his freedom.

Charles, a fellow judge, appeared in the doorway of Gilbert's room. "Help, I need amusing conversation, Gilbert. Something light, to take my mind off this appeal that I'm hearing. I have a court room full of experts, trying to out-expert each other."

"Come and sit-down, Charles. Let me tell you what I have learnt about bawdy Southwark in the 16th century. I'm trying to get a feel for what it was like when Saunders and Archer were alive: the accused men in this transferred malice murder trial that I'm researching. Did you know that Southwark was London's most disreputable district then, with as many as twenty-two inns along the riverside, theatres such as The Globe, and bull and bear baiting. There were public baths with naked bathing which were a cover for prostitution. Closed in the mid-16th century to stop the spread of disease, they were called 'stews' because of the hot sweaty bathing rooms. That's where the expression 'to stew in your own juice' came from: to suffer with the consequences of a visit to a stew."

"I only shower, much cleaner," Charles said jokingly.

"What is now Bankside, used to be the Liberty of the Clink: seventy acres of land controlled by the Bishop of Winchester. The Clink was the Bishop's prison. He made a nice living from licensing and taxing the eighteen brothel owners and three hundred and fifty prostitutes who were his tenants."

"Sounds like the side hustle of some of our boys in blue, and plain clothes."

"Southwark's popularity was due to these sorts of disreputable activities being banned by the City of London, just across the Thames. On the one hand, the Bishop's people justified prostitution as a means of letting off steam for good Christian men who might otherwise commit sodomy or masturbate. But on the other hand, a prostitute who dared to have sex with a man without charging him, who might have been her lover, would be sent to prison as a punishment."

"Have to keep the hamster money-wheel turning."

"The prostitutes were called Winchester Geese,

possibly because of the uniform that they had to wear as licensed traders under the Bishop's protection. Catching a venereal disease was referred to as being 'bitten by a goose'. The swellings which were a symptom of the disease were called 'goose bumps.'"

"That's true, Gilbert. In Shakespeare's world 'goose' was a term he used for a prostitute. In Romeo and Juliet, for example, Romeo jests with Mercutio about Romeo's 'wit' being a 'sweet meat' which 'serves a sour sauce into a sweet goose.'"

"'Wit', Charles, oh, does that mean?"

"Yes, think aubergine emoji, Gilbert."

"That is rude of the Bard of Avon. I'm impressed with your knowledge and literary recall, Charles. The street names in the Liberty of the Clink, which signposted what went on there, were a bit more obvious: Slut's Hole, Whore's Nest and Cock Alley,"

"Estate agents wouldn't like that. Not good for house prices."

"Good enough to line the Bishop's pockets, yet these women had ignominious deaths. They were buried in the Cross Bones Graveyard: unconsecrated ground and a favourite hunting place for the body snatchers who sold unearthed corpses for use in anatomy classes at the nearby Guy's Hospital."

"Now you've cheered me up, how about a sandwich, Gilbert? I'll nip to that nice deli around the corner. What would you like me to get you?"

"Sally usually fetches my sandwiches because I can never decide what to have. You choose for me, Charles."

The next day, Kate set off for Oxford Circus underground station. She walked past basement stairs with a handwritten notice on a door at the bottom. She read *new model* when a man blocked her view as he came up the stairs to leave. She imagined the woman down below, washing her hands and tucking into the remains of a take-way meal before the next customer. She walked through Berwick Street market. The street was emptying as the stall holders were packing up, whilst the early Saturday evening good-timers picked their way through the abandoned fruit and veg and cardboard boxes.

In the 16th century, when Saunders and Archer had conducted their murderous plot, the area around Berwick Street, where Kate now lived, was known as the 'killing fields of London'. But it was hares and foxes, not humans, that were chased to their death by huntsmen calling 'so-hoe' to their harriers in what was then a Royal Park. It wasn't until the Victorian era that Soho toppled Southwark as London's most popular entertainment centre.

Kate was going to the home of Ray Millan, a notorious villain who lived on the South bank of the Thames in what used to be the Liberty of the Clink. Ray was throwing a party to celebrate that crime does pay.

He expected her to be there, Kate having worked as part of the defence team which helped Ray's illegal call-girl empire to avoid justice and Ray to escape being sent to the clink.

Ian Blake sat in the main bar of The Fastidious Fox (known locally as 'The Fox'), a pub in London's Vauxhall. He was heading for the same destination as Kate. Ray was a criminal client of his. The *Sunday Splash* newspaper had described Millan as *London's call-girl king* when they reported how he had escaped prosecution.

Ray owned Kiss, Plaisir, Lace, and Dream of Me, four online glamorous businesses offering escort and massage services throughout London. The galleries on their websites showed countless revealing pictures of foxy women. Ray's wife Patsy had wanted to use a classier name for one of the businesses, such as *Suarium*, which she explained to Ray was Latin for 'passionate kiss'. Ray said that the name made him think of an aquarium with mermaids swimming around. "No mermaids: they lure men to their death."

Months before, whilst preparing Ray's defence, Ian had visited the 'engine room' of his businesses: a hi-tech basement with multiple phones and computer screens, where calls or messages from eager clients were answered by a team of women called 'angels'.

A twenty-four-hour staff rota framed with lipstick-drawn hearts was pinned to a notice board on the wall. A circular shaped clock with large hands and a promotional message on the face *scratch that itch* dominated another wall. Ray's mission statement was lit with blue neon on a third wall: *live your life without limits*.

The angels chatted in between answering calls.

"I added 'I'm vegan' on my dating app."

"Rachelle, nobody wants to make eyes at a vegan. Not a turn on."

"That's not true, I read that compassion for animals is sexy."

"Sexy vegan? Sounds like an oxymoron."

"Are you calling me stupid?"

"No, Rachelle, it's a figure of speech, two opposite words next to each other. You'd spend the date arguing about where to go for dinner."

Ray also controlled at least fifty websites from the engine room, each displaying a personalised loving message from a model-like woman who claimed to be an 'independent' escort and masseuse. These women did not use their real names. Instead, they went by professional names, to create identities which were more alluring than their personal lives.

Ray and his staff offered a one-stop shop. He recruited the women, trained and dressed them, put them in an online window, prepared the menus of services on offer, set their working hours, negotiated their charges, instructed them where to meet their clients and had drivers take them there. The angels had access to flats and hotel rooms if a caller could not receive a woman at their own accommodation. He insisted on online payments from which he would take a percentage cut. There was a ready supply of women for the angels to send in response to the clients' requests.

The engine room was in Ray's modern four-storey town house in Bankside, near the Globe Theatre. Ray thought it was an appropriate location: "a lot of ham acting goes on here as well," he would joke, referring to his angels selling their wares to the callers. The police suspected correctly that the house functioned as a giant emporium: sourcing, controlling and marketing the women for sex.

"He's debauched," Annie had complained to Ian. "Why do you feel the need to socialise with him?"

"He's a good client and refers many of his business associates to us."

It was too early to arrive at Ray's. Ian was happy to pass the time with a bottle of Thirsty Fox, sitting in an armchair in the main bar of The Fastidious Fox. In the late 13th century, the Head of King John's mercenaries had owned Faulke's Hall, a large house in the area. It was later known as Fox Hall, the inspiration for the pub's name, and eventually Vauxhall.

With its own microbrewery, The Fastidious Fox was always busy. The microbrewery's owner showed devotees around, proudly telling them, "This fox is scrupulously clean, and our head brewer is very fastidious about how our speciality beers are produced." T shirts with *I am a zythophile* across the front, "means a lover of beer", the owner would explain, were on sale at the end of the tour.

Relaxing, as the beer triggered his feel-good hormones, Ian compared Ray's sophisticated operation to what sex in Soho used to be like: a rash of clip joints which had long since disappeared from the Soho scene. Ian visited Girls Galore when he was much younger. For a £5 entrance fee it offered a 'no holds barred' striptease. A wag had changed the 'd' into an 'e' on the sign. Lacking an alcohol licence, he was forced to pay an extortionate price for some 'nearly beers' for himself and mocktails for the hostess. The advertised striptease never took place as the stripper turned out to be busy elsewhere. No clothes were ripped off that night, only Ian and his wallet.

It was Saturday night. On the way to the party, Kate had to make a detour and deliver a file of witness statements to

Ian. His solicitors' firm was doing its best to help Maxine, languishing in a women's prison, accused of killing her partner Brent. Brent was violent towards Maxine, and she felt unsafe because his abusive behaviour worsened following the birth of their child. As a precaution, Maxine would take a knife to bed with her and hide it under her pillow.

What triggered Maxine's fatal reaction was when Brent raised both his legs in the middle of the night, when her restlessness had disturbed him, and kicked her so hard in her side that she flew out of bed and hit her head and body on the night storage heater. She got to her feet, took out the knife and stabbed him to death. To show how badly Maxine had been provoked in the past, Kate went from door-to-door to find neighbours who had seen her bruises and black eyes or had heard her screaming as he assaulted her.

The underground train made its way noisily to Brixton, where Ian lived. Away from the station, the wet pavements emptied, and people were replaced by lines of parked cars. Kate turned into a leafy residential street of smart looking terraced Victorian houses, symbols of gentrification. A Ford Transit van looked out of place, parked clumsily on the corner. An Alsatian dog sat behind the steering wheel, keeping the seat warm for the driver.

Kate answered Mary's phone call. "Saturday night, I'm putting the kids to bed. Bet you're out having fun."

"Off to a work-related party. Should be free flowing alcohol."

"You're not driving, are you? Tell me you're not."

"Public transport. Why, are you worried about me?"

"It's just I had this mum today. Told me she didn't drink much. Then I saw her police record: three recent convictions for drink driving, the second whilst on bail for the first and the last whilst disqualified for the second. She's on a suspended prison sentence now, luckily for her she wasn't locked up."

"Stop thinking about me like I'm one of your clients. You know I don't do excess anything."

"Yes, sorry, got to go turn the kids' bath water off, have fun."

Kate stopped outside a late 19th century Victorian terrace house, built when the railway transformed Brixton into a middle-class suburb. In her mind, the authenticity of its building materials and the timeless charm of its design symbolised British family life.

Kate rang the bell. Annie answered the door.

"Hi, sorry it's late. I'm Kate Sullivan. I work with Ian as an investigator. I've brought a file of signed witness statements that he needs. Is he in?"

"I didn't realise when he talks about the investigator that you're a woman. Is that bad of me?"

"No, quite a common reaction. Is he about?"

"He's at a police station somewhere. He was called out earlier: another client in urgent need of his services."

Two children in pyjamas joined Annie at the door. She introduced them to Kate as Maisie aged ten and Jack aged eight.

"Sorry I can't stay to chat."

"I'll make sure that he gets them." Annie took the file of papers from Kate and left it on the hall table for Ian.

Ian had recently bought a motorbike, to boost his flagging forty-something ego. It had been raining and there was a dry shape left on the road outside the house where the covered motorbike had been. The shape reminded Kate of the chalk-marked silhouette of a body in a crime film.

Described by some as 'ballsy', Annie worked as a maths teacher in a challenging secondary school. She enjoyed regular visits to the gym and jogging in the local streets in the evening after the children were in bed. She supported Ian in his work, which she considered important: giving a voice to people who were inarticulate; ensuring that their legal rights were respected; and holding the police to account. She was realistic about what to expect from their marriage, which was satisfactory and comfortable, and she didn't need to fantasise about having an affair. She assumed that Ian felt the same as her.

It took her by surprise when her friend Martina made a remark during the coffee break at the women's self-defence group: "I need to have many different friends, so why do I have to make do with only one lover. It's a welcome change to spend time with someone who appreciates me, and I feel anything but guilt."

"Have another glass of bubbly." Ian had never seen Ray so expansive. "Have you met the girls? Sam, Louise, Chantelle, come and meet Ian, a gentleman, and a scholar." Ray rattled his jewellery as he spoke. Whenever Ray had visited Ian in his office, he had worn a double-breasted pin striped suit and had behaved in a quietly obsequious way. Now he was loud, and wore leather sandals, white trousers, and a very bright Hawaiian shirt draped over his large stomach.

Ray gestured to a tall blonde-haired woman, aged in her mid-twenties, beckoning her to join him and Ian.

"Ian, this is Sandy. Sandy, Ian's my lawyer. He's celebrating our good fortune with us, aren't you Ian?" Sandy offered Ian a hand to shake. Ian smiled at her politely. Sandy made some small chat then went back to join Chantelle and Louise, and the women continued to talk animatedly in a corner. Ray called them all 'girls', regardless of their age. Ian was introduced to Ray's accountant, his driver, and a woman named Rita who was his office manager. Patsy, Ray's wife, and the kiddies were away visiting her mother.

Ray's empire was not a part of Victor's network of protected businesses because Ray had refused to pay him. Victor needed to show results for the Vice team and had worked to close Ray down. When they investigated Ray, undercover officers used false identities to pose as clients and purchase the services of the women he promoted. They arranged to meet them at hotels and tried to record the encounters. The Court of Appeal in *Regina - v - Woodhouse and Hall* had given the green light to this practice by deciding that an offer of sexual services to a police officer was not hearsay and could be given as evidence at trial as proof that the offer had been made. DS Carly Bonetti and DC Steven Stant, from C15, Victor's team, worked together.

With the help of the mobile phone companies, the phone user data on the various websites all pointed to Ray's house and C15 decided to investigate him. Stant was tasked to contact the women to see whether full sex, rather than just dinner or a professional massage, was on sale. For the first time, he dressed up as an Arab sheikh and from a bedroom in a four-star hotel, The Runway at Heathrow, requested Amie and Nina to give a 'four-hands experience'. Bonetti hid in the bedroom wardrobe with her recording device. When the women arrived, it did not go according to plan.

"It's £300 for one hour. You must pay now," Amie demanded. Stant paid her.

"What would you like us to do?"

"What do you do?"

Before she could explain the various options, DS Bonetti sneezed helplessly inside the wardrobe. Amie pulled open the wardrobe doors and saw her crouched there.

"He's brought some woman to hear us do it, the fucking pervert, I'm not staying here with him." Both women left the room in a hurry, keeping the £300.

"That's the cost of the hotel room, my Arab gear hire and £300 with nothing to show. Bonetti, you're a goose. How are we going to justify all that on expenses?"

"Bonetti pulled a miserable face as she looked into the hotel bathroom mirror. "Who'd shag this?" she asked herself disparagingly.

The police finally raided Ray's house. Besides what they were looking for, they found a full-length one-way mirror between Ray's private study and the unsuspecting au pair's bedroom.

The law had changed so that merely profiting from prostitution without any element of control was no longer an offence. The Sexual Offences Act 2003 required proof of control of the women for Ray's activities to be classed as illegal. The investigators targeted the women who were featured on the websites and some of them were 'persuaded' to give evidence against him. They agreed to say in court that Ray had encouraged them to offer sexual services; and that he had promoted, directed and instructed them whilst keeping most of their earnings for himself. Following Victor's instructions, the investigating officers had coerced them to co-operate with threats and intimidation. Even though the women were not committing crimes, as they mostly worked on their own, the investigators led them to believe that any refusal to co-operate would be met with searches of them and their homes; arrests on trumped-up charges such as dealing drugs; and for the single mothers, any child they had would be put into temporary foster care.

Ray was surely bang to rights. He was charged with conspiracy to control the activities of prostitutes. But in Ray, Victor had met his match. Just before the trial began, the Public Prosecutor wrote to Ian that the case was dropped. The investigating officers had been caught out having sex with the women who were going to give evidence for them. The officers and the women were all now considered unreliable witnesses, and the prosecution case was tainted. The investigators, trapped in a honeypot of Ray's making, later faced misconduct charges.

To make matters worse, Ray complained that Victor had demanded protection money from him and claimed that he had been targeted by the Vice team because of his refusal to pay them. Victor received a dressing down for bungling the investigation and was moved from C15 to Major Crimes, working out of Union Street Police Station investigating homicides. DC Stant and DS Bonetti, who had not fallen victim to the escorts' embraces, were moved from C15 to keep an eye on him.

"Shadwell can't mess up with dead women, well not so that it would cause our investigations a problem," Detective Chief Superintendent Drake said to the Commander when recommending the transfer.

3

Seduction

At the party, Ray was jubilant at having triumphed over the police again. "Makes a change when we trap them, doesn't it?" Now he was celebrating to mark the occasion.

The investigation and trial preparation had wasted many thousands of pounds and caused the police great embarrassment. They had since turned their attentions away from Ray and left him free to continue.

Ian asked Ray to excuse him and went to the downstairs toilet. As he walked to the toilet door, Kate found herself behind him, heading for the same place. She recognised him from the back and was about to call out 'hi' when he disappeared through the door. She heard the lock click shut. *He must have finished his police station visit, or not told his wife the truth about how he was spending Saturday night*, she thought. *He told me he wouldn't be at the party because his wife didn't approve of Ray. Must have changed his mind. Wish he'd said, could have saved me a visit to his house.*

Kate was aware of a woman in the corridor, waiting in front of her by the toilet door. She was another of Ray's escorts. She ignored Kate. *She looks gorgeous* Kate thought.

The lock on the door clicked open, but before Ian could come out, the waiting woman pushed in through the open door and the lock closed again. *Well, well*, thought Kate, *what is going on here?*

The toilet was large and gaudy, with a shell-like wash basin, gold taps and coloured lights. Ian had turned the lock, about to leave, when the door opened from the outside and a woman entered.

"Sorry," she said, locking the door behind them, "I'm bursting." She pulled up her dress, pulled down her expensive knickers and squatted on the toilet. Ian looked away politely.

"I'm Stella, you're Ian, Ray's told me all about you. He thinks very highly of you. You're better looking than he described. Don't go, I'll finish in a minute, then we can talk some more."

Stella washed and dried her hands, checked herself in the mirror and took hold of Ian's hand.

"Let's go somewhere quiet, the top floor."

Kate watched from a discreet place as Ian came out of the toilet, together with Stella, who led him away. *That's a bit risky*, Kate thought. *He must have known that I'd be at the party.*

Stella led Ian into a bedroom and sat on the bed. She patted the duvet for him to sit next to her. "So, what little bit of legal magic did you sprinkle on his case?" she asked, as she kicked off her expensive shoes. "Must have been something special."

"Not really," Ian said modestly. "The girls felt threatened by the investigators, and they asked me if the police really could fit them up if they refused to give evidence against him in court. I told them, 'You need protection against the police. Try to get the officers to repeat their threats, somewhere you can record it.' So, they arranged further meetings with the officers in discreet-looking locations. The detectives were canny enough not to take the bait and threaten them again, but alcohol flowed and, almost to a man, they got into bed with their witnesses. Just couldn't resist it."

"Who's a clever boy?" Stella asked.

"It was only afterwards that I learnt that Ray was paying the women a special bonus for helping torpedo the criminal case."

She told him to undress her. Then she lay invitingly on the bed. Ian grinned stupidly. "Ray asked me to give you a little thank you present: so, what turns you on?" Stella asked him.

It was October, and Stella sat on a bar stool in The Fastidious Fox, next to Victor.

"How's Margaret?"

"Still smiling."

"Why don't I come with you, the next time you visit? Beechcroft House isn't it?"

"Better not, the sight of you would give the old boys there a heart attack. Spies tell me you've been hanging around with that smirking scumbag Ian Blake. What's that about? I thought that outside work you like tall pretty boys with toned physiques who can deliver fireworks between the sheets."

"My life is just work. No time for those sorts of hobbies. Not that it's any of your business. Ian's besotted with me. Ray asked me to entertain him and now Ian can't get enough. He insists on meeting me after his work so we can get drunk together and go to my apartment, then he's back early the next morning with coffee and croissants. It's exhausting. Honestly, he's like a teenager on heat. He's married with kids. Men have no shame."

"I love it, he's such a self-righteous hypocrite, banging on about police misconduct all the time. He's no different from anyone else, easily tempted."

Stella broke off the conversation as she looked at her phone whilst sliding off the bar stool.

"Got to reply to this message."

She soon perched on the bar stool again.

"My favourite hotel in Park Lane, new gent. Must go home soon and transform myself into somebody who is irresistible."

"I'm surprised that you take Ian home. You have never let me, or any of your other visitors, go there."

"My neighbour would object if she had a trail of men passing her door. Anyway, it's a regular thing with him. Too expensive to find somewhere else to go together. Ian likes it and it saves me having to get out of bed in the morning. He says he wants to get to know me better. How well do you know him?"

"Only professionally, he's the enemy. What's it like, doing 'the business' with him?"

"Necessary, I've got expensive tastes. He's very generous. He doesn't pay me by the hour. Instead, he's given me a credit card, to use however I like, no limit. And Ray doesn't take his usual cut. Says it gives him a hold over

Ian which could be useful as Ian is about to be promoted to a 'pillar of the establishment.'"

"I didn't know. What pillar's that then?"

"Just a fucking judge."

"Doesn't he mind, you know, what you do? He looks like the possessive type."

"We don't talk about it. Out of sight, out of mind. Anyway, it never bothered you. Why should he be different?"

"Well, we have what's called a utilitarian relationship, with a common bond: screwing people and making money."

That evening, Ian was relaxing with a large glass of wine. He and Stella were in a bar around the corner from her apartment. Ian looked soulfully into his glass. "There are some benefits to getting older," he said. "One of them is realising that there's only one life and it's short, so don't have any regrets."

"Is that piece of advice for me or are you trying to convince yourself about it?"

Ian topped up Stella's glass from the bottle in the cooler by the table.

"Je ne regrette rien," Stella continued.

"Another is knowing the importance of saying what you think, straight talking with no bullshit," Ian said, ignoring Stella's attempt to lighten the conversation. "Know what you want and go for it."

"I already do that," Stella replied abruptly.

Ian topped Stella's glass up again. She was getting bored with all his introspection, and the wine bottle was empty.

"Shall I get another bottle?" Ian asked.

"I'm sure you've got lots more pearls of wisdom for me, but can we talk about something else? Anyway, I need the ladies' room."

"I'm with Ian. I can't take any other bookings tonight," she said into her phone as she sat in the toilet cubicle. "What? Who calls him the 'bed blocker'? That's a bit rude. I do have space for other men. He can be irritating, like now, but he's a good client."

The following evening, Annie confronted Ian. "You were home extremely late last night. You know that I try to go running after I've put the children to bed. Why didn't you answer my calls or messages."

"My phone was on silent in a meeting, and I forgot to put the sound back on afterwards. I need to work late these days, sorry."

"Are you having an affair?"

"Are you mad? I won't dignify that question with an answer."

"Don't be angry with me. You seem distracted, it's like you're not here, what's wrong? It makes me anxious."

"I'm under pressure at work at the moment."

"Anything you want to tell me about?"

"Just very busy with a big case."

"You used to tell me about your cases. How long do I have to wait until you're working regular hours on the bench?"

The next evening, Ian was sitting in a living room with Miss Phelps, Stella's neighbour. Stella was late coming home and Miss Phelps, seeing Ian standing at the door to

Stella's apartment, had invited him in and offered him a cup of tea.

"You must be in love, Ian," Miss Phelps said, "you're here virtually every day."

"I am, it's like an illness, Cynthia."

Charlie, Miss Phelps's dog lying in his basket, opened one eye and then closed it again.

"Love or lust?" Miss Phelps asked.

Ian looked surprised at the question.

Miss Phelps smiled, "I was a good looker in my young days. I had plenty of young men after me."

"It's both, to be honest."

"She's a stunner and you seem like a nice man, you are both lucky to have each other, but you're married, aren't you?"

"How do you know?"

"You're wearing a wedding ring."

"Oh yes, I've worn it for so long that I don't notice it anymore."

"Does your wife know about your feelings for Stella?"

"God no, but it's becoming difficult to keep it from her and spend time with Stella. I know that it's a horrible thing to say and I feel guilty just thinking it, but sometimes I wish that Annie, my wife, wasn't around so that Stella and I could be together properly."

"Yes, Ian, that is a horrible thing to say." Charlie gave Ian a withering look.

Miss Phelps went into the kitchen to make the tea whilst Ian picked up her copy of the *Daily Splash*. He read about middle-aged men who feel the need for risk and danger. Instead of mountain climbing or potholing they lead double lives involving drugs, gambling, drinking and casual sex. They think they are unassailable until they suffer the inevitable calamitous end. Ian did not recognise himself.

Just then he heard Stella putting her key in her door lock.

Miss Phelps came back into the room. "Don't wait for your tea, you must go to your lover," she said dramatically. "One day, if you are a good boy, she might give you a key of your own."

It was early December and Kate's studying was interrupted by the door buzzer. A woman was standing on the pavement four floors below, trying to make herself heard over the noises from the street.

"Hello, is that Sullivan's Detective Agency?"

"Press the door hard, top floor. There's no lift I'm afraid."

The four flights of stairs gave Kate at least sixty seconds to straighten her clothes, brush her hair and try to look professional. But she couldn't hide the fact that this was also her home and that she had not read Marie Kondo's book *The Life-Changing Magic of Tidying Up*.

Kate led Annie into a room that doubled as her office. Annie took off her scarf and coat. She went to sit in an armchair that Kate motioned towards. The springs were worn, so that she sat further down than she expected. She gasped in surprise and then laughed as her legs briefly went up in the air. That broke the ice, as the embarrassment of the situation and the thought of confiding in a relative stranger had made her feel nervous.

"Sorry, I meant that you should sit in the other chair. I would have warned you about that one. It's wonderfully comfortable though, once you've sunk down in it."

"I didn't know who else to turn to. I don't know any other private investigators. I was a bit unfriendly when I met you on the doorstep in the summer. I thought that you and Ian might be, you know, more than just friends."

Kate laughed at the suggestion. "No chance, no disrespect to Ian."

"I'm being paranoid. I can be a bitch sometimes. It's just that he talks so enthusiastically about the brilliant work his investigator does. And I pictured you as a retired policeman, overweight and going grey on top, wearing a suit with a loosely tied tie, the top shirt button undone because the collar is too tight."

"I could tell you all about the history of women PIs. And I like to be called a professional investigator."

"You are a professional then?"

"I'm licensed, even though it's not required by law yet, if that's what you mean."

Kate recalled her sighting of Ian at Ray's party and guessed why Annie had come to see her.

"I don't really know where to begin."

"Can I help? You have suspicions about Ian, that he's up to a bit of extra-marital intimacy with someone. The doubt is nagging away at you. You want me to confirm it or put your mind at rest. At least you can cross me off your list of suspects."

"He's being very preoccupied and secretive. It's been going on since I met you. He's also abrupt with the children, and that's not like him. He used to be a 'home bird' but now he's constantly rushing off, saying that he must work late. Sometimes, he doesn't come back until I'm asleep. He's behaving in a weird way. It's like he's had a personality change. I just want to know the truth and that I'm not imagining things. I've been thinking that maybe the gym and my running has knocked some of the femininity out of me and he doesn't find me attractive anymore."

"I feel for you. But you know that this is to do with him, not you."

"I looked at the search history on his laptop and the messages on his phone, but there was nothing unusual or suspicious."

"He's probably using another phone. What do you want me to do about it?"

"Find out what's going on. And sorry again for jumping to the wrong conclusion about you. When I saw that you are an attractive woman and younger than me, I put two and two together and made five. Bit sad that, especially as I'm a maths teacher."

"Obvious question, have you asked him whether he's seeing another woman?"

"I have, but he just snapped back at me that I was being ridiculous, as if it's me who's in the wrong. Made me feel guilty just for asking him."

"That's so unfair, Annie. I think it's time to kick some arse."

4

Peeping Tom

Kate has a spare room which she rents to Chihiro Fukuda. "Call me Chi," Chihiro said when they first met. "*Fuku* pronounced *Fookoo* means good fortune and *da* pronounced *dah* means rice field. It's a traditional family name in Japan. Chihiro can be the name of a boy or a girl, so people don't always know what to expect when I turn up. I'm like an older version of Chihiro in the film *Spirited Away*, full of energy and positivity and using my wits to survive. *Chi* means thousand and *hiro* means search or seek, so it literally means a thousand questions. I've only two questions: which is my room? and when do I start work?"

"Chihiro *Fookoodah*," Kate practised.

"Well, Kate is short for Katherine and means pure. In the Middle Ages the name was often given to girls who were expected to lead a virtuous life. So, my parents got that wrong. And Sullivan is an Irish name. Not as fascinating as the etymology of your name."

Chi, twenty-seven years old, from Shinjuku, the 'anything goes' entertainment district in Tokyo, was in London on a two-year working visa. She was now one month into her new job, working for Kate. "Company HR policy," Kate told her. "We don't say you work for me; you work with me."

"But you're still the boss," Chi added for reassurance. "This is all still new to me."

Kate looked for Chi in her room but all she could see was the onigawara, a statue of a fearsome beast with an ogre's face, watching her from the dressing table. Kate called it spooky. Chi said it made her feel at home.

Kate found Chi in the kitchen. She was eating her usual breakfast: steamed rice with a raw egg on top. Chi was slim and short in stature. Her jet-black hair, pulled tightly back into a ponytail, framed her oval face with its delicately shaped eyes, nose, and mouth.

Kate showed Chi a picture in a magazine of knitted tea cakes and tarts, titled *Guilty Pleasures*. "Artwork on exhibition by an inmate of a women's prison," Kate explained. "Good isn't it. I told you about Maxine. Her guilty pleasure was killing her violent husband. If we can show the jury that it was a sudden loss of self-control, she'll be sentenced for manslaughter instead of murder.

"I wanted to ask you about my niece Claire. She's been here a few times. Do you remember her? She's fifteen and she met a friend of mine's son, Henry, at a school charity disco. Henry is sixteen and goes to the boy's school next door to Claire's."

"Uh huh," Chi said, trying to sound interested.

"Claire said that Henry is acting a bit weird towards her. He keeps messaging her and saying inappropriate things. Should she be worried about it and do something?"

"Aren't all sixteen years-old-boys a bit weird around girls? you know, testosterone driven and socially awkward. What does her mother say?"

"Mary? Claire hasn't told her yet, too embarrassed. But you're right. I'll tell her to ghost him. Hopefully, he'll take the hint. Changing the subject, I've got a job for you: watching my client's husband to find out whether he's cheating on her, and if so, who with and how serious it is."

"In the absence of a love life, I will be watching other people at it. Sad isn't it. Give me the details."

"My client is Annie Blake. She was here last night but you were out. This is a photograph of Ian Blake. He's your subject. This is one of him with Annie, so that you know whom he should be out with. She seems nice. She called me attractive, so she's got good judgement. As for Ian, he can't have sown enough wild oats when he was young, and now he's making up for lost time. This is a picture of Stella Godley, whom I suspect he is spending that lost time with."

"Wow, look at her. No wonder."

"She's an ambassadress for Ray Millan. That means she's special, classy, expensive and clients are selected for her.

"This is a folder with a map and details of his home and office, and the location of Stella's apartment. Here is a mobile phone on which Annie has installed a tracker for his phone, to help you know where to find him when his phone is switched on and he's not working. You will watch him, and keep an observation log of times, places, actions, and his companions. Take photographs of him in the company of any woman other than Annie. I've a special camera film for night-time that you can use."

"I know what to do. I've been reading this American guide to surveillance. It recommends keeping observation from the back seat of the car; taking binoculars, a change of clothes and a wig in case you have been spotted; wearing soft-soled quiet shoes; and carrying a dog's lead so that you can say you are looking for Buster."

"Buster? Looking for Rover more like. This is England not America," Kate pointed out.

"Or Pochi, a popular dog's name in Japan."

"Yes, but we're not in Japan. When was that guide published?"

"Latest edition 1991, the year of my birth. That's a sign isn't it, that I was meant to do this work. How much will you pay me?"

"Usual rate."

"It sounds like it's going to occupy most of my evenings, what about my social life?"

"All right, plus a bonus of twenty per cent of what Annie pays me if you get results."

"It's a deal."

"Take the Beetle. Don't forget the usual: drinks and snacks, your music, and something to read. Wrap up warm but don't go to sleep on the job or you might miss him." Kate knew that it could be cold and tedious work, sometimes with nothing to show for it.

"What do I do if I need the loo?"

"First rule is prevention and anticipation."

"That's two rules."

"Pay attention. Prevention: stay hydrated with water and avoid spicy foods, alcohol, caffeine, chocolate, and carbonated drinks."

"Hey, that sounds a heap of fun, not."

"It's so you don't irritate your bladder. And anticipation: don't wait until you have to go, go when you have the chance. Lastly, if all else fails, I've got a special plastic funnel. I take my GoGirl to pee at music festivals, it lets you aim and go standing up. It's here, in the cupboard."

Chi squirmed as Kate handed her a plastic funnel.

"It's been washed," Kate said, noticing the face that Chi was pulling. "Why don't you practice? But only in the shower please, we don't want any accidents. Aim for the drain thingy."

"Hit the target, first time," Chi called out from behind the shower door minutes later. "I've always wanted to do this and pee like a boy."

"Way to go, girl," Kate called back.

Chi sat slumped down in the rear seat of Kate's VW Beetle. She wore a baseball cap pulled over her long hair, with her ponytail sticking out through the back. She was on the phone to her friend Mai. Mai was visiting from Japan and excited about the fact that Chi was conducting surveillance.

"It's like being a spy," Mai said.

"It's boring," Chi replied.

They had exchanged gossip about what their mutual friends in Japan had been up to, discussed the popular programmes on Japanese TV and Mai had told her about the latest scandal involving Japanese politicians in the sale of public land at a huge discount.

Chi had a well-thumbed copy of *Shukan Gendai* (Modern Weekly) on her lap, with chatty stories about celebrities in Japan.

"Last night, me and my boss Kate went to this private member club, Obsession," Chi said.

"To meet men? Hey, you could have invited me."

"No, for work. Anyway Kate, my boss, isn't into men. The club has a licence for alcohol and entertainment only, but the local council received a complaint that there was nudity in a room called The Playroom. So, they paid us to go along and investigate. We pretended to be a same sex couple, paid the door attendant to get in and took pictures.

"*Kuso*" (shit), Chi said. Ian had walked past the Beetle on her side of the road, without Chi having noticed. He crossed the road and entered Stella's apartment block. Chi rang off.

The exquisite six storey 1930s art deco building in yellow brick, boasted a crescent shaped façade. The original Crittall windows and balcony doors added to its classic appearance.

Chi had watched Hitchcock's *Rear Window* countless times. She was keeping observation on an apartment like Jeff Jeffries (James Stewart), but there the similarity ended. She was not in a wheelchair with her leg in plaster, although sitting cramped in the back of Kate's Beetle she might as well have been. Instead of a sweltering summer, with people throwing open their windows so that the noise from inside their apartments was audible outside, this was near Christmas and people kept their windows shut and curtains drawn. And Chi was watching the apartment's front windows. Stella's living room and bedroom were on the first floor, above the entrance to the block.

The silence was interrupted occasionally by rowdy drinkers coming out of a nearby pub, either to stand around together in a group and have a smoke, or to go home. Sometimes there would be loud continuous barking from somewhere, or cars would drive past with music blaring.

Chi did see a disturbingly intimate scene. One evening, she heard a woman cry out, "Don't!" from Stella's building. She saw the woman pull the curtains apart and look out of a window in the floor above Stella's. It was as if she was searching for someone to come and save her. A man stood behind her. The woman turned to face him, and he put his hands around her throat. The woman didn't make a sound. After a couple of seconds, he released his grip and shouted something at her. Then he looked out from the window. He looked down and noticing Chi he paused, then roughly tugged the curtains shut. *That was no ordinary look he gave me*, she thought.

One night, she saw Miss Phelps come out of the building with Charlie. *It would be more fun if she lowered him down in a basket, like in the film,* she thought. Miss Phelps walked him to a communal grassy patch outside the apartment block. As Charlie concentrated hard on emptying his bowels, someone opened a ground floor window and shouted out, "Dirty dog, not outside my window, take him somewhere else." Then they threw a bucket of water out of the window at Charlie. "Stop that. You don't know the meaning of the word neighbours," Miss Phelps called back. "Neighbours like each other and talk to each other instead of hurling insults." The ground floor window shut.

Chi regularly saw Ian and Stella together and would watch them go into the apartment block. Shortly after,

Stella's living room light would come on and Chi would see her take her coat off and stand talking to Ian. Then the bedroom light would come on and Chi would see them both embrace near the bedroom window. Stella would look out to the street below, as if she knew that Chi was watching, and then draw the curtains. Ian would leave for home much later.

Chi told Kate what she had seen. "I know it's my job, but it makes me think of *Rear Window*. I can't help feeling like a voyeur, watching others in their private worlds without their knowledge or consent."

"What I don't understand in that film is why Jeff is playing hard to get with Lisa who is practically throwing herself at him. Grace Kelly is a beauty, and James Stewart isn't even able-bodied."

"Lisa said that Jeff was seeing things that he shouldn't and called it a disease."

"A peeping Tom? I don't think there's a similar name for a woman since women don't peep. Peeping Thomasina doesn't sound right. Keyhole Kate from *Beano* is the best I can do."

"But is it okay to spy on Ian and Stella and their neighbours like this?"

"Don't forget that Lisa joined in the spirit of Jeff's 'window shopping' eventually and helped to solve the murder. You're well paid, it's not illegal, and it's our job, it's what we do."

Chi followed Ian and Stella when they were together. She stood in the cold outside restaurants and bars, her face pressed up against the glass to get a look at them, as they drank and dined in the warmth inside, holding hands, kissing across tables, and whispering in each other's ears. Chi pretended that she was vaping or on her phone, in order not to look out of place and attract attention.

On Christmas Eve, Chi watched Ian and Stella sit together across the corner of a table. Ian leant towards Stella, whispered in her ear, and then kissed her drunkenly. She smiled and they got up to go, holding hands. *Kusoyaro* (what a shit), Chi thought, as she pictured Annie and the children at home without him, his presents neatly wrapped under the Christmas tree.

Philip Royal is in his forties. Once a photographer on the *Sunday Splash,* he now depends entirely for his livelihood on the studio in his flat where he takes glamour photographs of eager young models who wish to build a portfolio for their agents.

Good at taking teasing and suggestive pictures, Philip no longer works for the newspaper. His downfall and sacking had been sudden. Sophie, a model, was posing for a full-page topless picture for the next edition. The session started well enough, and Sophie was giving Philip cheesy grins. Uninvited, he walked over and tweaked both her nipples, claiming that he needed to make them hard for a sexier picture. Sophie, who had already suffered at the hands of other photographers, walked off the shoot. She complained to her agent who told her to "get over it." Then she told her boyfriend who said that he would "kill him." Finally, she told her dad, worried about what the boyfriend would do, and he insisted that she report the matter to the police.

It wasn't the first time that Philip had taken liberties with a model and because of his past record this latest assault landed him in prison for a short spell. To add to his woes, the editor of the *Sunday Splash* promptly dismissed him for behaviour in breach of his contract and for bringing the newspaper into disrepute.

Now recently released, Philip was in the bedding department of a large store in London's Oxford Street, buying pillows for his flat. Tessa, the shop assistant, was helping Philip choose. She wore a tightly fitting pencil skirt as part of a smart grey suit. "These," she explained, holding up a pillow, "are made from Hungarian down. Down is a layer of fine feathers found under the tougher exterior feathers. Young birds are clad only in down. The Hungarian down is from young birds which are still alive. The birds are not killed, unlike in China, where most down comes from. There, the down is taken from older birds which have been killed for their meat."

Tessa turned her back on Philip and stretched to replace the pillow on its shelf and select another type.

"Young birds, I like the sound of that, I'll take them."

It was early January when Annie was back in Kate's flat, summoned by a brief telephone call. She looked at Kate and Chi and read the concern on their faces.

"Basically, he's infatuated with her," Kate summarised. "We've been tailing him for four weeks now. He meets her and goes to her flat daily and their time in public is spent talking intimately or locked in an embrace. There's no doubt that you should be giving him a piece of your mind."

"Maybe it's just sex?" Annie asked hopefully.

Chi put her straight: "It's not what we call 'pillow business' in Japan. He is not meeting her discreetly, once or twice a month after lunch, in a hotel where she rewards his high spending on her with sexual favours. Instead, their behaviour is bold and without shame. He is obsessed with her, and she has him firmly in her clutches."

"But who is she?" Annie asked desperately.

"She lives in Vauxhall, a block away from the river. She's tallish, dark hair. At night-time I could mistake her for you. Just a younger version, with more bare flesh. Her name's Stella Godley. She works as an escort for Ray Millan. He's big time. She's a chancer and she'll take what she can. She's clever and a survivor. In short, she's a formidable opponent. It's not likely to be free love as Stella doesn't come cheap."

Kate looked at Annie's sad face. "Is there anyone you can confide in, who may be able to support you? A relative or someone at your work?"

"There's his brother Dave. We've always been friends, but he's just got over his own problems. I don't want to trouble him with mine. I'll think about it. Thanks for caring."

Annie was given a neat file documenting in writing and pictures when Chi had seen Ian and Stella together, times, places, what they were doing and how much fun they were having.

When Annie got home, she locked herself in the bathroom and read Kate's report. "I could kill him," she said aloud, "the lying, cheating, bastard. And as for that trollop, I can't believe she did that to me. No excuses, she's a selfish bitch, and she's not getting away with it."

The next day, after their self-defence class, Martina caught up with Annie in the gym café. "You're looking serious, what are you reading?" She looked over Annie's shoulder at the open page.

Have you ever thought of killing your cheating partner? If so, I recommend poison. But would you know which one to use and in what quantity to be effective but avoid suspicion? Agatha Christie used at least fourteen different poisons to murder her victims. A kind horticulturalist in Kew Gardens could help you to identify gelsemium elegans, a rare Chinese flowering plant, nicknamed 'heartbreak grass' because it can trigger a cardiac arrest if ingested. Or a walk in the woods could provide you with amanita phalloides, the so-called death cap mushroom which looks like the edible variety. As little as a half of their pale green cap is enough to kill. Mushroom soup anyone?

"Hey, girls, Annie's going to poison someone," she called to the others. "The book is called *The Final Curtain*."

"It's like an instruction manual for someone who wants to bump off a love rat," Annie explained to them all.

"'The push' where he falls from a height is surely quicker, and more satisfying," Martina said. "And no telltale evidence left behind."

"No, I'd choose poison, least messy, apart from the occasional vomit. A woman pushing a man who is bigger than her, risks him grabbing hold of her and taking her down with him. He might even manage to fight her off," Annie replied.

"Or there could be an eyewitness," Martina added.

"In which case you say that you slipped and accidentally pushed him over," another gym buddy volunteered helpfully.

"How can we cash in on him?" Victor asked. "That public school smug clever-dick lawyer." He and Stella were back in The Fastidious Fox, drinking together. "He could well be the goose that lays the golden eggs for us."

"Oh, very Aesop's fables. He's comprehensive school, not that it makes any difference. Anyway, he's already paying my bills and buying me things."

"No, not like that, big money. That house of his must be worth a couple of million. Imagine what we could get in exchange for naughty pictures of you and Ian, your lovely bodies in various positions, cavorting on that leather sofa you told me about. Well, your lovely body, he's no Adonis."

"Are you serious?" Stella asked, after a long pause.

Victor mocked the surprised look on Stella's face.

"Your greed will end badly one day," Stella continued. "It's not even a class thing: working class lad takes from entitled solicitor. You grew up in a detached house with a garden."

"You exploit wealthy gullible men, and work for a crime baron," Victor replied. "What's the difference between that and a bit of sextortion? You could make a sex tape together and we could use it."

"He wouldn't agree. I suggested a sex tape to him once, but he's too self-conscious with his boxers off. He'd insist on hiding his face. It would be a disaster."

"Is there somewhere which overlooks your lovely sofa? I can take some pictures and a video."

"I've a balcony outside my living room."

"I'd enjoy watching you perform with someone else. I'm due to start my shift. We'll talk tomorrow." He eased himself off the bar stool and left.

Sitting in his car, Victor took a call from a colleague. "That Bryan Western," the man said, "he's still missing. Do you know what has happened to him? I'm getting a bit nervous about his next move."

"It's dealt with. He's history. He was stupid for a former cop."

5

Fightback

"You man stealer, whore." Annie waved her arms and shouted as Stella approached. She had been waiting for her outside the entrance doors to Stella's apartment block.

"Are you addressing me? Who are you? Why are you screaming at me?"

"I'm his wife. How can you do it, you bitch?"

"His wife? Does he have a name?"

"He's Ian, you know what you're doing. You're having an affair. Why are you playing games with me?"

"I wouldn't call it an affair, it's more like an arrangement. He pays me, I take my clothes off and *voila*, result. Now clear off."

"That's disgusting. You're disgusting, you're a prostitute. What I mean, you slut, is how can you destroy a marriage and a family?" Annie burst into floods of tears.

For Annie it was not going to plan. Her intention was that Stella would be humiliated in front of the neighbours. But the street was empty and not a curtain twitched as she confronted her. Annie wiped the mascara that was running down her face.

"Come inside and calm down," Stella said, opening the entrance door. "You're only making a fool of yourself out here. We can sort this out."

Briefly distracted by the stylish stained glass front doors, she tamely followed Stella up the stairs to the flat and sat on the sofa, facing her.

"Let's get something straight, I didn't force him. Men can say no. They do have brains you know. To be quite honest, he didn't even hesitate. I only had to smile at him, and it was like watching an alcoholic reach for the whisky bottle. I'll ignore that you called me a prostitute. I take his money, provide him with sex and company and try to make him happy. Just like you, only I don't cook for him or do his laundry."

"How long has this been going on?"

"Since the summer."

"I'm going to have it out with him and really make him suffer," Annie said bitterly.

Stella had to think quickly about this. She hadn't expected Annie to find out about her and Ian. It would blow her and Victor's plans out of the water if Annie told Ian what she knew.

"You want to know the truth?" Stella said, thinking quickly. "Ian has pursued me relentlessly from the start. I knew that he was married, with children, but lots of my clients are married, and dating me helps the relationship with their partner. Puts a bit of spice back into it."

Stella stopped as Annie looked distracted. "What?"

"I wondered why he's been suggesting that we try new positions. I thought it was probably from his watching porn."

"I was beginning to feel a bit suffocated by him," Stella continued, unfazed by Annie's comment. "When he's drunk, he tells me how he loves me, and that he wants to live with me. Rest assured, that last one's not on the cards. And his declarations of love: I'm sure it's only the testosterone and drink speaking."

Normally, Annie would rush to Ian's defence, but this time she listened in silence as Stella described how she and Ian were spending their time together. "What, you did it on this sofa," Annie shrieked, and jumped up as if she could catch a disease from sitting there. She felt sickened by what she heard. "I feel utterly betrayed. It's as if I have never really known him. Our life together must amount to nothing in his eyes. I can't bear to spend another night under the same roof. He disgusts me."

"If you tell him to leave, where will he go? He can't stay here."

"I don't know. His brother Dave's. I don't care."

"Have you got any money?"

"I've got my job, but everything else is in his name."

"Would he agree to leave you in the house, give you custody of the children and support you financially?"

"Not without a fight. He's a lawyer so he knows what to do. He's going to be a judge and will soon have influential friends. Annie get your gun."

"Whoa there. You don't need to kill him."

"No, I'm not planning to shoot him. Did just cross my mind though. What would I have done if I had caught you both together *in flagrante*? My girlfriends and I used to belt out that Brandy Clark song *Stripes* about a woman who was cheated on and her itchy trigger finger.

"Do you know the 1950s musical *Annie Get Your Gun*? My parents loved it. I'm sure that I was named after it. But he doesn't deserve a quick kill. And I'm not a sharpshooter like Annie Oakley. I'd miss."

"I have a much better idea: blackmail," Stella chipped in. "A long, lingering, and embarrassing punishment for him with rewards for us. You turn the tables; it's what he deserves. You're a different woman now that your eyes are open. You're looking after number one. Go home and act normally. We can plan it together and split the money. Then you kick him out and divorce him. We get sexy pictures of me and Ian on the sofa here and throw in a video. Ian's a very eager lover. I can tell him to wear the Judge Dredd t-shirt I bought him. That will give it a judicial theme and add to his fear when we threaten to show it all to his friends, work colleagues and bosses. Who can we get to take the pictures?"

Annie sat in silence for a moment, turning the idea over in her head. *I've never seen Ian having sex with someone else. I've not even imagined it. I'm not sure that I could watch, sounds so indecent. And I'd be watching Stella having sex as well. Grow up Annie. Girl power, stop being a helpless damsel in distress.*

"I'll do it. I'm going to crush him. He'll be sorry that he ever met me. It's war. And I'm a good photographer."

"You can stand on the balcony outside the living room window. I'll make sure that a bit of the blind is pulled to one side so that you can see in. Lover boy will be too busy looking at me to notice. I'll have to disguise my voice on the phone to demand the payoff. I'm not good at amateur dramatics though."

"I'll do that, make the calls. I'll enjoy getting my own back," Annie said spiritedly. "I can do a good South African accent after a few drinks. I'll think of some things to say which will really scare him. But can I call him from your flat? Just your presence there will give me courage."

"How much is he worth?"

"He's about to leave his firm. The other partners must buy his share of the office building from him. They've had a valuation, and he reckons that they'll pay him at least £350,000."

"Well, that's a good start for our first demand, a taster with more to come."

"Then there's his partnership capital account, that's the profit share that he's not taken out yet. And he owns a flat that he rents out. He can raise money by increasing the mortgage on it or selling up. There's also a savings account, but I don't know how much is left."

"Well, you're a real cracker, I'm impressed, so cool and practical about it. It'll have to be cash, so that the payments can't be traced. I wouldn't recognise a crypto coin if one jumped up and bit me."

"He'll have to tell his partners that he needs to draw that money now. But will the bank give him all that cash?"

"That's his problem."

Annie was too drunk to drive home. Stella put her in the spare room after Annie had messaged Ian to say that she was staying with a friend. As Annie lay in a strange bed, she received a phone call from Kate.

"Sorry to call you late, I was a bit worried about how you're coping. Have you managed to come to terms yet with what we told you? For your mental health's sake, you have to find a way of dealing with it."

"I have."

"Oh, good. Have you talked to someone?"

"I have."

"Who, if you don't mind my asking? Only, I know a good counsellor if you haven't found one."

"I talked to Stella."

"Oh, I didn't expect that."

"We're both dealing with it. I'm taking his money, as reparation."

"What, have you spoken to Ian?"

"No."

"Well, don't do anything illegal."

"It's better than killing him."

"Annie, have you been drinking? Only you sound a bit different from usual."

"Tomorrow, I start kicking his arse."

The next day, Stella started to panic when she thought about what she was getting herself into. The fact that she liked Annie was making it more difficult to double-cross her. She needed something to help her keep calm. She scrolled down her contacts list and made an order.

You all right, can you meet me?
Yeah, what you after?
I want four twenty white. Can you do me the deal?
Whereabouts are ya?
What about you come to outside the City Lofts?
Fuck, it's hot around there now. I'm not bait.
Well, could you meet me in the car park of The Fox?

How much cash you got on you now?

You think I'm stupid. I'm not telling you that. It's enough. I'm ready to go.

Shortly afterwards, Stella got into the back seat of a matt black VW Golf that had pulled into the pub car park. She didn't know the three young men inside. She hadn't dealt with any of them before.

"Who's in charge, who's the dude?" she asked.

The driver spoke. "It was me you was messaging on the phone."

"Here you are, usual rate," Stella said, passing him the money.

"Thanks, babe, nice doing business with you."

"Maybe you and me could do some other kind of business together," the rear seat passenger said, looking at Stella.

"Marlon there's got an awesome tool. Show it to her, Marlon," the front seat passenger said jokingly.

Stella looked down as Marlon stroked something in his lap. It was a small handgun.

"She's sweet," Marlon said, referring to the gun as if it was his pet. "Here feel the trigger. It's not loaded. It won't bite."

He pushed the gun towards Stella. She knew that they were messing with her. She held the gun briefly, to pretend to them that she was not scared, and passed it straight back to him.

"Boys, just give me my whites," Stella said impatiently.

She didn't want any trouble with them. They were members of the notorious Fox Hall Mercenaries gang, the FHM, who controlled the drugs supply in the Vauxhall area.

"Bet the babe's hot in bed," the front seat passenger said, turning his head and looking at Marlon. "Unlike your sister."

"Fuck off, Carl, don't you disrespect my sister," Marlon replied angrily.

"He already has," the driver said, looking at Carl. "Here, you can watch the video, don't look like she's enjoying it though, waaa." The driver held up his phone. Stella saw pictures of two young people on an unmade bed, both naked below the waist. It showed Carl, grinning and facing the screen whilst holding a phone in his outstretched arm to make the recording. Then it focused briefly on the girl's anguished face.

"Fuck you," Marlon screamed as he recognised his sister.

"Cool it, Marlon," the driver said, "the babe's watching." He hurriedly passed the wraps to Stella.

There was a loud bang and the front seat passenger slumped down as a bullet passed through the back of his seat. Stella gasped.

"She shot him," Marlon shouted, dropping the gun on the car floor.

"He did!" Stella screamed and bolted out of the car.

Stella ran towards the road, where she hoped to find safety.

She turned her head and saw them dump Carl's body unceremoniously on the ground.

Tyres screeched as the VW Golf took off, narrowly missing Stella at the car park exit. Were they driving *at* her? she asked herself in a panic. She could hear police sirens. She didn't want to ditch the wraps that she had bought, so she ducked inside a café and tried to look calm. She sat at a table away from the window and slid them under a pile of out-of-date magazines.

Her brain was racing about what had just happened. *If they catch him, Marlon will try to pin the blame on me for the shooting. How do I prove that it wasn't me if the others say that it was? If they find the gun, my DNA is on it. I had no motive, but they'll say it was an accident and I'll be charged with manslaughter.*

The police cars raced past the café and turned into the side road leading to The Fastidious Fox. Not long afterwards an ambulance followed. Stella ordered a cup of coffee and sat drinking it quietly.

A uniformed officer came into the café. "There's been a shooting at the back of The Fox," he said. "Did anyone hear or see anything suspicious?" Stella looked down and kept her shaking hands underneath the table. The other diners remained silent.

"Well, if you remember anything, just speak to one of the officers guarding the scene."

When the officer had left, the woman behind the counter spoke to her customers. "You can bet it's that gang, the FHM. You know, the Fox Hall Mercenaries. This area's not safe anymore. They'll shoot you as soon as look at you, but nobody dares to stand up to them. I had one in here. He paid for his breakfast with a bent twenty-pound note. I took it and gave him change for a tenner." Everyone laughed.

Stella retrieved the wraps from under the magazines and left. She could see the blue and white chequered police tape, across the car park entrance.

Ian and Stella had a late dinner together in their favourite restaurant. Stella had drunk more than usual, trying to relax after the earlier incident at The Fastidious Fox and to psych herself up for the play-acting required of her later that evening. She kept topping up Ian's wine glass to get him in a pliable mood and so that he wouldn't notice Annie, already in place on the balcony of her flat.

"Keep up with me," she said to Ian, "so that I don't feel so bad about how much I'm drinking."

As they walked back to her apartment Ian bought a bottle of superior quality fizz, at Stella's request. He was in the living room, pouring the champagne into two glasses, when Stella appeared from the bedroom naked. Ian took one look at her and put the champagne glasses down in a hurry. Without speaking, Stella pushed him onto the leather sofa. She took off his glasses and undressed him. He couldn't keep his eyes off her and enjoyed her taking the dominant role.

"Put this on," she said, pulling the t-shirt emblazoned with *Judge Dredd I am the Law* over his head.

"We can turn the lights off, Dredd has bionic eyes and 20/20-night vision," Ian joked.

"Leave the lights on, I want you to look at me."

"I've always wanted to be police, judge, jury and executioner," he said, laughing.

Stella turned on her music to hide any noise from Annie.

"*I am The Law* by Anthrax, this has a good tempo for what we're going to do," she said.

Annie had to put her hand over her mouth to stifle a laugh as she watched Stella singing aloud to the lyrics about Judge Dredd, while she pumped away on top of Ian, writhing around as if she was riding a bucking bronco. Ian looked totally consumed by her and would not have noticed if Annie had been standing in the room next to them.

First Stella was on top, then Ian was on top, then Stella was on her hands and knees, then they were just a tangle of bodies. Whichever way up they were Stella was the star of the show and Annie was not disappointed by Stella's performance. Watching Stella as she moved this way and that, under, over and around Ian, Annie forgot her embarrassment at watching him perform with another woman. The sex romps were punctuated by the occasional sound of sweaty skin sticking to the leather sofa.

Ian climaxed with a long-drawn-out agonising moan. Annie had been embarrassed at school by a group of girls playing a male orgasm audio on one of their phones under a desk whilst she had her back to them in the classroom. Ian's utterances sounded remarkably similar. Stella the actor, not wishing to be outdone, erupted in "fuck, oh fuck" followed by a guttural scream. It was fake of course and signified to Annie that this was the end of the show.

Weeks earlier, a smart white embossed envelope had arrived at Ian's home, marked *Private and Confidential* with a black inscription *Justice Department*. As Ian had opened it, he had guessed correctly what the letter inside would say. It confirmed that all the time he had spent, in court and out oiling the wheels of the criminal justice system, had paid off. He was to leave his firm and be appointed a judge.

Ian broke out into a sweat every time he remembered his interview with the selection panel. It was all going swimmingly until the pinch-faced lay member of the panel spoke. "Mr. Blake, what are your values? What is your belief system?" she asked, looking at him intently, trying to trip him up no doubt.

Ian's head went into a spin. He was not religious and had never asked himself this question. Desperate to answer her, he could only think of sounding wholesome: "I go to bed at 10pm; I don't drink alcohol; I meditate; and I enjoy wild swimming, ice baths, growing vegetables in my allotment and trips to the local garden centre." None of which was true.

The other panel members visibly relaxed and smiled. "Well, that's all right then," the chairperson said kindly. "Remind me to ask you later about problems with my rhubarb."

At home, a new email arrived in his in-box. It was from an address that he did not recognise. The subject line said *surprise, surprise, you have been a dreddfully naughty boy!* There were attachments which Ian opened gingerly. To his horror, they were close-up pictures and a video of him and Stella having wild and energetic sex in various positions. He recognised Stella's living room. It didn't take long for him to work out that they had been taken from the balcony. Someone must have been out there, watching them.

Later that day he received a telephone call. The woman had a strong South African accent, and it was difficult to understand everything she said. "We want £350,000. If you don't pay, we will send the pictures and video of you and your tart to your wife and the newspapers, post them on social media and tag all your friends and work colleagues. We will recommend to the Justice Department that they watch you on YouTube, dressed as Judge Dredd. Oh, and don't think of going to the police. You have three days to raise the money. We will send you instructions about how to pay."

"Who are you?" Ian asked desperately. But the woman hung up.

Stella had been distant with Ian for more than a week. That didn't stop him from calling her and leaving messages about what had happened.

"I've got nothing against South Africans," he said, "but it was hard to understand everything that she said. She sounded a bit drunk."

Stella called him and said that she was frightened, having received similar pictures and a phone call in which a woman with a South African accent told her that she was to collect the money from him in three days' time, otherwise she would have acid thrown in her face and her career would be ruined.

"Ian, I'm really scared," Stella said, "you've got to do what they say."

Ian went to Stella's apartment later that day.

"I've had another call," Stella said. "It's the same woman. You've got to use unmarked notes and put them in an overnight bag. Then I must take it to the Serpentine Café in Hyde Park on Wednesday at noon. Someone will be watching and will phone me with further instructions. You must not go with me."

"I won't pay a penny," Ian said. "I will tell Annie about us and go to the police."

"That will cost us both much more," Stella replied sharply.

Ian was desperate for someone to confide in. He could only think of his younger brother David.

"Dave, I need to talk to you."

"Be quick, I'm at work."

"Not on the phone, I need to talk to you properly. It's important."

"What have I done wrong, now?"

"Nothing, not you, it's me. Can we meet?"

"OK, I'm working in a house in Kennington. There's nobody else here. I'll text you the address."

Later, David pulled a dust sheet off the living room sofa, and they sat down next to each other.

"I'm in a spot of bother."

"Go on."

"I've been seeing a woman."

"Not Annie then."

"You won't tell her."

"Why would I do that?"

"Well, she's always had a soft spot for you."

"You don't deserve her. So, who is this new woman?"

"Stella, she's like a fatal attraction."

"What, she's obsessed with you? Unlikely."

"No, the other way around."

"So, what's the problem?"

"Someone's threatening me, us."

"How?"

"If I don't pay, they've got photos, and a video. You know, the embarrassing sort."

"You idiot. Didn't know you had it in you. Just don't show them to me."

"You don't need to see them. What should I do?"

"Go to the police."

"They said not to."

"They would. Anyway, why are you asking me? Do you even remember, Ian, how you didn't care when I was having a tough time? Fat lot of good you were to me then. At least Annie tried to help me. Now go, I've got work to do."

6

Contract Killer

Ian was at Union Street Police Station advising Frederick Bundy, a troubled man who had wanted to get revenge on his ex-partner. Frederick had drunkenly knocked on his ex's neighbour's door by mistake. When nobody answered, he had kicked the door open, caused some damage and left behind a photograph of himself to remind her of him. It didn't take long for the police to identify him.

Ian found Victor in his office, feet up on the desk.

"I need your advice. Can I talk to you off the record, man to man?"

"Bit rich, you coming to me for advice. My advice is stop helping your scumbag clients. But I hear that you'll soon be banging them up instead."

"I know that we don't always agree with each other's methods. That's because we're on opposite sides," Ian said, to appease Victor.

"I nick bad people, and for some crazy reason the government pays you to get them off. Is that what you mean? Go and ask Inspector Cranshaw for advice, he's a wet liberal like you. Or that brother of yours, David, at least he's got a proper job."

"I don't think Cranshaw would approve of my situation, and Dave's no use."

"So, why me? You know I don't like you."

"I thought you wouldn't judge me."

"Depends on what you've done."

"I'm being blackmailed."

Victor gave a low whistle of surprise. "So, Mr high and mighty has been a bad boy. Now this gets interesting. Okay, go on."

"I thought that you would know what to do. I've been having an affair with Stella Godley. They want £350,000 in cash by Wednesday. If I don't pay up and go to the police they will ruin my life, my wife's, and hers."

"I am the police, or had you forgotten?"

"I've just been appointed a judge. I'm a family man with a reputation to keep. This is a nightmare."

Ian told Victor everything that had happened.

"Show me the pictures. So, I can see how serious this is."

Ian had the pictures and video on his phone, and he handed it to Victor. Victor took his time flicking through and studying them. He gave a grunt of appreciation. "They're good. She's hot, not sure about you though. You need to go the gym, lose a bit of weight. What's this Judge Dredd look? Judge Dudd more like."

"For God's sake, take it seriously, it's a tragedy for me."

"Don't report it. This place is like a sieve. Once the plods know that you're involved, they'll be on the phone to the press within minutes. Any chance of keeping this out of the newspapers or investigating this properly will be scuppered. The South African will get wind and who knows what she'll do. We can't give Stella 'round-the-clock protection."

Ian told Victor about the caller's instructions to Stella.

"I'll manage it myself for ten per cent," Victor said. "How can you raise the cash?"

"I can tell my partners that I need my departure money urgently."

"I'll put a tracking device in the overnight bag," Victor said. "Then you tell Stella to do exactly as the South African says. I'll go in with hired muscle and get the money back as well as the pictures and the video."

Ian returned to Frederick. As a protest at being held in custody, he had urinated against the cell door and when woman police officer Pressel had gone to check on him, exposed himself to her.

Ian apologised to everyone on Frederick's behalf. "It's the combination of the alcohol and the drugs. He's not feeling himself today."

"That's not what Pressel said," PC Clark replied, laughing.

Victor made a phone call to Stella. "That was a clever move, getting Annie to take the photographs and make the calls. The more we implicate her, the better we can control her.

"On another subject," Victor continued, "why are you so interested in that Fox shooting? We found the car that the young man was shot in, burnt out of course. Didn't find the gun. They will have taken that with them, need to return it to whoever lent it to them. Our intelligence shows the car was being used by the FHM for drug dealing. It looks like a case of gang members falling out with each other. You don't know anything about what happened do you? Hope not, for your sake."

Ian was back at Victor's office on the Thursday. It was the day after Stella's visit to Hyde Park with the money. Victor told him to wait outside.

Victor called Stella again. "About that FHM murder since you're so interested. An informant has told us that there were three men in the car, doing a drug deal with a woman. He gave us the name of a suspect, and we arrested a Marlon Walters.

"He won't admit that he was there. We tried to bluff him, saying that we'd spoken to the woman, and she would be able to identify him. He said, 'go on then, where is she?' We searched Walters' bedroom; he lives with his granny, poor soul. He's an FHM soldier with form for possessing a knife, grievous bodily harm, and robbery. He's a nasty piece of work. Anyway, we didn't have enough to hold him, so he's been released under investigation. If you know something that you're not telling me, now's your chance. Whoever that woman is, she needs protection."

Victor called Ian into his office.

"I tried to call you last night to find out what happened. You didn't get back to me," Ian said. "I'm panicking."

"I've got other fish to fry, besides yours. I don't know where your money is because the tracker stopped working. It may be defective; it's been in the equipment store for some time."

"The South African woman, I'm sure it's Stella. The same woman called me this morning for more money. She threatened Stella with an 'acid facial', that's what she called it. Then I heard a dog barking and her neighbour's voice, Miss Phelps, in the background. Dog must have been out on the landing. The South African woman said, 'oh fuck', and hung up."

Victor was taken aback. It took him seconds to regain his composure. "I did have my suspicions, when she said that you had to give the money to her to deliver."

"Added to that," Ian said, "there's no way out onto the balcony where the photographs were taken from, except through her living room. Then there's how she arranged that we would have sex on the sofa, in front of the balcony window whilst she had the lights on and music, to hide the sound of someone moving about. We usually go into her bedroom. That leather sofa can be cold on naked flesh this time of the year. What do I do? She's still got the pictures and my £350,000 and she'll be back for more."

"In my experience," Victor replied, "there's only one way to get people like Stella off your back for good. You need to take her out."

"What do you mean, take her out? Take her out where?"

"Finish her."

"What do mean finish? I'm not sure that I follow." Ian hoped that he had misunderstood Victor.

"Eliminate her, neutralise her. It's the only way that you'll know for certain that she won't come back, pursuing you again. She's most likely working in league with others, an organised crime gang. You've got to show them that you won't be messed with. You want your money and pictures back, don't you? They'll be keeping their distance from her now, whilst they assess whether she's under suspicion. She hasn't had time to move the money, to wash it."

Ian swallowed loudly. "I don't know who could do it, take her out, or how it's done. I might be caught. This conversation alone is conspiracy to murder."

"Only the stupid ones get caught. All it needs is a plan."

"What sort of a plan? I've never planned to kill someone."

"I'll show you what else it needs." Victor pointed out of his office window, towards Southwark Bridge. "A bit of guts. See that church over there? Can you read what's written in stone just below the roof? At times like this it inspires me."

Ian joined Victor at the window. It read *all may take if they dare.*

"I dare, you see, and so I take," Victor told him. "So should you."

"You're not reading it properly," Ian replied. "Look at the rest of the creed: *all may take if they dare lead a glorious life and death*. It means you must be worthy to get your reward."

"Anyway, you need a contract killer," Victor said, ignoring Ian.

"Oh, and they advertise their services, do they?"

"No need for sarcasm, I'm trying to help you. And don't get stressed, it'll make people suspicious. I'll make some enquiries if you agree."

"I'm tempted."

"I'm not surprised. Stella's hot and Adam couldn't resist taking a bite."

"No, I mean I'm tempted to agree."

Ian quizzed Victor briefly the next morning. "You said you'd find someone, have you got a name and phone number yet?"

"You need someone who is cheap but reliable. He's in Amsterdam, Pieter Jansen: he comes over, does the job and straight back to the Netherlands."

"So, how do I contact him?"

"You must go over and meet him. Pay upfront in cash and tell him what you want. He works at the De Vries bookshop as a cover. He'll charge you £15,000."

"If I go to Amsterdam, how do I know he'll be there and that he'll see me?"

"Tell me when you're travelling, and I'll make sure of it."

"Why can't I just speak to him on the phone. Or hold a zoom conference meeting, or message him?"

"He's old school. He doesn't know you and will need to assess you. He'll take you to a bar, ask you some questions, and make a deal over some beers if he thinks that you are trustworthy and won't blab about him afterwards. He needs cash so the transaction can't be traced, and he needs it up front to hire a gun."

Stella sat with Victor in the back room of The Fastidious Fox. "You are up to something bad," she said. "I know that cold smile. What are you planning? Just don't kill our golden goose."

"We could 'take out' Annie and keep her share of the money. Then make it look like her body is yours and claim on a fat life insurance policy on you that I will obtain. I'd have to insure both of us, so it looks less suspicious."

"Are you serious? You'd never carry it off, surely. Would you really go that far with Annie?"

"You like to think you're hard, Stella. Your face is a give-away: it's gone a whiter shade of pale. That was my parents' song, Procul Harem 1967. Never did understand the words though. I know 'trip the light fantastic' but what's a 'light fandango'?

"Dad told me what he and Margaret got up to during the Summer of Love 1967 in the toilets of a club in Soho. They went there on his Lambretta motor scooter to see them play."

"You always change the subject, Victor, when the talk gets awkward."

"In answer to your question, sometimes it's necessary."

"You're poisonous and mad. Would they even pay out if the person named in the policy was murdered, especially so soon after the policy started?"

"They won't pay anyone who is found to have been involved in committing the murder. But we won't get caught, so they'll have to pay. We may just need to wait for the money until the dust settles on their investigation. Just think what we could do with the millions of insurance money and Ian's £350,000 to top it up. No more of you having to compete with younger models who are willing to do things that you draw the line at.

"We could buy a beachside bar, near to my apartment in Marbella. You would be your own boss, with me as a silent partner. Let's face it, nobody's going to miss you. Your poor parents are both in the ground; you have no siblings; and your uncle Ted lives in Australia and never contacts you. The fact that there's no one close to you couldn't be better for us, and I'm not being ironic."

"If you don't mind, in my mid-thirties I'm in my sexual prime. Ask any of my clients. And those 'younger models' you spoke of are too coarse and uneducated for most men's tastes. They don't prep with *Finance Weekly* so that they can make intelligent conversation.

"Anyway, there's a problem. I've got a police record still from a deception case. I never asked for the data to be removed when my conviction was overturned. DNA from Annie's body would come up as a match to me."

"Okay, I'd overlooked that. Leave it to me. Another reason for us to do this, that Fox murder. If that was you in the car, it's just a matter of whether my lot or the FHM get to you first."

"Look, Victor, I know what you're capable of. They never found that Bryan Western, last seen with your ex-Janice eating lunch at a riverside pub near London Bridge. What did she know? Was he really going to expose you? Is that what you have in mind for Annie, push her in the river?"

"Western should have known better than to meddle. He fancied a dip. He just hadn't reckoned on the current and the cold water."

"And where is Janice? I'm told that she went off radar a few days after Western disappeared. I know what you're saying, but honestly, Victor, I don't know if I can do this."

"It's nothing personal about Annie, just a good plan. Where's the money Ian's paid so far?"

"It's at my apartment, Annie keeps pestering me for her share."

"I've sent Ian to see Pieter, in Amsterdam."

"That Pieter, the one who put on the murder mystery

for the C15 works outing to Amsterdam? Why would you send Ian to him?"

"So, Ian can give him £15,000 and Pieter can share it with us. When he's finished with Pieter and lost his money, he'll be willing to pay me a lot more to sort it for him."

"It's one scam after another with you."

"And I know someone we could use: Yuri Prokonova, a Russian who works for me and for nightclub security. He's a bit of a rogue, but dependable enough. He needs the money and owes me for not reporting him and his false documents to Immigration Enforcement. He's an illegal.

"I also know where we could do it. That pervert Philip Royal, whom you find it amusing to wind up in The Fox. His flat, near the river at Tower Bridge. He's on the first floor of one of those swanky converted warehouses, all industrial chic. We can get Yuri in there with Annie, and make it look like a sex game with Philip gone wrong. My having put him away for the sex assault on a model means that if Annie's found on Philip's bed, with his criminal record we won't go looking for anyone else. I'll do a check, see where any cameras are. Ian defended him last time, so Philip's bound to ask for him again. It'll be a real inside job."

"Poor Phil, he's already a sad loser."

"It might not be too bad for him. If Ian does his job properly, Philip could be done for manslaughter rather than murder. He might even get a suspended sentence."

"Phil knows what I look like. If there's a trial, he'll see in the crime scene pictures that the body's not me."

"He's not done any glamour shoots with you. He only knows your face, not your body and he doesn't know

Annie. You're about the same height and build as she is. If I can hide her face in the pictures, she could pass for you. Get your hair cut the same length and style as hers. He won't be able to tell the difference. I can give you a picture of her to show the hairdresser. And he may always accept the inevitable and plead guilty to manslaughter."

"I still don't know. It's so risky. Anyway, I like Annie. She's never harmed anyone. And she's got spirit. You make it sound so ordinary. Like putting out the rubbish."

"Oh, look at your face. Toughen up, don't go all soft and sentimental on me. This is just business. Over two hundred people die each day in London, it's nothing unusual. We are all mortal. I'll have that engraved on my tombstone."

"That is such a stupid thing to say, about how we all die. I do wonder about you mentally, Victor."

"You're a hypocrite, Stella. Ever taken a long look at yourself? You play with men like a cat plays with mice."

"Well, I'm not saying yes, *yet*. But if I did, how would we get her in there?"

"We tell her that Yuri is a friend of yours who is holding her money, and that she needs to go to his address to recover it. Just before she is due to meet him, you make a move on Philip in The Fox, get him drunk and drugged up on something, take his keys and give them to me. I'll let Yuri into the flat whilst you keep Philip occupied. Philip's at the pub most nights."

"When would we do it? If I say yes that is."

"The sooner the better. As soon as Pieter's done with Ian in Amsterdam, Ian will come running to me to sort it, and he'll pay my price. I'll tell him to get me the money so that I can hire Yuri and we're game on."

"Get me a double of something strong, Victor, I need some Dutch courage."

"That's my girl."

"I don't want to go to prison, Victor."

"Most murders go unsolved. And we've got Philip as backup."

Victor phoned Pieter that evening. "Pieter, you like acting. You and your brother were brilliant in that *Find the Murderer* you staged."

"You want another? You boys coming over again?"

"Not quite. I'm sending a friend to see you. He thinks that you're a contract killer."

"You've lost me, Victor."

"You told me that you want to give up working at the bookshop and set up full time putting on these 'whodunits' for tourists. I'm offering cash for you to play the part of a contract killer. But you don't have to kill anyone, just convince my gullible friend that you would. You take his money and share it with me."

"Victor, I don't look or sound like a hit man."

"You're an actor. Use theatrical makeup: put a scar on your face and a fake tattoo on your neck."

"That won't work at close quarters."

"I was joking. Don't shave for a few days, think 'I am a killer' and act hard. And don't mention your cat. Hit men have big dogs."

7

Faking It

Ian was nervous at the start of the Eurostar journey to Amsterdam. As he sat in the vast waiting hall in St Pancras International Station on a Friday evening, he imagined that people were looking at him, and whispering. He was surely the only passenger who was on a mission to hire a killer.

The train increased speed as it began its journey through France, as if it sensed the urgency of his task. He looked out at the neat and tidy villages and small towns, surrounded by countryside, and contrasted them with his messy life.

It was Easter time in the centre of Amsterdam, and he was overwhelmed by the many tourists and the silent bicycles which sped up without warning from behind and threatened to cut him down. How could any confidential business be conducted in the maelstrom of these crowds? It quietened down as he walked further away from the station and found his hotel in a peaceful canal street.

His small room was at the top of very steep stairs. The walls were paper thin, and he could hear the excited conversation of the young couple in the next bedroom. He sat on the single bed and tried to map his personal journey in his mind: from a risk-averse student at university, who would watch over his friends as they experimented with different drugs, to the present madness.

The next day, he waited for Victor to call him to say that he should go to the bookshop. It was after lunch when Victor finally phoned. The De Vries bookshop was in a residential area, just five minutes' walk away, across two bridges. The shop was on the ground floor of a typical tall and narrow 17th century merchant's house. The building tilted slightly, due to the degradation of its timber foundations next to a canal. It had a typical hoist to the attic, and a bell-shaped gable at the front of a steeply pitched roof. At first, Ian moved around the shop awkwardly, pulling books randomly from the shelves to open and browse, trying to look like the other customers. He watched the man behind the counter. Was he Pieter? Did he look like a contract killer or more like a librarian?

"Pieter Jansen?"

"Who's asking?"

"Ian, Victor sent me."

"Yes, I was expecting you," Pieter replied, staring coldly at Ian and curling his lip as he spoke.

In the Union Street Police Station DC Stant and DS Bonetti faced each other across a desk.

"I finally agreed to speak to Bryan, as long as I could remain anonymous," Stant said. We arranged to meet, and he didn't turn up. A long time has passed, and he hasn't phoned or messaged me or returned any of my calls."

"I never took Shadwell's money either," Bonetti replied.

"He would leave it for me in an envelope on my desk, bold as brass. I just gave it back. Made me unpopular. He stopped trying after a while. I was never one of his gang."

"Like you, Carly, I never felt safe speaking out. I wouldn't know who to trust. Who could I talk to in confidence? I'm sure that the place is full of Shadwell's spies. But if we ever find an opportunity to nail him, I'll take it."

Ian waited nervously until Pieter had completed a sale with a customer. "I finish in one hour. I'll meet you at Plezier, the bar on Niewgracht," Pieter snarled at him.

The bar was on a corner next to a bridge, at a crossroads of a canal street and a wider road with tramlines. The exterior was covered with brown glazed tiles, beneath a Heineken sign. He noticed that there were only male customers in Plezier. As Ian waited, sitting at a table in the corner, he tried not to make eye contact with the other drinkers.

Pieter arrived shortly after him.

"How do I know that you are not full of shit?" Pieter asked roughly.

"You can trust me. Victor can vouch for me."

"Victor said that you are new to the rough stuff."

"Not my cup of tea."

"That expression, so polite, so genteel, such an understatement, so English. But your compatriots were so ruthless and violent. You stole Kenyan land to grow tea; turned Chinese people into opium addicts for tea; stole tea plants and seeds from China; and enslaved labourers in India to cultivate tea. Who am I to 'take out', as Victor puts it so delicately? Give me the name and the money."

Ian produced a printout with several pictures of Stella. He had attached details about her to the back.

"She is the one?"

"You can see her in one of the pictures, coming out of the Work-It Gym in Vauxhall, near the Thames in South London. She goes there every Monday, Wednesday and Friday evening at 6pm, without fail, and then returns to her apartment, seen here, through this poorly lit subway under railway lines."

"I don't like public places."

"She's used to men contacting her through this website." Ian showed Pieter Stella's webpage. "You could arrange to meet her somewhere private."

"But she'd take precautions, as she doesn't know me. Some women even want references from other escorts."

"You could go to her apartment dressed as a delivery man. It's on the first floor, where the arrow points in this picture. If you go there with flowers on Valentine's Day, she'll buzz you in. She gets lots of flowers."

"Guns N' Roses, my favourite band. Hope she'll soon be *Knockin' on Heaven's Door*." Pieter laughed at his own joke. "I said give me the money."

"It seems like a lot for just a day's work."

"Are you joking with me? I must hire a Walther with a silencer. Then there's the hotel and travel to pay for. I take all the risks. So, pay me or you go now."

"It's just, she used to be a friend."

"You are full of shit, wasting my time. Do you want her dead or alive?"

"Sorry, yes dead of course." Ian passed a package containing the money across the table.

"I will give you advance warning so that you have an alibi for when I eliminate your problem. And I leave the body where it falls. Not dispose of it, I don't do removals. That costs a lot extra."

Pieter went somewhere private to count the money.

As Ian waited anxiously for him to return, a hand gripped his shoulder. He looked up in surprise at a large man in police uniform standing over him. Where was Pieter? What had he done? Had he informed on Ian and run off with the money? It was all suddenly out of his control.

"Can I buy you a drink and sit here?" the man asked.

Before Ian could reply, Pieter returned. "Stop bothering my friend," he said to the man.

Pieter put the pictures and money in his shoulder bag, and they walked to the door.

"Who was that man in uniform?" Ian asked. "He makes me nervous."

"That's Diesel, so called because he's toxic. He likes to dress up and startle everyone. He's nothing."

As they stepped outside, a black car pulled up suddenly and a man dressed in a suit got out.

"Inspector Willem De Groot, Amsterdam Regional Police, get in the back of the car." He flashed a warrant card at them.

"We're fucked," Pieter said. "Just do what he says. He'll have back up nearby in case we try to run, and our police are armed."

Ian reluctantly did as he was told.

"We know your dirty business, Jansen. We have been conducting surveillance on you. What's in the bag?" Pieter handed it over."

De Groot took out the Stella brief and the package with the money and examined them. "I have your customer," he said, pointing a finger at Ian. "And your very attractive victim," he held up the pictures. "And your payment of course," he waved the money at them. "Give me your ID," he barked at Ian.

Ian handed his passport to De Groot who flicked through it.

"What do your British police say at a moment like this?" De Groot asked, handing the passport back. "Bang to rights? You will both be detained."

"Please let us go, we can make it worth your while," Pieter begged.

De Groot put the money inside a briefcase on the front seat and passed the shoulder bag back to Pieter. "Get out of my car and consider yourselves lucky this time."

Ian and Pieter did as they were told. De Groot drove off, with the money.

"Is that it?" Ian asked Pieter. "Have I just been robbed? What happened? Stop and talk to me."

"Shit happens," Pieter said. "Don't try to follow me." He walked off hurriedly.

The next morning, as he travelled back to London, Ian phoned Victor from the train. "Was I set up?" he asked miserably. "Why did De Groot speak in English from the outset, before he even knew where I was from?"

"Pieter's never let me down. But I've heard of De Groot. He's a bent Dutch cop. Going to complain to the Dutch police, are you? No point in dwelling on it when there's nothing you can do. It'll cost you £30,000 now. Give me the money and I'll set it up."

"That's double. This is madness."

"You don't have a choice."

"I don't want to be involved in this sordid business."

"Just pay me, keep your mouth shut and you won't be."

Within twenty-four hours, Ian had withdrawn a further £30,000 from the firm's account and paid it to Victor.

"Ian gave Pieter the money, and Pieter's brother Willem then took it off them. Like candy from a baby."

Victor was sharing his drinks cabinet with Stella, having invited her to his home so that they could talk in private.

"We're sharing it between the three of us. Ian came back with bedbugs instead of an agreement. Better still, the life insurance broker has arranged a five-million-pound policy on each of our lives that pays out on a death within the policy term. He said that it's more than usual, but I told him that we're getting married, and that you earn big money in the entertainment industry, so we can afford to pay the higher premiums. He was disappointed that you weren't with me. Turned out he's seen some of your films and was excited to get your autograph, even if it was just on that paper you had to sign. He wanted the commission and didn't look too closely at the tax returns and bank statements that I cooked up for him."

"That's a lot of money. Won't someone smell a rat?"

"There's a contestability clause where the company can investigate any claim made within one year of the policy start. But if we do our jobs properly, they can probe as much as they like, they won't find anything."

Stella's behaviour became more strident as she continued drinking victor's spirits. "Don't think of double crossing me, you've got a big insurance policy too." Stella pointed two fingers together at Victor and blew at the end of them, imitating a gun. "You must know it, Macey Gray, *Strange Behaviour.*"

"Now that my alcohol has loosened you up, I need you to help me execute my plan."

"I thought we'd already planned my execution," Stella said, laughing at her quick wit.

"This is important, so concentrate and try to be serious for a moment. I need to tape Philip admitting to the crime."

"Oh, and how will you persuade him to do that? He's not supposed to have done anything yet, besides which you're always complaining about your suspects protesting their innocence."

"I need you to phone Philip. Try not to sound tipsy. Use this phone so that I can record it and the number can't be traced back to me. Here's the script. I haven't decided yet whether to have AI copy his voice or use this tape we're about to edit."

"And when, sir, do you want the actress to perform?"

"No time like the present."

"He'll recognise my voice and know it's me."

"I've installed a real-time voice changer app."

"Can I choose my voice? I want to be a sultry female."

"No problem."

Stella dialled Philip's number.

"Hello, Philip here, who's calling?"

"Sorry, who am I speaking to?"

"You should know, you called me. Philip Royal."

"I'm a bit nervous, Philip, excuse me. I'm Chloe and I hear that you do edgy photo shoots."

"That's right, Chloe. No need to feel nervous with me. What do you have in mind?"

"I thought maybe sex play gone wrong type pictures. You don't mind a bit different, do you?"

"I'm sure I could do that, if the money's right."

Stella pulled a 'so far so good' face at Victor and rubbed the phone speaker against her clothing.

"Sorry, Philip, not a great line. What could you do?"

"Sex play gone wrong. Not done that before, but there's a first time for everything."

"Same here," Stella said off script.

Victor shook his head at her.

"Can you make it look like she's dead, me I mean, as the model?"

"I'm sure that can be arranged."

Stella rubbed the phone speaker against her clothing again.

"Sorry, bad line, do what?"

"Make it looks like she's dead, you that is."

"I've got butterflies now, Philip. Where is your studio?"

"No need for butterflies. I'll put your nerves to bed. I'm at Number two Tea Trade House, Ceylon Street, Bermondsey. My name is on the doorbell."

"I'll call you so we can arrange a date, Philip and talk about your fee."

"Looking forward to it, Chloe. You have a very sexy voice."

"Why thank you kind sir."

Stella put the phone down and burst out laughing.

Victor called Ian, "It's tomorrow night around 8pm. Make sure that you have a good alibi. You don't need to know anything else. Just make yourself available at Union Street later, Philip will need your legal advice. If they offer manslaughter, tell him to plead guilty and make sure he doesn't cause problems for us."

"I must get into Stella's apartment before the police do; see if I can find my money, the pictures and video and anything that suggests she was blackmailing me. No point in my trying to pretend that we hadn't been seeing each other. They are bound to ask Miss Phelps if Stella had visitors and she will tell them about me."

That night, Ian dreamt that he was standing in a courtroom dock. His Honour Judge Nemesis was passing sentence on him. Nemesis spoke, *Pride goeth before a fall: the Book of Proverbs 16:18. You have shown overconfidence, pride and arrogance and you are guilty of hubris. Blinded by a woman, you have lost contact with reality and your behaviour has led inexorably to your downfall. I must now exact retribution.*

8

Switcheroo

"First, put two of these white pills in his beer. These are the old ones, without the dye." Victor gave Stella a packet of Rohypnol that he had taken from the exhibits store at Union Street Police Station. "They won't show up in his drink. Give them thirty minutes or so to get working. You've got a window of about four hours before Philip starts to recover.

"Next, dump him by the Thames in a place where there are no cameras. Throw his phone in the water, so that his movements can't be traced. You could always push him in the river. It would look like he committed suicide after killing you."

"Push him…. you must be joking. One death is enough for me to have on my conscience."

"I'm going to do the job with Annie myself instead of asking Yuri. Might as well keep all of Ian's money. You know what you must do when you arrive at Philip's."

"Okay, I'm going to scatter my clothes on the bedroom floor and then undress Annie's body and take her clothes away. I'll bring all those things we agreed that identify her as me, and those two items that we bought in the sex shop."

"Anything else?" Victor asked.

"And the wipes. Oh, it's Valentine's Day today," Stella said. "If we weren't doing this, I would have been busy tonight, top fee."

"You'll be able to stop work altogether after this. I trust that you've done what I asked: taken your website down; deleted all your social media; and removed any pictures of yourself in your apartment. We don't want anyone comparing a picture of you with the body."

Stella entered The Fastidious Fox. Philip looked sharp, wearing a black jacket with a black shirt and skinny white tie. He was sitting at the bar with his laptop open. Stella slid seductively onto the bar stool next to him.

At first Philip seemed unresponsive to her charms. He walked off, saying "I need a pee." Victor came over, keyed in a search on Philip's laptop: *how do I prevent asphyxiation from resulting in serious injury or death?* and left for the back bar.

Kathleen, who was serving behind the main bar, came over to speaks to Stella. "Two goons from the FHM were in here earlier, asking questions about a woman they're looking for. They gave a description. Could be you? Be careful, they're not nice people."

"Don't worry," Stella reassured her, "it won't be a problem for much longer."

Philip came back and joined Stella. "I thought I saw Shadwell. Hope he's gone, good riddance." Philip sat back on the bar stool. Stella pointed her legs at him and pressed her knees against his.

"What's your poison?" he asked, finally responding to her approach.

"I could murder a dirty Martini."

Philip smiled and went off to order her cocktail. She popped the pills into his beer.

After a while, they moved to a sofa in a dimly lit corner of the bar. "I'm a huge admirer of your body of work," Philip said. "I've seen all your films more than once. That Hungarian, down on you in *Budapest Naughty Nights;* was that a real *petite mort?* You were screaming."

They didn't notice that two young Japanese women were watching them.

"I hear you do glamour portrait shots. I bet you could up the 'likes' on my website," Stella said, putting a hand on his knee.

Philip was soon acting tipsy and had Stella in a clumsy embrace. She ran her hands over his pockets to find his keys. They were in a trouser pocket. Philip soon had his head slumped on her shoulder. She moved, so that he fell across her. She slid a hand into the pocket and lifted out the keys.

"Now it's my turn to pee," she said, removing him from her. She met Victor in the back bar and gave him the keys.

"That took long enough, you're losing your touch," Victor remarked.

Mai had seen the main sites. Clutching her copy of *Sekai No Arukikata – London* (How You Can Walk the World – London), she had visited Big Ben (just like the picture in her schoolbook); London Bridge (disappointing, just a bridge); Buckingham Palace (no-one at home); Trafalgar Square (fountains to put your hot feet into); and Camden Town (for Camden Market).

Chi told her that she needed to see the alternative

London, the 'real life' places that her work for Kate took her to, like The Fastidious Fox. She took Chi there on Saturday night.

It was stand-up comedy night. *Barking Mad Tonight* the poster announced at the entrance to the back bar. "Foxes bark at night, but it's a reference to mad dogs," Chi explained as they joined the regulars in the busy main bar. Two elderly ladies sat at the table behind them, deep in conversation. Chi couldn't help overhearing them.

"My husband died last week. I was at his bedside. He took my arm, pulled my face down to his and tried to say something to me. His head jerked and he was dead. I stayed with him for a couple of hours."

"Oh, I didn't know."

"Our son came to the house the next day. He hardly ever comes to visit."

"That's nice for you."

"We don't get on. He said 'I've come to see dad. Where is he'?"

"You hadn't told him then."

"I said 'he's dead'."

"That must have been a shock for him."

"He said 'well that was a wasted journey then. What's he left me?'"

"He doesn't hang about then."

"I said 'nothing, you waste of space.' It wasn't true, but I was buggered if I was going to give him any good news."

Chi looked startled, nudged Mai and pointed in the direction of a sofa near to where they were sitting. Mai had insisted that they always speak to each other in English to help her language studies, but when they could be overheard and wished to keep a conversation private, they always spoke in their native Japanese.

"*Anoko yo* (that's her)."

"*Dare* (who)?"

"*Hora, 'Aijin' yo* (the lover) *Stella.*"

"*Masaka* (you don't say)."

"*Iisho ni iru no ha dare* (who's she with)?"

"*Kare totemo hen ne* (he looks really creepy)."

"*Watashi wo totteru yoni, kare no shashin totte* (take a picture of him, pretend you're taking a photo of me)."

"*Kanojo nani shiteru* (what's she doing)?"

"*Kanojo dakitsuite, Kare no pocket kara nanika toro to shiteru mitai* (she's all over him, looks like she's trying to pick his pocket)."

"*Kare nonderu? Yaku yatteru yoni mieru* (is he drunk? He looks doped)?"

"*Dokka iku yo? Tsukeyou,* (where's she going? Let's follow her)."

They went into the back bar.

"*Ima kanojo, sumini iru hito ni nanika watashita yone* (she's handing something to that guy in the corner)."

"*Kagi kana* (looks like a set of keys)."

"*Waraukara ano hito no shashin mo totte oite* (take a picture of him as well, I'll stand in front and smile)."

Stella returned to the sofa and stood over Philip. "Let's go somewhere private, like yours," she said aloud, picking up his laptop to take with her. "He's had a few too many, just my luck, hope he's up to it," Stella called out to the regulars, so that they would pay attention to her and Philip leaving together. One of them helped her walk him across the floor of the bar to the exit.

Annie was reluctant to visit Yuri on her own. She tried messaging Stella: *I want you to go with me. I'm coming over to your apartment now.*

Not long after, she left another message for Stella: *You're not in. Now I have to call a cab and go it alone.*

Stella stopped her car by the river Thames. Philip had his eyes closed and was lying across the back seats. She helped him out and laid him on a bench close to the water. *If he rolls off and drowns himself, that's not down to me*, she thought. "You really know how to give a girl a fun time," she said to his comatose body. She threw his phone in the river and drove off to Philip's flat, leaving him there.

Ian was in a hurry to get into Stella's apartment, and he parked where he could watch her leaving. He sat low down in the driving seat, so that she wouldn't see him.

He glanced at his copy of the *Daily Splash* to pass the time. *Police increasingly involved in sex abuse: the Police Standards Board reports a disturbing increase in the number of police officers who are caught procuring women and young girls who are victims of crime, for sex. Some officers are taking large amounts of money to turn a blind eye to organised and serious crime. The report entitled State of Corruption concludes that significant efforts must be made to tackle this disturbing trend.*

A car pulled up outside the apartment block and the driver hooted and waited. A woman who had been waiting by the main doors got into the front seat of the car. Ian couldn't see her face properly.

Strange, Ian thought to himself, *Stella said that she would never get into the front seat of a minicab after a driver had once leant over and tried to kiss her. 'And I was paying him, what a cheek,' she told me.*

He suddenly wanted to save her. He called out "Stella, Stop!" and waved his arms at the car as it drove off, but he couldn't be heard over the noise of a passing delivery van which temporarily blocked his view.

Ian went straight to Stella's block and pressed the buzzer for Miss Phelps.

"Stella's just gone out, but she forgot that we're supposed to be having dinner here together. I messaged her and she said she'd be back shortly, and I was to ask you if I could use the spare key and wait for her in the flat."

"Of course, come up, dear."

Ian met Miss Phelps on the landing, and she gave the key to him.

"It's 8.15pm," Ian remarked to her pointedly, looking at his phone.

Once inside, the flat looked different, as if Stella had moved out. Most of her clothes and personal possessions were gone. He couldn't find her laptop or any evidence that she had ever known him.

It still isn't too late, he thought. He sent Victor a message: *stop it now.*

He called the restaurant, and their food arrived twenty minutes later. "It's 9pm," Ian told the delivery driver, who took it as a complaint. Ian laid the table and poured two glasses of wine. *A clever alibi*, he thought. *I am miles away, at her flat, waiting for her to come home to a special dinner I have ordered for us.*

It was sometime later that he had a reply from Victor: *stop what?*

He knocked on Miss Phelps's door. "It's 9.30pm, she's not back, and she's not answering her phone. I don't think she's coming home tonight. Please take this food I ordered; it'll spoil otherwise." She took the food containers, and he handed the key back to her.

Victor was waiting in Philip's flat when Annie pressed the bell at the street door. Victor buzzed the door open and told her through the intercom "First floor, come up." He met her at the flat door.

"Are you Yuri? Where's my money?"

"You must be Annie; don't believe in pleasantries, do you?"

"Have you got my money? I'm in a hurry. I don't want to be here."

She followed Victor through the living room into the bedroom.

"It's in that bag." He gestured at a black holdall on the floor next to the bed.

"Well, pass it to me then."

He put it on a chair.

She unzipped it. It was full of old newspapers.

"This isn't…."

Before she could finish her sentence, Victor held out his warrant card. "Annie Blake, I am arresting you for the blackmail of your husband Ian Blake contrary to section 21 of the Theft Act 1968." Victor cautioned her. "I have to handcuff you." She noticed that he was already wearing police issue blue protective gloves.

"How did you know? You don't understand. It's all his fault. It wasn't even my idea to begin with."

Annie looked confused and upset. "Hang on, before you put the handcuffs on, how do I know that you're legit? what station are you from?"

"Union Street," Victor said casually, taking hold of her wrists.

"Why are you here on your own? Something's not right."

"There's a van coming in a minute, we'll wait for it downstairs, after I've cuffed you."

"Get your station on the phone, so I can speak to someone there and check who you are and that this is official." Annie tried to sound assertive and pull her hands away.

Victor gave her a sudden push back on to the bed. Annie's self-defence training came to her rescue. As he leant over her, she kicked him hard between his legs. Victor howled with pain. Then she went for his eyes, jabbing a finger into his right eye. Victor yelled with anger and clutched his face.

The buzzer sounded from the street door. Annie climbed off the bed. She thought of running out of the building, now that she had a chance to escape, but was concerned that Victor might be speaking the truth, and she would have to confront officers from a police van arriving at the street door. She picked up the intercom and listened.

"It's Stella."

"Thank God it's you, come up quickly please, something terrible has happened."

"What have you done?" Stella asked as she saw Victor crouched down, holding his face. "You've assaulted a police officer."

"I know, it was just instinct, a reflex."

Stella looked at Victor. "Your eye is very red."

Victor stood up. He didn't speak, but lunged at Annie, who was caught off guard. He scooped up her legs and bundled her body on to the bed so that she was lying on her back. He climbed on top of her, sat on her pelvis and held her wrists with one hand. He went to reach for the pillow with other hand. As he stared down at her angrily, she did what she had practised in her self-defence class: she took a deep breath down into her abdominal muscles, exhaled and screamed at him, "Stop!" Victor froze.

"Finish it," Stella said urgently, but he didn't move. Stella picked up the Hungarian goose down pillow, placed it over Annie's startled face and applied pressure. "I'm sorry," Stella said lamely.

Annie could see only pitch black. She tried to breathe but could not take in air. She tried to move her arms to tell Stella to stop, but Stella pressed down harder with the pillow. Her lungs were empty now and as the pressure on her eyelids increased, she saw stars and psychedelic-like patterns and flashes of colour dancing around her field of vision. It wasn't long before she stopped resisting, lost consciousness and her limbs became floppy. Only then did Stella let go.

"She could have blinded me," was Victor's only response to Stella's quick action. "Clean her hands carefully. You may need to clip the nails. She'll have my skin on her, and I don't want anyone to find that."

"You couldn't do it," Stella said mockingly. "It's true, about the female of the species being deadlier than the male, like in the Rudyard Kipling poem: she shouted at you, and you turned aside."

Stella had brought Philip's laptop, together with a bag containing items to leave behind: her purse with a debit card for a bank that she hardly ever used; store cards; a gym membership card; and a driving licence with Stella's name and Annie's photograph which someone from a site on the dark web had produced for Victor.

"Do you have that saucy postcard from Brighton that I got Yuri to send you?"

"It's in the bag."

Victor took it out to check that Yuri had written what he'd asked.

Hi Stella. I'm enjoying day out by beach. Good yeh? I saw boobs on card and thought you. That Phil man sounds bad news. If he tells you again play games with him to pay for pictures tell him get lost and call me anytime on new phone 08754884931 Your dear friend Yuri Prokonova xx

Victor put the card in the bag that they would leave behind.

Stella undressed Annie and carefully folded her clothes, making sure not to drop any loose items which would help to identify Annie's presence. She put them in a bag to take away, along with all of Annie's other possessions.

"Did you bring the pink fluffy ones?" Victor asked, "to make it look like playtime."

Stella handed Victor a pair of boudoir handcuffs and he put them on Annie's wrists, arranging her arms above her head. He left the pillow covering her face.

"Did you bring the baby wipes?"

Stella wiped Annie's body down, then took off her own clothes and scattered them around the room to give the impression that they had been removed hastily. She dressed in a spare set of clothes that she had brought. Meanwhile Victor sat casually on the bed and smoked a cigarette.

"She's dead instead of me. Feels weird, no feels worse than bad. Shit, why did I do it?"

"Knowing her, she's probably donated her organs, so we've done someone a favour."

"It should have been you. I'm such a mug. Did you freeze on purpose?"

"Just needed to ensure you'd remain loyal to me. Of course it was on purpose, what do you take me for? Your shoes, leave them as well."

"These high heels cost a fortune."

Victor stubbed the cigarette out on the sole of his shoe, leant over and placed the butt on the bedside table, intending to dispose of it later. "Got to use the bathroom." He went and examined his bloodshot eye in the mirror.

"He's got nice equipment," Victor said when he returned to the bedroom. He took a camera down from a shelf.

"Polaroid 600 Land Camera. It's vintage eighties. I need a memento to remember the dead." Victor pointed the camera at the body on the bed and pressed the button.

"That's sick," Stella said.

"Did you bring the magazine, to make it look as if they were playing around together?"

Stella pulled a copy of *Full Throttle* from her bag and handed it to Victor.

"You do know that this is an American biker magazine," he said, flicking through it.

"Well sorry. I grabbed it from a shelf in a specialist

magazine shop. I saw the title and the bikini clad model on the cover. I didn't have time to look inside."

"Leave it anyway."

Victor handed the magazine back to Stella, who without looking laid it down on the table by the bedside, inadvertently covering the butt.

"You ever tried that sort of game: hands on the throat?" Victor asked.

"Only if it's his throat and my hands. But then I'm too lazy for even that. If a guy asks me about my favourite position I'll say 'awake, apart from that I'm not really bothered'."

"Make sure you ditch her phone and delete any messages that she has sent you. And book that Airbnb in rural Wales in a made-up name. You don't exist anymore, remember?

"Everything's done then. It's 'Goodnight Vienna' for both of us."

They sat in Victor's car as he dialled the emergency services and played the heavily edited recording of Philip to the female police operator: *Philip Royal - sex play gone wrong - not done that before - but there's a first time for everything - sorry looks like she's dead - Number two Tea Trade House Ceylon Street my name is on the doorbell*

9

Camel Butt

"Victor, you the boss on this job?" DC Stant asked.

"Yes, I have the honour of being the Senior Investigating Officer."

"I've got a 'PJ' for you, get me a packet of ciggies love," Shadwell said to DS Bonetti. "Twenty Camels, I've run out. If I don't have a smoke, I get the hump. It'll spare you the anguish of witnessing too much of this unsavoury scene. She may be a tart, but you are all sisters under the skin."

"Smoking at a crime scene? Surely not," Stant said in surprise.

"I'll go outside." He gave Bonetti a twenty-pound note.

"So, this is what I became a detective sergeant for?" Bonetti said to Stant. "He'll be asking me for a cup of tea next." She gave Shadwell an annoyed look as she left the room.

"Keep your hands in your pockets when you're not using them for something useful," Shadwell told the officers present, "to avoid leaving unwanted prints. That shouldn't be difficult for you, Shawcroft, it's like you're working a Punch and Judy show down in your trouser pockets. Has the crocodile got the sausages?

"Don't, as DC Stant so helpfully pointed out, smoke, chew tobacco, use the telephone or toilet, eat or drink, move anything, open windows or doors, touch anything unnecessarily, litter or spit. Remember that the entire flat is a crime scene."

Uniformed officers from a fast response police car were first on the scene. A resident of another flat in the building buzzed them in from the street. They checked for but couldn't find a pulse.

DC Stant and DS Bonetti from the Major Crimes Unit at Union Street were next to arrive. The duty sergeant at Union Street arranged for Dr Black, the on-duty forensic medical practitioner, to attend and certify that the woman was dead.

Shadwell was off duty but had still picked up the call somehow. Happening to be in the vicinity, he had insisted on attending.

DC Stant looked for identification. In the woman's bag was a driving licence, bank and membership cards but no mobile phone.

"She's Stella Godley," he told DS Bonetti. "Her phone's missing. Whoever did this, must have taken it with them."

The initial crime scene processing did not take long, and DC Stant had completed it before Shadwell's arrival. The visual picture that greeted him was of a naked woman, lying on her back with a crumpled pillow covering her face and handcuffed with a bondage toy. There were no signs of forced entry to the flat.

He scanned the crowded dusty bedside table, pulled on protective gloves and lifted the *Full Throttle* magazine. Underneath was a cigarette butt, easily recognisable as a

Camel by the iconic camel logo on the paper near the filter. He paid particular attention to these items as they were next to the bed and the body. He recorded them in his pocketbook and placed makeshift markers next to them so that one of his uniformed colleagues wouldn't accidentally 'plod' over them and contaminate any DNA on their surfaces. When forensics arrived, they lifted them gingerly and placed them in exhibit bags, then urgently got to work, looking for traces of somebody else on the body.

Shadwell had entered shortly after the forensics team. "Pictures of the scene in the same way that we found her, and don't move the pillow, its position on her face is key," he told the photographer.

Bonetti returned in time to watch the woman's hair combed for trace evidence and her fingernails scraped and clipped. "A bit late for a make-over," she said to show that she may be female, but she was still one of the lads.

Last to arrive was Dr Ian Snowden, 'Snowy' to those who were used to working with him, recognisable by his overgrown white hair, a Home Office duty pathologist. After a few minutes, Snowy put away his magnifying glass and head torch and announced his findings. "I can tell from the conjunctival haemorrhaging on her eyelids and eyes, which are the results of increased pressure on the veins in her head when her airways where obstructed, that she was asphyxiated. Smothered by this pillow no doubt, whilst handcuffed. No signs of a sexual assault. Seems he hadn't progressed beyond the foreplay. I'll see you at the post-mortem Shadwell."

"I'll bag up the bed sheet, pillow and the handcuffs as well as the rest," Stant said. "They'll have to go off to the lab together with her clothes."

"Can I keep those shoes?" Bonetti asked jokingly. "Must have cost a month's worth of my wages." She examined the label on the pillow. "Hungarian down, his weapon of choice. I've got those pillows in my bedroom, but I've never thought of killing anyone with them."

DC Stant was unable to tell Shadwell about the cigarette butt, as Victor was busy chatting to Sarah, a recently qualified forensics officer. "What's a pretty girl like you doing in a job like this?" Victor asked. He waved Stant away imperiously: "Not now, Stant, can't you see I'm busy?"

"Why's Shadwell wearing dark glasses?" Stant asked Bonetti. "Looks like Miami Vice. And why's he walking like he's just got off a horse? And what happened to the ciggies?"

"They didn't have Camels, so I got him Marlboro. I thought he'd like them. You remember the adverts. He acts like a cowboy. Even more so than usual with today's funny walk. What's a 'PJ'? That's a new one on me."

"A private job, a personal errand carried out by a police officer doing shit, to be precise."

"Oh, thanks very much. The name Stella Godley, does that ring any bells with you? I'm sure that I've heard it somewhere."

"I'll do a search for her on the database. Talking of searches, I heard that Western's mum went to his flat, with a spare key she had. The place was a mess, like it had been searched untidily. There was no sign of Western."

"That's not good. I worry about what's happened to Bryan. Whatever he had on Shadwell may never be exposed now."

"Gather 'round, team," Victor called out to Stant and Bonetti. "This case is open and shut: he confessed to the emergency operator; he's a known sex offender; and we found her naked in his bed, smothered with his pillow. That's good enough for me, so let's not waste time on it.

"Just tick the boxes to satisfy anyone who asks that we've done our job: door-to-door, check whether anyone heard or saw anything suspicious; search her address and see if you can find her laptop and phone; speak to her neighbour and ask about her visitors; find out if she owns a car and search it if she does; find out where she works and see if anyone there can paint a picture of her for us; and contact the card providers, see if they can add to our information about her.

"I'll contact this Prokonova guy, see what he can tell us about this Ms Stella Godley and if he will come to the mortuary to identify the body."

"It's Philip Royal at the street door," an officer called up from downstairs. "He says he's lost his keys. From the way he's behaving, looks like he's lost his memory as well."

"The final piece of the puzzle: killer hands himself in," Victor said to Stant and Bonetti. "Very considerate of him."

Bonetti went down to the street door and took hold of Philip by his arm.

"What's happening?" Philip asked. "I know you."

"I've arrested you before. I'm DS Bonetti from the Major Crimes Unit at Union Street." She showed her warrant card.

"What are you doing here? Get your hands off me, you can't push me around."

"Philip Royal, a woman named Stella Godley has been found dead in your flat and I'm arresting you on suspicion of her murder. You will be detained so that evidence can be preserved, and an investigation conducted. I'm taking you to Union Street for interview." Bonetti cautioned him.

"Your sort are not to be trusted."

"My sort? What sort's that then?"

"You women call it empowerment, but I call it revenge, arresting me when I haven't done anything."

"'I haven't done anything.' That's what you said last time. Jury didn't agree, did they? I am aware of your unfortunate history with women. Unfortunate for them that is."

"Keep him down there," Shadwell called to Bonetti. "If he comes up here, he'll disturb the crime scene."

The Custody Officer opened the cell door. Philip was wearing a white paper 'onesie' and had a grey blanket draped over his shoulders.

"Philip," Ian exclaimed, "Why, oh why? Lucky that I just happened to be here, seeing another client. As soon as I heard your name mentioned I told the Custody Sergeant, 'He's an old client of mine. Needs my help.' So here I am."

Philip stood up. "I didn't kill her; you must believe me. She came on to me in The Fox and we had drinks together. I don't remember much after that."

"But, Philip, you were the last person seen with her alive, in the pub. You went home with her, and she was found dead, naked on your bed, asphyxiated, next to a copy of *Full Throttle* and restrained with fluffy handcuffs. You called the police to say that you had killed a woman during a sex game gone wrong. And there is a postcard from someone saying that you photograph her in return for sex."

Philip put his head in his hands and groaned.

"They want to interview you, Philip. My advice is to go 'no comment'. You know what to do, just don't say anything. They'll ask you 'time of day' questions at first, just to try and get you talking."

"I'm not paranoid, but that Sergeant Bonetti, who was at my flat, she's out to get me. I know her type, hates men and assumes that we are all rapists. I've been stitched up by a woman before. I didn't kill her. I want you to get me off. I know I had my keys with me. Stella must have taken them. Someone must have seen us. It was *Barking Mad* night. The pub was packed. Why would she do that? Do you think that she gave them to someone so that they could steal my stuff whilst I was out? I'm sure that I saw that creep Shadwell there, hanging around unwelcome, like a turd in the toilet that won't flush away. He's a detective, do you think that he saw anything? You could ask him. I had my laptop with me in the pub. How did that get back to my flat before me? I've never used handcuffs and I don't read *Full Throttle*. I don't go in for that choking or domination stuff. And I've never taken pictures of her, she's never been near my flat."

"Philip, you're getting carried away. How will you deal with the fact that you can't remember what happened? There's at least a couple of lost hours that you can't account for."

"In the interview, shouldn't I tell them about the keys?"

"I think that we should keep that to ourselves. If you start talking in the interview and say that you remember some details but not most of what happened, it will sound as if you're hiding something and make it impossible for you to produce a believable account for a jury. I can't tell you what to say at your trial, but you might later remember that she brought the frilly handcuffs and magazine with her and asked you to cuff her up and smother her with the pillow. You'd agreed a safe sign, but she didn't give it and you didn't realise that she had stopped breathing. When you lifted the pillow, you panicked when you saw what you'd done. You could do much worse than plead guilty to manslaughter."

"You're just making up a story, you're as bad as the police. I've never pleaded guilty to anything and I'm not starting now. I should have a blood test. She may have drugged me. That would help, wouldn't it?"

"If we test you, the prosecution must be told the results. They could be negative. Better you just tell the jury you believe that you were drugged, then the prosecution can't disprove it."

"Nobody cares about the truth."

"Philip, I care, trust me. I have another client here who needs to see me now, I'll be back to you before they question you."

Philip was charged just after midnight with Stella's murder.

Chi and Mai were sitting on stools at the counter of the G Spot night club. Chi had found it amusing to say to Mai, "Let's hit the G Spot," and when they got close by to ask any good-looking young man, whilst pulling an innocent, serious face, "Excuse me, do you know where the G Spot is?" She enjoyed his embarrassment as he gave her directions.

Chi said loudly to Mai, above the music, "*asoko no*

futari ga kocchi miteruyo (those two guys are looking at us)," confident that they would not understand her.

"*E-mendokusai* (what a pain)."

"*E- kinpatsu no hou ikemen dayo* (the blonde one's quite cool)."

"*Uh wow, kocchi kuru* (they're coming over)."

"Hello ladies, where are you from?" Grant asked. Grant was in his late twenties, tall, with neatly trimmed blonde hair and boyish good looks.

"*Bimyo jan* (some chat-up line)," Mai said, looking disinterested.

"*Chotto kurai ii desho* (give them a chance). I'm from around here, like you no doubt," Chi said. "Where did you think I was from?"

"Can we get you both a drink?" Grant asked, taken aback by her forthrightness.

"Alright," said Chi, trying to hide her interest in him.

"*Kyomi nai te itteyo* (tell them to go away)," Mai said.

"What would you like?" Grant asked, moving closer and perching on the next free stool.

"*Takai mono tano mo* (make it expensive)," Mai said.

"A bottle of champagne will do," Chi replied.

Grant's friend Bradley looked concerned. "Is she for real?" he whispered to Grant.

"*Wakatte nai mitai*" (he doesn't get it)," Chi said.

Grant's expression did not change. "Of course, coming up," he replied.

"*Okane tsukawasete nige yo*! (we'll let them spend their money, then get out of here!)" Mai said.

"*Sore wa dokana* (I'm not so sure)."

"*Nani ga?* (about what?)"

"*Omoshiroi ka do ka desho* (it depends on whether he can make me laugh)," Chi said, nodding towards Grant.

"*Kare ha okaikei mite bikkuri suru yo* (won't be laughing when he sees the bill)," Mai added.

Kate had a phone call about Stella's death from an upset sounding Ray. He asked her to come in and see him. "She meant a lot to me. Not just as a business asset. I liked her and I looked after her professionally. She was always very careful with men. I can't bear to think that she may have suffered. I want to know what happened and I don't trust the police to find out. I want justice for her. That DCI Shadwell, always cosying up to her, what is his game?"

"I don't know," Kate replied. "I've been working on behalf of Annie Blake, Ian's wife. Ian's defending Philip Royal, the accused."

"Is he? You've worked for him as an investigator. Is he using you in this case?"

"No, there's a conflict of interest if he asks me. I've just finished a job for Annie, reporting on his shenanigans with Stella."

"Oh dear, my fault for playing matchmaker. Even more reason why I should get involved and hire you to help sort this mess out. I'll pay you. I don't understand why Stella was in Philip's bed. She wouldn't waste her time normally with rubbish like him. Her clients were all 'A list', he's a 'D' or an 'E'. Let me know what you can do."

Kate, unsure about whether she should take Ray's money, phoned Jacqui. She told her about Ray, his trial collapsing and Stella's murder. "The problem is that I know the exploited women who make his money for him."

"A bit late to be moralistic about it. Ian took Ray's money as his solicitor and paid you out of it to work on Ray's defence. What you do now for Ray would be in a worthy cause, to get justice for Stella," Jacqui said.

10

Double Your Money

It's the murder steeplechase with some fat brief fees at stake. The barristers' chambers in the running are 5 Century Buildings, with clerk Bradley, and 1 Stack Court, with clerk Grant.

Which barristers are the lucky riders? It's Monday morning at 5 Century Buildings. "Good morning, sir," Bradley greeted Robert Montague (Monty) Bell QC their most senior barrister. "I've got a nice brief for you, Regina v Philip Royal, worth a big fee. Murder of an escort girl; you're prosecuting; it's a dead cert."

"That's the ticket. Who's my junior?"

"I thought I'd give Cecilia a chance, sir."

"Good choice, just the break she needs."

It's Monday morning at 1 Stack Court. "Grant, this Philip Royal murder brief does not have my name on it," Guy Hammond QC called out crossly.

"Ian Blake, sir, he's the solicitor and he has demanded that Benjamin does it."

"But nobody wants to brief Benjamin anymore. He's a nice enough chap and all that, but he has *issues* and he's past it."

"Sorry, sir, couldn't persuade him out of it and Mr Blake does give us a lot of work."

"Who's the junior?"

"Felicity Crabtree, sir, at least he left that choice to me."

"Well, I suppose she makes up for Benjamin's shortcomings."

"It's a loser, sir, I've probably saved you the embarrassment of failing to win over a jury for once."

Grant hit the G Spot with Chi. It was their first date. On the way there she played her usual trick. She spoke to a woman behind the counter in a shop. "Excuse me, my boyfriend and I…can you help us, we can't find the G Spot and I'm getting rather impatient." The woman looked at her uncertainly. "Or maybe it doesn't exist?" Chi asked. Grant stood by, looking embarrassed.

"The G Spot Club," he added hastily.

"Spoilsport," she said outside. He really couldn't make her out sometimes.

Inside the club, they found a sofa away from the stage. "What is it that you said you did?" Chi asked.

"I didn't say."

He was desperately thinking of how he could impress her. Barristers' clerk at 1 Stack Court wouldn't clinch it.

"I'm an investment banker." There, it was, out. He at once regretted the lie.

"Are you good at it?"

"I take people's money and multiply it many times. If you gave me £20,000, I could double it with a few deals." Grant was unnecessarily adding to the lie, confident that

Chi didn't have anything like £20,000 to spare and would not call his bluff.

Chi looked interested and smiled sweetly.

She likes me Grant thought.

Soon they were hitting the G Spot again. "You remember telling me about the tricks you could do with money," Chi said. "Well, after finishing university I wanted to save to start my own business. So, for five years, as well as my daytime job, I worked evenings as a hostess in Club Leo in Kabukicho in Tokyo."

Grant thought *Christ, she was a bar girl*. He had met them in Bangkok. He was trying to work out whether this was something in her favour or not. On the one hand, she would have lots of bedroom toys and pleasing sexual techniques. On the other, she must have been with countless men. He suddenly felt insecure. How did he measure up, literally, to all the men she'd known. She might be bored with straight sex. She might be 'bi', many of the bar girls were. Before Grant's imagination could run away with him completely, Chi put him straight. She must have noticed the keen but confused look on his face.

"It didn't involve actual sex. Just looking attractive, talking to older men, smiling sweetly, laughing at their jokes, and serving them alcohol. And knowing how to keep on the right side of the yakuza. Also having dinner dates with customers, but nothing else outside of work. I understood the power play between them and us and that it was a game of sexual politics we all played: they had the money; and we were their sexual fantasy. I was skilled as a *cabakura* and I brought new customers to the club. I made good money and I want you to invest it for me. Here, write down your bank details where I can send it." She pushed a piece of paper and a pen towards him.

Grant hesitated. How much money was she going to send him? He felt her hand on his leg. *Mustn't blow it now, she couldn't have saved that much*, he thought. He did what she asked, trying to look casual about it. He passed the paper back to her.

"I want you to double it for me, or even treble it if you're clever. I'm depending on you."

When Grant did his online banking at breakfast the next day, he found that she had transferred £50,000 to him. He dropped his spoon in horror splashing full fat milk and granola across the kitchen bar.

Bonetti and Stant sat around a table with Victor in his office, going through a list of the forensic material found at the crime scene.

"We've hardly any budget left for forensic analysis so, only the essential submissions and send them to the police lab, not some fancy private lab, and mark them 'non urgent' or they'll charge us extra," Victor told them. "Am I clear?"

"A Camel butt was found at the scene," Stant said. "I should include that."

"Waste of money," Victor replied, "won't help us build the case against Philip. What's next?"

"The *Full Throttle* magazine. Could show us who's been looking at it."

"No point, we know it's Philip's. Pages probably stuck together anyway."

When they had finished their meeting, Stant took Bonetti aside. "What should I do with that butt and the *Full Throttle*?"

"I'll send them anyway. It could be important and Shadwell's using tunnel vision as usual, looking only for evidence that proves a case against Philip. He makes it impossible for us to do our job professionally. I'll avoid the police lab and use Dr Alfie Slincott at Forensic Answers and mark it 'urgent, Carly off record'. He'll invoice me directly. It means that I don't require Shadwell to sign off on it. I usually find a way to pay that doesn't affect Shadwell's pathetic forensics' budget. Alfie's better than the police lab and has access to our database. We don't have to tell Shadwell about it if it comes to nothing. Oh, and don't get too excited about *Full Throttle*, it's a biker mag."

Later, Victor had a message from Stella: *that picture you took, play safe and destroy it*. Victor messaged back: *will do*. Then he went into the exhibits storeroom to deal with the Camel butt in the 'not for submission' material only it wasn't there.

That same week, Bonetti found Stant on his own in the police station canteen. "I've got the forensics back from Slincott in the Godley case."

"Anything interesting?"

"Shadwell left that cigarette end. Strange that, I didn't see him smoking there. When he arrived, he said that he'd already run out of cigarettes. Do you remember, he made that silly joke about getting the hump? They matched it with his reference DNA profile kept for elimination purposes. He didn't have any Camels, I bought him Marlboro, you remember, the cowboy's favourite and you reminded him not to smoke at the scene. The *Full Throttle* matched data they had for Stella, so no surprises there."

"So, her biometrics must be on our system for Alfie to get a hit for her. That's interesting. We need to see what info we hold about her. She must have been convicted of something. That cigarette end was there when I arrived. Apart from the uniform boys, I was first on the scene, before Shadwell. He must have left it before I got there. I'll ask him."

"I don't trust him, better caution him first."

"What?"

"Joke."

Stant confronted Shadwell in his office. "The Camel butt went off to forensics by mistake. They've matched it to you."

Victor replied without looking up. "Must have had a cigarette outside and dropped the butt when I went in. Go on, tell me off for being careless, Stant, slapped wrist. Get Bonetti in, team meeting."

Bonetti gave Stant a 'what did he say?' look as she sat down opposite him in Victor's office.

Stant shook his head with a 'not now' in reply.

"Bonetti, you start us off."

"Right, so what do we know? No signs of forced entry. Royal's keys must have been used to let Ms Godley into his flat, or he opened the door to her. He is a glamour photographer, and we know his reputation. We can check to see if he has taken any pictures of her. There is a postcard from Yuri Prokonova suggesting that she was paying Royal with sex for photographing her. Bank card: she hardly uses that account. Regular visitor to the gym. What were they playing at? It's known that intentional asphyxiation leads to cerebral hypoxia, starving the brain of oxygen, inducing hypoxic euphoria, and carrying a serious risk of accidental death."

Stant took over. "No doorbell or nearby camera footage. Neighbours didn't hear or see anything. I visited her address, no phone or laptop. Maybe that's why he left his flat. If she had brought them with her, Royal may have gone out to ditch them and anything else incriminating him. Then he panicked, realised how bad the situation was, didn't know what to do with the body still on his bed and so in desperation he made the phone call to emergency services mistakenly thinking that sex game gone wrong is still a defence. I spoke to her neighbour, Miss Phelps. Seems she only had one male visitor, a man named Ian. She doesn't know anything more about him, except that he's married. Oh yes, on the night of the murder, he was at her flat preparing a romantic meal for them both. Sad isn't it."

"That rules him out then," Victor added.

"No traces of another person on her body," Stant continued. "To stop her breathing, Philip, if it was him, must have been on top of her and pressing down hard. There were signs of phenoxyethanol, which is the cleanser in baby wipes. Must have been used to clean her skin. That may be why he left no traces on her. She would have fought back, but Royal has no self-defence injuries."

"She's been working as an escort but little interaction with her co-workers," Shadwell said as he took over. "I've spoken to Yuri. Seems that they met on holiday in Greece and kept up the friendship when they both returned to London. Nothing suspicious about him.

"Thanks, team. We all know that Royal's our man. So much circumstantial, I can't see him wriggling out of this one."

"I'll run Godley's name through our system," Stant volunteered.

"Leave that to me," Shadwell replied.

Kate and DS Carly Bonetti were in Only Girls Allowed. It was the evening. They had entered the club through an unobtrusive door in an alleyway off the street near to Kate's home in Soho. They were good friends through work, and they shared a social circle.

Kate was a member of the club. It was Carly's first visit and she looked at her surroundings as she entered the bar area: rich red velvet wallpaper, gold framed mirrors, black ceiling, good looking women.

"Do you come here often?" Carly asked, surprised by the plush interior, which was in complete contrast to the stark looking entrance.

"Is that your chat up line?" Kate replied, laughing. "It's convenient, and safe to walk home from on my own when it's late. And the food's good when I can't be bothered to cook."

"Do you usually come on your own or bring a girlfriend?"

"Are you interviewing me, Detective? Chi comes with me sometimes. She likes to be hit on, boosts her self-confidence, but that's all it does for her.

"Carly, you wanted to see me. I'm flattered, of course, but I guess that it's to do with work, not pleasure. You know my hourly rate," she said, jokingly. "Let's go somewhere more private."

The chill room was darker and more relaxed, a place where couples could go to talk without being overheard.

"What's the problem, girl, and how's Henry?" Henry was Carly's sixteen-year-old son.

"Am I a good mother?" Carly asked. "Henry is angry much of the time. He argues with me and says hurtful things. He won't help me around the house or do what he's told. He won't let me in his bedroom, so I've no idea what he gets up to. I don't think he cares if I live or die."

"You're a diligent, clever detective, who is doing her best to hold down a full time, challenging job, whilst bringing up a teenage son on her own."

"Henry's dad is not interested in him, and the poor boy knows it. Henry pretends that it doesn't bother him, but I know that it does, and he feels rejected by his dad."

"I'm sure that's why your Henry's acting up. Teenagers can be a nightmare. Look at my fifteen-year-old niece Claire. Didn't she have a brief dalliance with young Henry? I'm worried about pictures that she sent her now ex-boyfriend, Rupert. The silly girl took intimate pictures of herself and sent them to him. Now Rupert's got a new girlfriend Lily, and he showed them to her. Lily confronted Claire and called her a slag and a slut. She is jealous of Claire and now Claire is afraid that Lily may pressurise Rupert into putting the pictures on social media to humiliate her. I don't know what to advise her."

"Claire is only fifteen. In law she's a child, and anyone who possesses or distributes erotic pictures of her is committing an offence. Her mother's a social worker, she should know that. Do you want me to speak to Rupert and Lily to warn them off?"

"Thanks, it would be a real weight off my mind. She's only just told her mum. I'll send you Rupert's details."

"Can we talk about work now? That's why I came to see you. No budget to pay you I'm afraid. I'm investigating the Stella Godley murder. The officer in charge of the investigation is DCI Shadwell. Something odd's going on and it's bothering me. I can't tell Shadwell about it or make it official because he's the problem. He's always a problem, he's poisonous." She explained about the murder investigation and finding Shadwell's cigarette end at the scene. "He must have been in Royal's flat before the murder, but how and why? He won't let us investigate fully and he wasn't even on duty the day the body was found, yet he turned up at the scene and took charge."

"I'm glad you confided in me, Carly. Chi, whom I think you've met, has been following Stella on behalf of a client, Ian Blake's wife. You know Blake as Ray's solicitor. Blake's been having an affair with Stella. Now his wife Annie, my client, has gone missing, but Blake's not reported it. And he's now defending Royal for murdering Stella. You'd think he'd want Royal convicted and locked up for life. Your DCI Shadwell was seen by Chi with Stella in The Fox on the night of the murder. Stella was also with Royal that evening and Chi's convinced that she saw Stella remove Royal's keys when he was drunk and give them to Shadwell. She's shown me photographs that she took of them. Royal looks completely out of it."

"That would explain how he got into Royal's flat and left the cigarette end," Carly said. "If he knew Stella and met with her, why didn't he say so at the scene?"

"When Ray Millan's trial collapsed, there were rumours about Shadwell and Stella Godley being an item. This is bad. What can we dig up about Shadwell?"

"I can ask around at work."

"A good start, if you are trying to find out about someone, is to look in their wheelie bin."

"Much as I'd like to, a police officer can't search Shadwell's bin. He lives in a gated mews, and I don't have sufficient reasons to apply for a warrant to go in there. Applying for one would also tip off Shadwell."

"I could have Chi do it, immediately."

"Thanks for the offer, but I've got to find a way of paying Alfie for the work he did on the butt and *Full Throttle* before I can commit to paying for anything that you do for me."

"Ray has offered to put me in funds to find out what I can about what happened to Stella. We can pay Alfie and Chi with his money. Where does Shadwell live?"

"I'll get the address for you."

Kate's phone pinged and lit up. "Oh," Kate said, smiling. Carly leant over to look at the screen.

You are my favourite kind of deliciousness baby.

"It's Jacqui, she's rather emotional," Kate explained. "She's my account manager at the bank. I've been seeing her since I went there for a loan."

"What bank's that then? I should try it."

"It's not just a one-nighter."

"Not just a brief encounter then."

"I love that film. I can hear the stirring Rachmaninoff piano concerto now."

Kate's phone pinged again. They both read the message. *My heart begins at your fingertips.*

"Aaaahhh," they said in unison.

"She assessed me in bed last night."

"You don't rate each other between the sheets, do you? That's real pressure to perform."

"No, not that. She asked me questions from my course notes: trace evidence and types of marks; imprints and impressions; safe handling; secure packaging; sealing and referencing of samples; continuity; storage and preservation; completing the scene examination form; being properly briefed. Shall I go on? You know about my forensic science and crime scene investigation course. It was your idea that I sign up for it. I've got an exam tomorrow. You'd find it a doddle."

"I should hope so. You've brought Jacqui here?"

"Yes, she's new to the scene and it's part of her education."

The next morning in Union Street, Carly asked Dale, one of the team's support staff, to run a check on Stella as she didn't trust Shadwell to share anything that he found out. "See what info we have on her," she instructed.

Dale reported back that there was a police record for Stella when she was younger. "She's come out of a club late at night in Meard Street, Soho, approached a man and taken money from him to pay for a key to a flat where she said they would go to have sex. She told him to wait for her whilst she obtained the key. Of course she didn't return.

Police spotted her in Soho the next evening, and arrested and charged her with deception.

"You remember all the complaints we had about 'clipping' around that time. She was convicted after a trial. But her victim was a plain clothes police officer, a member of a task force out to catch 'clippers'. On appeal the court decided that because the officer knew that she was going to fleece him he hadn't been deceived.

"I was able to find all this information because she didn't request the deletion of her biometric data and record when her conviction was overturned. Handy that."

"Meard Street is just around the corner from where a colleague lives. I'm going there now. She'll be very interested in this," Carly said.

Carly and Kate arranged to have lunch together near Kate's flat. Before they met, Kate phoned Mary. "My friend Carly, the police officer, is going to contact Rupert and Lily and scare them off. How are things?"

"Thanks," Mary replied, "that puts my mind at rest. Don't ask me how I am. No time for lunch, applying for an Emergency Protection Order. Two young boys with recent injuries, including a cigarette burn to one of them. Dad's been seen to hit them and the mum. Both parents claim the injuries are accidental. Fat chance."

"Keep up the good work," Kate replied.

Over lunch, Carly mentioned Stella's conviction for clipping. "No surprises there," Kate said. "There's always been a club of one sort or another in Meard Street, like a goth club called Batcave in the 1980s. I took Jacqui to see the nose that an artist has glued to a wall there. Here, I'll show you." Kate leant over to share a photo of the nose saved on her phone.

"The street has some exceptionally fine early 18th century Georgian houses which escaped the bombing during the blitz. You can see them in this picture. And here is the sign that Sebastian Horsley, an artist, writer and dandy, whose home was in the street, put on his door for amusement: *This is not a brothel, there are no prostitutes at this address.* He once said, to *The Independant*, about Soho, 'the air used to be clean, and the sex used to be dirty. Now it is the other way around. Soho has lost its heart.'"

In Beechcroft House, Margaret sat with Joyce in the day room. Joyce had a pack of tarot cards laid face up on the table. "I don't see the point of this," Margaret said. "I've got no future, well none worth looking into. It's all behind me."

"It passes the time," Joyce replied. "That nice lady with the hat left them. Shame not to try them. Oh, look, this one's a thief."

"That makes sense. That'll be my Victor."

"Why don't you talk to him, Margaret? When he visits."

"He only comes to see if I'm still alive. He had to sell my house to pay the charges here. He thought he was going to inherit it. Instead, he just watches the money he got for it slip through his fingers. Buggered if I'm going to pass the time of day with him."

"Next card. Oh, Margaret, it's the Grim Reaper. You're not having much luck."

"Victor again, he'll probably try to put something in my tea to finish me off."

"Is Joyce's chair in the way?" another resident called out anxiously. "You'll have to move her if it is."

"Now, Agnes," a care assistant replied, "you know it's not in the way at all. Leave Joyce to get on with her cards."

"I thought she was in the way, just trying to help. She can get in the way you know."

"Daft as a brush," Margaret said loudly.

Chi had no difficulty finding Shadwell's home: a pseudo-Georgian house in a gated development near the newly converted Battersea Power Station. *The house is like Shadwell*, Chi thought, *pretending to the world to be something that it isn't.* Fibreglass pilasters, standing on each side of the door and pretending to function as supporting columns, were an example. The shoddy building materials throughout ridiculed the classical style which the house tried to mimic.

There was no need for her to work out how to drive in through the gates. The bins were all standing neatly in a row on the pavement outside, expecting their rubbish to be collected by the bin men at any moment, and they were all conveniently numbered according to which house they belonged. *If I had arrived in the afternoon, I might have been too late*, Chi thought.

Chi had already calculated that it would attract unwelcome attention to search them there and then, so she had brought her fluorescent yellow cycling jacket to the back of which she had attached a notice, 'Speedy Refuse Disposal'. It was mid-morning and she got down to work straight away, tipping the contents of Shadwell's bin into the black bags she had brought. She put the bags into Kate's VW Beetle and drove away.

That afternoon Chi had a phone call from her mother

in Japan, telling her that her father was seriously ill. She bought a ticket to fly home straight away and told Kate that she would go through the bags on her return. She left them in a storeroom on the ground floor of Kate's building with a note attached: *This rubbish is not really rubbish, so please don't chuck it away.*

An email from the prosecution with an attachment labelled *Crime Scene Photographs* arrived whilst Ian sat at his office desk. There would be pictures of Stella's dead body. He knew that it would upset him to see them. He forced himself to look. There it was, her naked body, lying on its back. He couldn't see her face because of the pillow. *Just as well* he thought. Then he realised, it wasn't Stella. Ian went into a state of shock as he recognised the familiar naked body of his wife. It couldn't be. Was this a joke? His mind was racing. Someone has mistaken her for Stella. Ian felt sick.

Ian's secretary Leanne knocked on his door and walked in. Ian got up from his seat, looked at her wild eyed, leant over his waste basket and noisily vomited into it.

"Are you alright, Mr. Blake? Can I do something?"

"Just go, Leanne, please." He vomited again.

He heard her talking in the corridor. "He's acting weird. I think he's taken drugs."

Ian closed the email. He began to realise the enormity of what had happened. Annie was dead and he was involved. He could not tell the police about his discovery as they would find out that he had paid for Stella to be killed. Did Victor know whose body it was? He was at the crime scene. He must have known.

Ian phoned Victor. "That's not Stella's body, it's Annie. You must have looked at her when you were there. You know what Stella looks like. What have you done?"

"What have I done? I was just carrying out your instructions. I didn't mess up."

"Well, someone did. How could they kill her, Annie I mean? What was she doing there?"

"Mistaken identity? It happens. Have you thought that she and Stella may have been in this together and Stella double-crossed her somehow."

"How can you be so matter of fact about it? She's my wife, or had you forgotten?"

"You're the one who forgot that she's your wife, when you got into bed with Stella. The first post-mortem should be finished today. Tell Snowy that you don't need a second one with your own pathologist and that the body can be released. Yuri will arrange the funeral and ask for her to be cremated. We don't want anyone digging up her grave, do we?"

"People will ask where Annie is when she doesn't turn up for work or go to the gym and when she isn't online, as usual. What do I say to them?"

"Make up a story. She has gone on a retreat in Wales. Somewhere which has a poor internet and phone signal. Park her car in a lock up and say that she's using it. If you don't look concerned, others won't be either."

Victor put the phone down on a distraught Ian. There had been talk about Victor and Stella being an item. Victor had set him up, big time. Stella will have gone to ground, using Annie's bank cards to give the impression that she was still alive.

Victor phoned Ian back: "Don't do anything to make people suspicious. We must avoid a missing person's inquiry. We don't want people here at Union Street asking lots of questions and checking CCTV and APR cameras for her."

"Where is Stella?" Ian asked lamely.

"Probably thanking her lucky stars."

11

Fuzzy Logic

'Stella's' funeral took place a week later. The only people in attendance were Bonetti, for the police, Ray her boss and Tracey and Kimberley, two of the women from Ray's agency. Yuri, Stella's 'closest friend' was a 'no show'. Annie lay unrecognised in the closed coffin. There would have been a good crowd there if people had known who was really being cremated. Ian stayed away, having been told by Victor not to advertise his relationship with Stella.

That evening, following up on Chi's information, Bonetti went to The Fastidious Fox to find if somebody else had seen Stella with Victor or Philip on the night of the murder.

Kathleen, the bartender, refused to talk to her, "I'm busy love, customers to serve."

Bonetti went over to a group of drinkers talking animatedly in the main bar. "Excuse me guys. I'm investigating the murder of Stella Godley. You may have known her. And you may know Philip Royal who's been charged with the murder. Did you see them here together on a Saturday night recently? They may have been with another man, DCI Victor Shadwell."

There was complete silence.

"Come on guys, it's important. Your information could help Mr Royal."

One of them broke ranks: "Buy us a round love, that might loosen our tongues." The others laughed.

Bonetti gave them a contemptuous look and went into the back bar to try her luck there. It was *Barking Mad*, the comedy night. The room was crowded. She recognised Charli, a new woman stand-up on the stage. Charli saw Bonetti come through the door and gave her a wave.

Charli: "I'm single and ready to mingle. Anyone out there interested?"

1st man shouting out: "Me."

Charli sounding surprised: "That was quick, are you excited?"

1st man: "Yeah."

Charli, shielding her eyes with her hand: "I can't see you properly, with all the lights in my face. Is he good looking?"

Woman shouting out: "He's got a good heart."

Charli: "He'll need it if I'm going to take him for a ride."

Women in the audience laughed and cheered.

2nd man shouting out: "Take me."

Charli: "Wow, he's got competition. Take it outside boys and let me know who's the winner."

Woman calling out: "They're brothers."

Charli: "Really? What are your names boys, Cain and Abel? If you really are Cain and Abel fighting over me, then I must be God. I always knew that God is a woman."

Women in the audience cheered.

Bonetti decided not to interrupt Charli's act and left.

After she had gone, the talk in the main bar was about Philip's photographic studio in his flat, and the scantily clad would-be models who visited there. An account of his sexual assault trial had occupied a full page of the *Daily Splash*. The same drinkers had lapped up every word of the article, whilst pulling mock scandalised faces, passing the newspaper 'round from one to the other.

Chambers are the rooms which barristers work from. They get together in a 'set' of chambers to share work, overhead expenses, a library, and the clerks who manage them. Each set belongs to an Inn of Court. The two pre-eminent Inns, with many sets of chambers, are Old Inn, with a long and distinguished history, popular with the traditionalists. And New Inn, which attracts the avant-garde, enlightened, modern type of lawyer.

Century Buildings and Stack Court are both London sets. Century Buildings, with its Liberty print curtains and wallpaper, Conran furniture and state-of-the-art IT, is in New Inn. Stack Court, whose members regard those in Century buildings as pretentious upstarts and posers, is a member of Old Inn.

Old Inn was set up in the 13th century. By the 16th century it had reached a golden age, when it was as famous for the revels, masques, plays and banquets which it hosted as it was for the brilliance of its teaching, and the influence that its members could bring to bear on the courts and the institutions of government. Saunders and Archer will have been defended and prosecuted by barristers from sets in Old Inn, where the trial judges will also have been members.

New Inn, in complete contrast, was founded in the late 20th century and its sets are accused of behaving towards the others like ungrateful children. The extracurricular activities of the barristers are managed on behalf of the Inns by Christopher Carruthers, known to everyone as 'CC'.

CC runs Barri-Bets, a betting syndicate which is open to members of all the Inns of Court, where they may wager on the outcome of any Crown Court trial. To join the syndicate, a judge or barrister must be introduced by two members who can vouch for their discretion. The odds are fixed by Barri-Bets and the pay-outs are based on the odds offered when the individual bets were placed. Called 'live odds', they can change, influenced by developments in the case up to the moment when the jurors retire. The bet is completed when the jury foreman announces their verdict and cannot be undone if the verdict is set aside on appeal.

CC is aided by an AI powered algorithm he calls Veronica to help him fix the odds. Fond of innuendos about Veronica, he'd say, "If you don't like the odds, blame Veronica, not me. She kept me up late last night, with her fuzzy logic."

CC, Veronica and all the members of the Inns have access to the Courts' Electronic Store. This is where, in a spirit of full disclosure, all the evidence to be presented at trial from both the prosecution and the defence must be deposited. Veronica's predictions are based on this information, and fuzzy data such as: 'give aways' from the behaviour of the punters placing bets; records of the success rates of the barristers in the case; any suspected bias of the judge; and the demographics of a jury which may show whether they are likely to believe police evidence or not.

All the profits go to fund a chain of rest and recuperation centres ('R and R' resorts) around the world where the members can stay at a heavily subsidised rate.

The head clerk in a set will sit down with any new tenant who is a betting novice, to explain how Barri-Bets odds are calculated.

Ryan, the head clerk in a set at Fisher Court, instructed two new tenants. "Listen up, I won't repeat this. Yes, do take notes. The odds are written as a fraction. The first number in the fraction is the Barri-Bets stake, and the second number is your wager. The fraction stands for the likelihood of an event happening, such as an acquittal. I'll call that event 'X'. If the first number in the fraction is bigger than the second, like 4/1, and Veronica considers X, an acquittal, unlikely, Barri-Bets will stake £4 for every £1 that you wager that the defendant will be acquitted. This is called 'odds-against' the acquittal. If the numbers are the same, then the chance of X is even. Any questions so far?"

"So, let's do some examples. I'll write them on the white board. 4/1 suggests a 1 in 5 (4+1) or 20% chance of X, an acquittal. So, its 'odds-against' X. Wager £100 on X and if you win, you will be paid £400 (4 divided by 1 = 4, so 4 x your stake) plus your stake. Lose any bet and you lose your stake. Does anybody have a comment or a question?

"It's obvious."

"Thank you, Mr Rivers. Must be the way that I tell it."

"Do you give tips?"

"I have been known to, Ms Brown. And I like Cuban cigars."

"Do the odds represent real probabilities?"

"Good question, Ms Jackson. No, Barri-Bets wants to win overall, and Veronica is programmed to adjust the probability slightly in their favour. You must take that into account, as well as doing your homework by comparing Barri-Bets likely outcome with your estimate of the real outcome."

Members of the Inns meet during their leisure time in the public houses near to the barristers' chambers. There is frenzied discussion amongst members about who or what Veronica is. Some barristers claim to have seen her with CC and that she's 'hot'. Several even boast that they have dated her. Their descriptions of her become increasingly outlandish as the drink flows. Ryan was able to put a group of them straight about her 'fuzzy logic': "It's an approach to computing using data and information which is vague and lacking certainty."

Gossip, rumour and inside knowledge about ongoing trials is traded in the public houses, including the inevitable complaints about a protagonist hiding information. Philip's trial was a simple two-horse race: guilty or not guilty to murder. There was no co-accused and Barri-Bets were not taking wagers on a manslaughter outcome.

Her Honour Judge Penny Winter sat in court number one, Riverside Crown Court. Felicity Crabtree had arrived to represent Philip at this, the plea and case management hearing. She entered the courtroom after speaking to him in the cells. "He gives me the creeps," she confided to the usher. Felicity sat patiently, waiting for Philip's case to be called on.

Winter looked up to acknowledge her. Then looked back at the Barri-Betts app open on the tablet in front of her.

Philip was brought into the dock. The court clerk read the charge to him. The betting opened in his case as he entered a not guilty plea to a charge of the murder of Stella Godley. Nicholls, the prosecuting barrister, asked Winter to remand him in custody. Felicity did not apply for bail and the hearing was soon over.

No contest: Veronica had decided he'd be convicted. The odds to bet he'd be acquitted were set at 20/1 against. Nobody was prepared to risk their money on the case. Grant looked at the odds and decided not to put Chi's money on a long-shot acquittal.

Ian sat with Philip in the late afternoon, waiting at HM Prison Gormley for Benjamin Hind QC leading counsel. Philip was concerned that he hadn't met the senior brief. Junior counsel Felicity was at home with flu.

Ian looked at his watch. Hind was late. Ian had to hand in his phone on entering the prison and was unable to contact him.

"That emergency services call, I've been set up," Philip said disconsolately.

"By whom, Philip, Chloe?" Ian asked, sounding sceptical.

"I don't know."

"It's definitely your voice on the recording."

"Yes, I said some of those things."

"What, 'it looks like she's dead.' Really, Philip, what's the matter with you?"

"I didn't say it like that."

"Now I don't know what you are telling me."

Before Philip could try to explain, Benjamin arrived. He was sweating profusely as he entered the legal visits room. He put his hand inside a bulging supermarket 'bag for life' and pulled out a pile of dog-eared papers. The brief was covered with overlapping circle-shaped red wine glass stains. *They look like the Rio 2016 Olympic games logo,* Ian thought.

"Don't worry," Benjamin said unconvincingly, "we'll beat this charge, we'd better get started…err," he opened and scanned the brief, "Philip."

When Benjamin had gone, rushing to catch his train, Philip looked at Ian.

"My God, where did you find that heap of compost?"

"He's very experienced."

"Old you mean, well past his sell by date and probably always available."

Bonetti admired the interior décor of 5 Century Buildings. It was like a five-star hotel. Shadwell was enjoying two weeks holiday in Spain and Detective Chief Superintendent Drake had sent her to the conference with prosecuting counsel. They sat with her around the table in a meeting room: Monty Bell QC the leader, Cecilia Lassi his junior, and Jack Couper from the Public Prosecutor's Office.

After discussing the overwhelming evidence against Philip Royal, Bonetti said that she had concerns that she wanted to share. Monty looked towards her. "Let's hear what's troubling you," he said, smiling at her in a patronising way.

"It's about DCI Shadwell, who's leading this investigation. The defence will have conducted their own research about his disciplinary record. He has enough misconduct notices to paper the walls of this room."

"He is a much-respected officer," chipped in Jack Couper. "I'm surprised and rather disappointed that DS Bonetti has chosen to drag her senior officer through the dirt when he is away enjoying a well-earned rest." Monty nodded, as if in agreement.

"Hear me out," Bonetti continued. "What worries me is that Stella Godley, the victim in this case, worked for Ray Millan, you know, the so-called 'London's call-girl king'. You must remember the bad publicity for the police when his trial collapsed. Rumour has it that DCI Shadwell was in a relationship with her. I accept that their liaison is unproven. Ian Blake was the solicitor who defended Millan. I have received information from an inquiry agent, Chihiro *Fookoodah*, who has been employed by Blake's wife, that Blake was having an affair with Miss Godley. Yet Blake is now defending Philip Royal, and he has instructed Benjamin Hind to lead for the defence."

"He's an old soak," Monty contributed.

"If Royal is convicted, he will probably have grounds to appeal, due to Hind's inadequate representation," Cecilia added.

"Her two former lovers are involved with this murder: DCI Shadwell is investigating it, whilst Blake is defending the man accused of it," Bonetti summarised.

"A bit incestuous," Monty agreed.

"I have also received information from Ms *Fookoodah*," Bonetti continued, "that on the night of the murder she saw DCI Shadwell in the company of Miss Godley in The Fox in Vauxhall. Royal was also in the pub that night and she saw Godley appear to take some keys from him and pass them to DCI Shadwell."

"She gets around, your Ms whatever," Jack Couper commented.

"What's more," Bonetti continued, refusing to be put off course, "DC Stant was the first Major Crimes officer at the scene, arriving before DCI Shadwell, who was supposed to be off duty. It concerns me that Stant found a cigarette butt with Shadwell's DNA on Royal's bedside table before Shadwell had arrived."

"Talk of a relationship between Godley and DCI Shadwell is just that, talk. I call it idle gossip," Couper said. We all know that DCI Shadwell was present at the scene and Stant could easily be mistaken about when he first saw the butt. It's not as if it's the find of the century. About the rest, it doesn't help to prove our case against Royal. And as for his choice of Ian Blake as his lawyer, that's up to them both. None of our business."

"These are serious allegations to make against a senior officer," Monty said. "Have you at least put them to DCI Shadwell, to see what he has to say?"

"He was asked about the cigarette butt and claims that Stant is mistaken about when he left it there. As far as the sighting in the pub is concerned, I found out about that later and DCI Shadwell is currently on leave, on holiday abroad, so, no, I've not been able to raise that with him."

"Have you approached Shadwell's boss, Detective

Chief Superintendent Drake about your concerns?" Cecilia asked.

"No, I haven't, not yet. He won't thank me for bringing him this mess to deal with."

Monty and Cecilia apologised for having to end the conference to deal with another prosecution case. Couper stayed with them. Bonetti left the room.

"If what she says is true, this cigarette butt item would have to appear on a schedule and be disclosed to the defence and they will parade it in front of the jury," Couper said. "We should keep it to ourselves. The defence would have a field day with it. It's all very unfortunate, but it's just a red herring. I don't want any of this on any disclosure schedules."

"Well, Benjamin's not going to probe," Monty commented. "He'll be too busy at lunchtime taking his medicine, the best red wine that the Whig and Gown, next door to the court, can offer."

"Ms what's her name works for Kate Sullivan," Couper added. "I have heard rumours that Ms Sullivan and DS Bonetti are 'close', if you know what I mean."

Monty and Cecilia looked at Couper blankly.

"I am not sure whether their relationship is only a work one. You know, I've seen them wearing 'rainbow badges'," Couper added, by way of further explanation, giving Monty and Cecilia a knowing look. They ignored him.

Later, when Couper had left, Monty Bell turned to Cecilia Lassi, looking quizzical. "The Detective Sergeant suspects that her boss can't be trusted to investigate this murder and may have some 'skin in the game'. We don't want to be dragged into their infighting. And there's a risk it could derail this case if we're not careful. I don't trust Couper's advice. I know that we need to win these good prosecution briefs that we get but there's something unprofessional about the man. What are the odds on this trial?"

"20/1 against his acquittal," Cecilia said.

"Those odds will shorten if some of this information leaks," Monty calculated, "but I still wouldn't risk putting any money on it, yet."

12

Unexpected Guest

Shadwell was on a beach in Marbella, which used to be known as the Costa del Crime. He received a message from Jack Couper, the gist of which was that Bonetti was digging up 'stuff' about him to do with the Stella Godley murder and that she could make problems for him. Couper signed off: *just a warning from an old friend.*

Shadwell went online and changed his flight home, bringing it forward by a couple of days. After his plane landed in London, late in the evening, he collected his Audi from the airport car park and drove straight to his girlfriend's flat. He hadn't seen the need to tell her of his change of plan. He assumed that she would be at home, although she was not expecting him.

Shadwell had been in a relationship of sorts with Ektrina Lavislova for almost one year. They met in the betting shop where she worked, close to Union Street Police Station. Ektrina was from Lithuania and was studying English. Shadwell was very possessive about her and didn't like the way customers in the betting shop would chat to her in an over-friendly way. He wanted to know who her fellow English students were and was jealous if she mentioned a male student's name.

Ektrina lived on her own in a split-level early 1970's concrete and brick-built council flat in Bermondsey. Shadwell parked in the estate car park and used a spare set of keys to enter her block. He went up to her floor. As usual, the lift smelt of urine and cannabis. He walked along the landing to her front door, passing a man in a white vest and jogging bottoms who was taking his dog out for a late-night toilet.

He opened the flat door and went into the hall. He was about to call out a welcome to her when he heard noises from upstairs. They were of a man and Ektrina. The man was grunting rhythmically in a deep voice, like a steam train going up a steep incline. Victor remembered the Burl Ives song *The Little Engine That Could* which 'moaned, groaned, huffed, and puffed' up the mountain. The bed was creaking and Ektrina was making a high-pitched whining sound. There was no doubt in Shadwell's mind that Ektrina was upstairs in her bedroom having full-on enthusiastic sex with a stranger.

Shadwell paused at the foot of the stairs. The coupling noises had stopped and instead he heard Ektrina's startled voice, "Shit, victor's back." There was pandemonium as Victor ran up the stairs and someone slammed the bedroom door shut and held it against him. He put his shoulder to it and burst into the room. He saw a naked, bald, dark-skinned man sitting on the side of the bed frantically trying to pull on his socks. Ektrina was holding the bed sheet around her. The man looked scared and Ektrina looked startled.

"Fazil, so you're the unexpected visitor, you bastard." Victor stood over Fazil Khan, Ektrina's betting shop manager.

"We're in love," Fazil said weakly, "she wants to be with me."

Victor looked at Ektrina. "It's true," she said bravely, "I wanted to tell you before. And Fazil is kind to me."

Victor's face hardened. He stared at Fazil. "Kneel down and say your prayers old man," he said coldly.

"Please let me go," Fazil begged, his eyes moist and his forehead sweating.

Victor pushed Ektrina down on to the bed. "You are disgusting," he said to her.

Fazil had pulled on his socks and underpants and made a break for the door. Victor rugby tackled him and brought him down to the ground, holding on to him by his legs. Fazil managed to get to his feet again and reach the top of the stairs. Victor took hold of him by his waist and using all his strength threw him down the stairs so that he went crashing to the bottom, breaking the bannisters as he fell and hitting his head against a heavy piece of furniture in the hall.

Victor followed him down and stood over a cowering Fazil. "I found you in my lady's chamber. I haven't heard you praying Fazil. You don't know any Anglican prayers. Should I torture and kill you?"

"Please no," Fazil mumbled.

"Get dressed," Victor ordered. "I'll throw your clothes down to you."

Victor went back to the bedroom and gathered up Fazil's belongings. He heard noises outside and then a fist banging on the flat door. "Police, open the door."

Victor fetched a bottle of whisky from the kitchen. He held Fazil's mouth open and poured as much of the whisky as he could down Fazil's throat. Fazil made choking noises. He then put the neck of the bottle in Fazil's hand. Victor dumped Fazil's property next to him and opened the front door. There were two uniformed officers outside, a man and a woman. Victor showed them his warrant card. They looked at Fazil, who was trying to get up.

"This is Fazil Khan," Victor announced. "He's outstayed his welcome. I'm afraid that he's very drunk. He was trying to sleep it off upstairs but needed the toilet and some more whisky and he has just fallen down the stairs."

The officers came into the hallway. "Your neighbour heard a disturbance and is concerned about the lady's safety," the male officer explained. They walked past Victor and helped Fazil to his feet. Ektrina, now dressed, appeared again at the top of the stairs. Victor stood behind the officers, facing Fazil and Ektrina. He looked at them both and drew his finger slowly across his throat.

"I'm sorry," Fazil bleated. "It's my fault. I'll get dressed and go now. I won't cause any more trouble."

The female officer went upstairs and took Ektrina back into her bedroom. Victor heard them speaking together. The officer came out of the bedroom and called down, "it's alright, Jason, she says the same, we might as well leave them to it."

"No more disturbance now," the male officer warned Fazil, "we don't want to have to come back." "Sorry guvnor," the officer said to Victor, "domestic violence protocol: we have to speak to the lady on her own." The police officers left.

Fazil was dressed and Victor held the front door open for him. His nose was bleeding, and he had a large lump swelling up on the side of his head. "Next time, I will carry you out in pieces in a bin bag," Victor threatened him.

"Now," Victor declared looking at Ektrina, "what am I going to do with you, you slut?"

Stant pulled Bonetti into an empty office in the police station. "Do I scream now?" Bonetti asked, shaking his arm off her.

"Shadwell's on the warpath and he's after you. Somehow, he's found out that you've been badmouthing him and making allegations over the Godley murder, be careful," Stant said.

"He'll be even more upset when he finds out that we, well Chi really, has been going through his wheelie bin. We'll see what she finds."

"You'll never make detective inspector this way."

"I'm not like Sarah Taylor. Since Police Training College she's been 'yes sir, no sir, three bags full sir.' She thinks she's going to be a commander one day. I'm not goose-stepping my way to promotion like her."

"You didn't hesitate when Shadwell told you to get him some ciggies though."

"I was taken aback. I wasn't thinking. Should have told him it's not my job."

"Before you cause too much upset, don't forget that you've got someone else to consider, who is reliant on you. How is young Henry?"

"Same as usual."

"My pal Jason, from Tower Bridge, tells me that Shadwell was engaged in a spot of bother last night. Jason was in the fast response car called to Shadwell's bird's flat. You must remember Ektrina, the tall slim attractive blonde number whom Shadwell brought to the Christmas party last year. He got drunk, they had a row and she left early. I felt sorry for her. Well, last night there was a drunk guy, Fazil something, who'd fallen down the stairs in her flat. They all said that it was an accident. She told Patsy, Jason's partner, that the man was her friend Fazil and that he'd drunk too much scotch. She was crying and he was almost naked."

"What was Shadwell doing back last night? He wasn't due until the day after tomorrow. He must have come back early without telling poor Ektrina. Calling her a 'bird' and a 'blonde number', Steve, really, explain yourself."

"Well, it's better than 'bit of skirt', the awful slang that PC Clark uses."

"You've given me an idea. Shadwell's slave, poor girl. She's had enough of him and wants a new life with Fazil. I think I'll pay her a visit. What about the results from the police lab?"

"They've only just sent them. Maybe it was poor quality DNA they tested. That would explain why they only found traces of Philip. No matches for Stella."

Back from Japan, Chi spread newspapers across the floor in Kate's kitchen and tipped the rubbish bags out onto them. The kitchen soon smelt like the bin. Chi held her nose at first, but then became accustomed to the pong. She opened a window, put on rubber gloves, and started rooting through the rubbish.

Her finds included empty bottles of spirits, a horse racing newspaper and an Arsenal programme. Coated in bits of roast potato and what looked like thick and creamy yellowish goose fat, she found a polaroid photograph which had been cut into many small pieces. *Why would he try to destroy it so completely?* she thought. *I'll see if I can put it back together.* She made sure that she had placed all the pieces of the photograph in the see-through exhibits bag.

That evening, Chi and Grant were eating out in The Grafenburg, the restaurant next to the G Spot and owned by the same proprietor. They studied the menu.

"There's a half roast goose, Hong Kong style," Grant said. "We could share it. It's been marinated in soybean paste, oyster sauce, sugar, salt and five spice powder."

"The goose reminds me of the contents of Shadwell's bin: shredded polaroid with goose fat and roast potatoes."

"Chi, that's weird, what are you talking about?"

"It's what I've been doing to earn a living, not very nice."

"I don't understand."

"I've been searching through someone's rubbish. I found a cut-up picture and used my dissectologist skills to put it back together. I hope it can be examined forensically. I may have discovered something important."

"Your what skills?"

"Jigsaw puzzle solving."

"Tell me more."

Grant encouraged Chi to tell him everything that she knew about Philip's murder case. Chi told him about Ian having a relationship with Stella before defending Philip;

about Shadwell's meeting with Stella on the night of the murder; and his visit to Philip's flat, using the keys that Stella had taken from Philip. She ended up explaining about the cigarette butt and the picture.

"We, that's DS Bonetti, Kate and I, think that Shadwell's involved somehow," she concluded. She didn't know that Grant was the clerk to Benjamin Hind QC and Felicity Crabtree, the defence team. She still thought that he was an investment banker.

Grant leant forward on the edge of his seat as she spoke, so that he would not miss a single word. She had never seen him so attentive and interested in what she had to say.

"Well, I never," he said, when she had finished. "You do lead an exciting life." *Century Buildings kept that to themselves*, he thought. Grant's mind was racing. *That'll blow the prosecution case wide open. Juries aren't interested in evidence and the obvious explanations, like Philip killed Stella, that's too easy. They like to play amateur detective and follow the scent put down by the defence team which leads away from the truth. They go home at night, during the trial, look things up on the internet and come back the next morning with their own madcap ideas.*

After their meal, they moved on to the club. "We should give it a go, the G spot, you know the real thing," Grant said tipsily, putting his arm around Chi.

"Just don't give up after ten minutes. More importantly, how are you doing with my money. Have you doubled it yet?"

Grant didn't answer her. *If I put some of Chi's money on his acquittal, before I tell Benjamin and Felicity what I know*, Grant thought, *I'll still get brilliant odds.*

"Grant, have you forgotten that I'm here? You seem preoccupied. You won't breathe a word to anyone about what I told you about the case, will you?"

Grant excused himself and hurried to the toilets. He locked himself in a cubicle and checked the Barri-Bets app on his phone. The odds were still 20/1 against Philip being acquitted. He scrolled down to R v Royal in the list of cases and tapped on it, keyed in £20,000 in the 'amount' box and pressed 'send' on the 'make a bet' option. *That'll start Veronica off,* he thought. *If she thinks that someone knows something about Philip's case that she doesn't, she may shorten the odds, then everyone will be speculating about what's happening.*

Grant sat back down and smiled at Chi. 'Always save the sweet things until last,' his mother had told him. "You have my undivided attention, let's go to mine," he said.

The morning after Grant had secured his bet at odds of 20/1 against, he told Felicity about what Chi had confided to him the night before. "Far too important to keep it to myself," he said, "a man's life is at stake." He hadn't bothered to inform Benjamin who wasn't answering his phone and was last spotted the night before, tucked up with a bottle of the best red wine in a local watering hole. Felicity at once grasped the significance of what Chi had told Grant.

After Grant had placed his bet, Veronica calculated that someone must know something in Philip's favour which she didn't, and immediately shortened the odds of Philip's acquittal to 15/1 against.

In 5 Century Buildings and in 1 Stack Court the communication lines were buzzing after the odds changed.

"Do you think that someone has blabbed about what Bonetti told us?" Monty asked Cecilia.

"They must have. They've listed a disclosure application tomorrow before Winter."

When Veronica found out about that, she reduced the odds of a jury acquitting Philip to 10/1 against.

The following morning, in court number 1 Riverside Crown Court, Felicity was making the application. She requested Winter to order the prosecution to disclose everything that they knew about DCI Shadwell's alleged association with Stella Godley, including information from a witness who had seen the two of them together shortly before the murder; the cigarette butt linked to DCI Shadwell at the murder scene; and DC Stant's notebook entries about the time when he found it.

Felicity arrived at court early so that she could discuss with Cecilia the items that she required to be disclosed. Couper was there and interrupted Felicity in a mocking and dismissive way: "you know diddly squat," he told her.

In court, Cecilia opposed the application. Felicity had decided not to refer to the polaroid photograph because she wasn't able to say yet how it could help her and was reluctant, if pressed, to explain to the judge how it was obtained.

"It's just a fishing expedition, Your Honour," Cecilia complained. "They don't know whether any of it is relevant."

HH Judge Winter was in expansive form. "The police, with their far greater resources, investigate on behalf of the defence as well as the prosecution, don't they, Ms Lassi? You shall have everything you ask for, Ms Crabtree. I won't have any secrets in my court."

Felicity looked across the courtroom at the dejected Cecilia. *That's cooked your goose* she thought. Winter left the court room in a hurry and put her bet, another £500, on Philip's acquittal at 10/1 against. It wasn't long before Veronica brought the odds down again to 5/1 against.

"It looks as if he's tried to hide something," Kate told Carly on the phone. "Chi has fitted the pieces of the polaroid together and cleaned it up. It's a picture of the crime scene, with the body on the bed." Carly went straight over to Kate's.

"This'll go directly to Alfie," she said to Kate. "Another of my 'Carly specials', courtesy of Ray. One of his experts may be able to capture it digitally and enlarge and enhance the image. There may be an important detail that we can't see now."

Carly phoned Stant from Kate's. "I've put you on loudspeaker. We're seeing Ektrina. Kate and I have a plan."

"Please don't tell me, I don't want to know. I hope that it doesn't involve a wardrobe," Stant replied.

"Don't remind me. We can do better than that," Carly said, and laughed.

13

The Sting

"If he thinks I'm looking at another man, he calls me slut or whore. If I leave phone on charge, he searches it to read messages. He phones constantly at work and says to go straight home when finish. If I am out with friends, he phones to find who I am with and what I am doing. If I am happy when I meet him having been with friends, he gets angry, because it shows him that I can be happy without him. He has imposed curfew, and phones me to check that I am keeping it. I told him I was depressed. I thought he might understand and help. Instead, he saw it as criticism of him and called me negative and said I didn't love him or care about him, screaming in face."

Kate and Carly had managed to persuade Ektrina to talk. She met them in a café, looking around nervously at first, afraid that Victor would somehow spot her with them.

"I was born Vilnius, the capital of Lithuania. I was educated under Russian regime. From school I went to work in office. Times were tough in Lithuania. I lived with parents and after father died found it hard, mother, brother, and I, to manage financially. Brother is disabled and cannot work. So, I came to London to earn money and send it home. I found job in betting shop because I am good at maths. I met Victor there, he was customer. We got on well. He was fun to be with first, always doing exciting things, spending money on me. Then he became controlling and cut me off from friends. He doesn't like me going home to see family. He says that I should only get pleasure from being with him.

"If I am using laptop, he wants to know what I am looking at. I may be embarrassed to show him and shut my computer screen. Then he will be upset and say I am trying to hide something and get angry and say he cannot trust me. I cannot keep anything from him as he knows all passwords. He insisted I tell him what they were and said we should have no secrets. I thought it was romantic."

"Was he ever violent towards you?" Bonetti asked.

"If I put hands to ears to shut out his swearing, he pulls them away. If we argue and I don't reply, he says I must be feeling guilty. If I stand up for myself, he says I am defensive. If I try escape from argument by leaving room, he blocks doorway, grabs arm, pushes me back into room and down on sofa.

"He is very jealous and once, when I was late meeting him, accused me of having been with another man. He grabbed bag from around neck to look through contents and hit my face with his hand, leaving bruise and swelling. When I wouldn't show him phone, he gripped wrist tightly, making me drop it and bruising skin.

"My confidence was so low I continued having sex with him only because I thought his happiness more important than mine. I realise now he is aggressive, jealous man and

I must put myself first or he will destroy me. My boss at work, Fazil, was very attentive and kind. I started seeing him behind Victor's back. You know what happened when he returned from holiday: he beat Fazil up."

"How do you protect yourself with him Ektrina?"

"You mean pull-out?"

"No, from Victor's aggression."

"Oh, when I first met him, he said he liked that I wouldn't say 'boo to a goose'. Now I have learnt to scream when he goes to hurt me. He hates my screaming, and it freaks him out. Neighbours don't like it either. I think his dad was bully when Victor was child, and he was frightened when mum would scream at dad to stop him."

"What he has done are crimes: assault by beating, and control and coercion. But you probably don't need to be told that," Carly said.

"Why is Victor called *pig*?" Ektrina asked. "He says they call me pig, so I'll act like one."

"It's what some people call police officers. We'd like to think it stands for Pride, Integrity, and Guts, but we know that it doesn't."

"But why?" Ektrina asked. "In my country we would call you names, like *milicija*, meaning military, *sikna,* that's arse, or *siknask*, that's arsehole, but never pigs, we love pigs."

"Sir Robert Peel, the founder of the police service in London, used to breed pigs," Kate explained. "American riot police officers, who wore gas masks when they tried to control anti-war demonstrations in the seventies, looked like they had pigs' faces. Pigs are said, unfairly, to stand for greed, gluttony, and uncleanliness. Even back in the

16th century someone who was heartily disliked would be called a pig. There's the expression 'pig ugly', or 'you can put lipstick on a pig, but it's still a pig,' or 'you can't make a silk purse out of a sow's ear,' or 'casting pearls before swine.' You're the pearl Ektrina."

"I like 'ducks and geese', the old cockney rhyming slang for police," Carly said. "And there's *plod* for a man and *plonk* for a woman; and *nickers*; but you get used to pigs. We get called *rashers*. When I was in uniform, I would walk down the street, and someone would say 'I smell bacon.'"

"The helmets that some police officers still wear on patrol," said Kate, "look like breasts and people call them *tit heads*. When my dad was a police constable and called in at home, we'd say *get that tit off your head*."

"I do smell bacon," Ektrina said, "but not you Carly. Can we get breakfast please?"

The three of them tucked into a cooked breakfast each, washed down with cups of tea.

"We must get down to business," Carly urged. "Ektrina, do you want to leave him?"

"Scared that he will follow and find and hurt me. He swore that if I left, he'd kill me. I'm sure that's what happened to his ex-Janice. Nobody knows where she is. And he beat up poor Fazil. He's not forgiven me for cheating on him."

"Well, the only way of keeping you safe is by getting him locked up, for a long time."

"I know how he makes money. But there are too many others involved, in police force. It's not safe for me to tell you. How would you get him behind bars?"

"We think that he is involved somehow in the murder of another woman. She was smothered with a pillow during sex."

"Oh my God no, I'm really terrified now. He likes to put hand over my mouth and nose as he's having sex with me. He likes to see panic. He says it should make me excited, but it doesn't."

"We need evidence that we haven't got yet. That's where you come in. Will you help us?"

"To get that bastard, what do I have to do?"

"We want you to ask him to tie you down. Tell him that you want to experiment. Say that it would make you excited to hear about the terrible things that he has done to other women. Ask him whether he has ever killed a woman. We need him to give you specifics, so that we know he's talking about Stella Godley. We will be nearby, listening to what he says and recording it. We'll make sure that he can't hurt you."

"Will he believe me, that I want him to tie me down?"

"I'm sure that you can play the part, if you want to get rid of him badly enough," Kate said.

"How will you keep me safe and hear what he says?"

"We'll be outside the flat in a car, linked up to a recording device which I'll hide in your bedroom," Carly explained.

It was late June, and Ian's mind drifted as he sat on a hard bench in the Main Hall of Old Club. It was the occasion of the annual Edward Crowden Memorial Lecture. The Lord Chief Justice, Lord Gilbert Osling, had chosen the title of the subject he was to speak about: How is the Principle of Transferred Malice Interpreted in English Law Today?

Ian tried to concentrate. He noticed Felicity sitting several rows in front of him. She turned around and gave him a wave.

"We owe a great debt to Sir Edmund Plowden," Lord Osling told the audience. "A brilliant lawyer, one of the first law reporters, also a member of this Inn. A brave man, who stuck to his principles. A Catholic, who in the 16th century turned down the best job in the law, Lord Chancellor, rather than deny his faith. He fearlessly defended Catholics on trial for hearing Mass. A layperson, who was an agent of the State, celebrated Mass so that he could catch and inform on Catholics who attended. Edward Crowden defended one of those Catholics. He declared, 'no priest, no Mass, the case is altered', and the Catholic was acquitted."

Ian's mind started to wander. How could he live with the fact that he had paid for Stella to be murdered or that he had brought about Annie's death? Raised a Catholic, guilt was ever present.

He had read in Graham Greene's *The Honorary Consul* that in a real love affair a man was interested in a woman who was someone distinct from himself. With Annie, bit by bit they had adapted themselves to each other, picked up each other's habits, ideas, even turns of phrase so that they gradually became a part of each other. And then what interest remained?

Greene wrote how a whore is the stranger in the bed that everyone needs.

It was good not to be fanatically correct in one's moral behaviour. Edmund Burke believed that people who hate vices too much love people too little.

But these were just excuses, to rationalise his behaviour. He could still get satisfaction from intimacy with Annie, his wife, despite indulging in a love affair with Stella, the stranger.

Lord Osling coughed, which brought Ian back to the lecture. "In 1575," he said, "Plowden reported the case of Saunders and Archer. Saunders wanted to kill his wife, so that he could marry another woman. He prepared a poisoned apple which he gave her to eat. His plan went awry when she gave the apple to their daughter Eleanor and Eleanor ate the apple and died. Saunders was convicted of the murder of Eleanor even though he had never intended to kill her. For transferred malice to apply, how important is it that the unintended victim was killed in the same manner in which the intended victim was meant to die, in this case by poisoning?"

Ian's mind drifted away from the lecture and his chin sunk.

"Have the courts moved away from this idea, so it is enough if simply carrying out the plan to kill the intended victim somehow causes the death of the actual victim?"

Ian's mind drifted off again. Later, brought to his senses by the hardness of the bench, he shifted his bottom.

Lord Osling concluded his lecture: "So, we understand from Plowden's report of Saunders and Archer, that where there is an accomplice, an important feature of the application of the principle of transferred malice is whether the accomplice knew the killer's true intention." Ian had missed Lord Osling's explanation for that.

He was a popular Lord Chief Justice and Ian applauded enthusiastically, along with the rest of the audience. Ian said "hello" to Felicity and other Old Inn's members whom he knew and left.

Kate and Carly had arrived by car, bringing plastic cups and a flask of hot coffee to keep them alert.

"We're early, Victor's not due for some time," Carly said. They sat in the car drinking the coffee.

Carly passed the time with Kate, telling her about Henry. "He always has money to buy things. He's got an expensive new phone. I don't know how he could afford it. His dad must be giving him money to make up for the lack of time he spends with his son. He said he hasn't given him anything, but I'm not sure I believe him, he's never been honest with me."

They went up to Ektrina's flat to check that she was still on board with the plan.

"He's due in half an hour," Ektrina said nervously.

"I've got the camera and audio recorder, just need to hide them somewhere," Carly said.

Ektrina wore seductive underwear and looked vulnerable and fragile. She placed candles around the bed to provide an ambience that she hoped would encourage Victor to engage with her.

Just then they heard a key turn in the flat door one floor below.

"Shit, it's Victor, he's early, what do we do?" Ektrina asked in a panic.

Fortunately, Ektrina had a large antique double wardrobe in her bedroom. Carly grabbed Kate's arm and pulled her towards it, indicating silence with her finger over her lips. They climbed inside hastily, pushing some clothes to one side. It took Kate back to the games of sardines she had played in dark rooms as a child, except that now they used the torchlights on their phones instead of battery torches to provide light when they needed it.

There were two large keyholes and as Kate viewed the bedroom scene through her keyhole, she wondered if it would be like a pier-end reel of *What the Butler Saw*, where the household's butler peeps through a bedroom door keyhole and watches the lady of the house partially undressing. The thought of seeing Victor's sexual antics was not a pleasant one.

Victor entered the room. "This looks more like a church than a love nest: all these candles. I got your message: you want to try something new and experiment with bondage. Well, I've never let a lady down yet."

"I want you to tie me down." Ektrina was laid on the bed. Victor stood there and looked at her. He didn't react, apart from taking off his coat and hanging it up. Kate and Carly were glued to the keyholes, hardly daring to breath.

"I've brought my special rope to tie you up."

'Tie me down, tie you up,' Ektrina did not seem to notice the subtle difference.

The recording device functioned silently in the wardrobe.

"I'm going to truss you up," Victor said.

She didn't realise that 'truss up' is one stage on from 'tie up'.

"Tell me all dreadful things you've done to women; I want to know. It will make me excited. Have you ever killed woman, Victor? I want to hear you say you have."

Victor started to truss Ektrina up.

"I'm not that sort of person."

"Please tell me you have. It must be ultimate thrill."

"Sorry to disappoint you."

"You can trust me. Was it Stella? I know you went with her. How did you do it, tell me please. I want to share your secret. It will make me feel special."

"I wish I could, but I can't, because it didn't happen."

Victor looped the rope around each of her ankles. He bound them together and tied a knot. Ektrina looked surprised. She had expected him to tie her legs so that they were apart, not together. Victor took the two ends of the rope up her body, under each arm and then across her chest, binding her arms to her torso. Then he brought the rope down the middle of her body. He fed it three times around each of her ankles. He pulled the rope tight, secured and knotted it and stood back and admired his work.

"I've used a double fisherman's knot. It's called a true-love loop because there are two knots which fit snugly together and cannot slip. It symbolises love, friendship, and affection. But you haven't shown me much of that have you Ektrina? Even if I told you that I had killed her, it wouldn't count for anything because this is clearly a sting. You've been with another man, and you've talked to a police officer who's causing me problems."

"I'm sorry. And I don't care about Fazil. I've stopped working with him."

Victor put on his coat.

"When are you coming back?"

"When you've learnt your lesson."

14

Poisonous Tree

Carly, Steve Stant, Kate and Chi were meeting in Kate's flat, so that Carly could brief them. "Okay team, Alfie has sent me a digitally enhanced high-resolution image of the polaroid photograph that Chi found in Victor's rubbish. I can show it now on my laptop screen."

"Alfie? I'm confused," Chi said.

"For those of you who don't already know Alfie, he's Dr. Slincott, a director at Forensic Answers. He gave the picture to a colleague, an image analysis expert who said it was easy to digitize the analogue polaroid with a flatbed scanner onto a computer."

They gathered around the screen and stared at the colour picture.

"It's a photograph of the crime scene, and I've got questions: who took it; why did they take it; when did they take it; what was Victor doing with it; and why did he destroy it so diligently? All we can be sure of is that it was taken with a polaroid camera. We can check if the picture was taken with a camera in Philip's collection."

Steve Stant spoke first. "There are no exhibit markers in the picture. I was first on the scene and placed two makeshift markers on the bedside table where I found Victor's butt and the magazine. Can you enlarge the tabletop in the picture, Carly? That's strange, you can see a butt, but no markers and the *Full Throttle* magazine isn't there either. Forensics binned my markers at the same time as bagging up both those items. Whoever took this picture must have been present at the crime scene at some point before I arrived, and I think we know who it was."

"Victor," they said in unison.

"If Victor took the photo," Steve continued, "he must have been present when Stella was lying on the bed with the pink handcuffs on. It's not possible to say from the picture whether she is dead. But she's in the same position, even with the pillow on her face, as she was when we found her."

"We know the rumours that Victor and Stella were close," Carly said. "But what were they doing in Royal's flat?"

"And why would Stella need to steal Philip's keys and give them to Victor?" Chi asked.

"Maybe she wasn't stealing them," Kate suggested. "Maybe they'd arranged for Victor to go to Philip's flat and wait for Philip and Stella to join them in a threesome."

"*Kimoi* (disgusting)," Chi said, pretending to be sick. "Those two perverts and Stella having kinky sex."

"Chi thinks it's disgusting," Kate explained to the others. "Chi, threesomes are not considered kinky these days. Get up to date."

"Alfie warned me that there is always a risk of contamination of the DNA on the butt sample," Carly stated.

"Those three are contaminated," Chi commented.

"Victor's DNA could have been transferred to it by accident," Carly continued, ignoring Chi's intervention. "If he had sneezed or coughed over it, for example. But there are no other traces present on it, as there would be in that scenario.

"Alternatively, somebody could have collected a cigarette butt smoked by Victor somewhere else and planted it at the scene. The fact that a DNA match has been found between a crime scene sample and an individual does not necessarily prove that the individual was present at the scene."

"Look," Steve said, "he doesn't deny that he might have left the butt there. Just claims that it was after he arrived officially and that he dropped it on the floor. I think that he's lying about that."

"Steve, do you remember how when he arrived, he said that he was out of cigarettes," Carly added. "He sent me out to buy some more for him and I didn't buy Camels. He's a rotten liar."

"Just as well," Kate commented.

"And when we saw him at the scene," Carly continued, "he was walking as if his balls had been in a nutcracker, and he was wearing dark glasses. Those could be self-defence injuries."

"The butt, the photograph, and the injuries all bear witness to Victor's crime," Kate concluded.

"How exciting, it's like *Silent Witness*," Chi said, "I've been watching it on the tele."

"I think that smothering with a pillow is definitely Victor's modus operandi," Kate said. "A bit of S & M that went wrong: out of control; pressed too hard for too long. Ektrina's told us that he gets pleasure from suffocating her during sex."

"Why did she stay with that monster for so long?" Carly asked.

"My sister Mary has told me all about these emotionally dependent relationships," Kate explained. "A vulnerable woman with little self-confidence clings to a violent man, fearful that no other man will pay her attention. She may even think, in a twisted way, that it's his way of loving her. The danger then is if she leaves him, she'll look for the same behaviour in her next partner, believing that to be love. I think we can help Ektrina to feel good about herself again and in control of her life."

The meeting finished and Carly sent a message to Henry.

I've left a jacket potato out for you, with ham and cheese. Put it in the microwave for your dinner and you can have the coleslaw in the fridge with it. I'll be home as soon as I can. I passed your message on to your dad and I'm sure he'll get back to you about it. Love you, mum.

She put her phone away and turned to Kate. "I spoke to Rupert and Lily. They both swore that they had never thought of sending the pictures to other students. Lily said that she doesn't like Claire and might have been a bit mean to her but wouldn't take advantage of her like that. I told him that he had already committed a crime by encouraging her to take the pictures and by being in possession of them, because of her age, and they both looked scared by that. I said that I would exercise my discretion and not take any official action this time, providing he deletes the pictures."

"Thanks," Kate replied. "Mary and Claire will be relieved when I tell them."

"Lily was writing in her diary when we met," Carly continued. "She closed it quickly when I looked over her shoulder, but I'd already seen what she'd written: 'Dear diary, my hormones are all over the place today.' She's still in that confusing in-between age, before good judgement kicks in."

Kate's phone pinged. She looked at the message and laughed. "You know who," she said to Carly. Carly leant across to look at the screen. *Let's continue this conversation in bed. My legs can't wait to hear what your hands have to say.*

Later, Kate typed in reply, smiling to herself.

Kate phoned Mary and gave her the encouraging news from Rupert and Lily.

"Do you believe them? I don't," Mary said. "Never liked that posh boy. And she doesn't sound any better. Nobody tells the truth and owns up these days. That woman I told you about, driving whilst disqualified. She told me, by way of an excuse, that she was rescuing a friend from a violent partner in the middle of the night. But she was on her own when she was stopped and told the officer that she'd been to a party."

"Are you sure that you should be telling me about your cases? You know, confidentiality and all that."

"Bit late to ask me now, but you won't tell anyone, and I need to get it off my chest. Anyway, to finish the story, she told me last month that she was not in a relationship, but the daughter told me that a boyfriend stays most weekend nights. Mum's answer to this was that it's only casual, not a relationship, and he turns up unexpectedly. Mum swore to me that she has never laid a finger on her daughter, but the daughter complains that mum is always whacking her. I'm fast losing faith in people."

"Probably not such a bad thing in your job," Kate said.

Bonetti went straight to Victor's boss, Detective Chief Superintendent Drake. What she and Kate had seen and heard in Ektrina's bedroom was not the hoped-for confession from Victor and so she didn't disclose their amateur attempt at a sting to Drake. But the information about Victor's meeting with Stella in The Fastidious Fox on the evening of the murder; the evidence of the cigarette butt; and the fact that he was disposing of a photograph that he had apparently taken of the crime scene before Stant's arrival, was enough for her to convince Drake that Victor was up to his old tricks and somehow jeopardising the investigation.

"Any developments with the missing person Bryan Western?" Bonetti asked Drake later.

"Western left his passport at home and hasn't touched his bank account or used his credit card since he went missing. You heard that his flat has been turned over. Nobody has heard from him for some weeks now. Seems like he was trying to do Internal Affairs' job for them. I'll deal with Shadwell about this latest issue. Thank you for bringing it to my attention."

Drake summoned Victor to his office. "I'm told by a reliable source that you were with Godley and afterwards in Royal's flat before you staged your very convenient arrival at the crime scene. And potential evidence in the

Godley case that could incriminate you, has now been found dumped in your bin. I don't want to know what you've been up to with Royal and Godley. I'll leave it to Internal Affairs to question you about that. Even if your relationship with Godley was entirely innocent, you should have reported a conflict of interest and declined to take the murder investigation on. You're now heavily compromised and I'm taking you off the case and you can stay at home and do gardening, or whatever else it is that you do in your spare time, until the trial is over. We can't avoid you giving evidence and no doubt the defence will have tough questions for you, so you'd better get your story straight beforehand."

An urgent conference took place at 5 Century Buildings. Drake attended with DS Bonetti.

"Let's not jump to hasty conclusions about DCI Shadwell which may be wrong," Jack Couper said. Bonetti snorted derisively.

"The evidence against Royal is still very strong," Monty said. "He confessed to the police operator that he killed her. We know that before the murder he searched on the internet about oxygen deprivation and that's how the poor woman was killed. He was with Ms Godley on the night of the murder, and she was found dead on his bed next to a suspicious magazine. There's also the postcard, although I don't know how we'd get that admitted in evidence. Nothing tells me that he didn't do it."

"The polaroid photograph must be significant," Bonetti stated. "Why destroy it unless you want to hide something captured in it? Shadwell has been concealing vital evidence. It can only be to protect himself."

"Wild speculation," Couper complained. "That's just the sort of fanciful explanation the defence would put forward. I expect better of you Sergeant, an experienced detective. Whose side are you on anyway?"

"Now, now," Monty said, "team work please. There's a plate of custard creams on the table which are untouched."

"Why does Bradley buy custard creams?" Cecilia asked, looking at everyone. "Nobody likes them, they're too dry."

"Because it's an iconic British biscuit," Monty replied.

"Well, I think that they are boring," Cecilia announced.

"I know that old favourites are supposed to remind us of happier times, and for the record my choice would be a Garibaldi, or a Milk Chocolate Hobnob, but can we discuss my worries about DCI Shadwell's part in all this?" Drake asked. "The defence will surely tear him and the prosecution case to shreds."

Cecilia looked gloomily at Drake. "The defence don't know about the photograph, do they?"

"We don't have to tell them," Couper said. "We know that it looks bad, but what does it add up to? It doesn't go to show that Royal didn't kill her or that DCI Shadwell did. It would just cause the jury unnecessary confusion if they found out about the existence of the photograph and that it was sent off to enhance the image. We should keep this to ourselves for as long as possible."

"It's too late to play hide the evidence games," Bonetti said. "Kate Sullivan's agent found the polaroid and its existence will soon be common knowledge. The defence are bound to ask for it."

Chi and Grant relaxed in their favourite corner of the G Spot, out of earshot of the other clubbers. "You'll never believe what the lab was able to show in the photograph," Chi said to Grant as she told him about the results of the expert's examination. *The odds are still 5/1 against Philip's acquittal*, Grant thought. *It's worth a punt of the rest of Chi's money.*

"That's amazing," Grant replied, "I've got to visit the loo." Inside the toilet cubicle he used his phone and placed the remaining £30,000 on Philip being acquitted. His confidence in Philip escaping conviction convinced Veronica to drop the odds even further and within the hour they were down to 2/1 against.

The next morning, Grant confided in Felicity about the startling result from the examination of the photograph.

Another urgent disclosure application was listed at Riverside Crown Court. "It's fruit from the poisonous tree," Cecilia declared dramatically. "The photograph was obtained illegally from DCI Shadwell's dustbin and so should not be admitted in evidence, and as a result cannot be relevant and doesn't require disclosure."

HHJ Winter shook her head. "You should know, Ms Lassi, that there is no rule in English law that says I must exclude improperly obtained evidence. It depends on the circumstances and what the interests of justice require. By 'the poisonous tree', you mean that the unlawful act from which the evidence was derived is poisonous and poisons the evidence obtained as a result. Well, DCI Shadwell had disposed of the photograph in a dustbin which was put out on the public pavement ready to be emptied. It could be argued that the photograph had been abandoned by him and that the collection of it by *Ms Fookoodah* was not illegal. How relevant and probative the photograph is and whether it is fair to admit it in evidence is a question which the trial judge, who may be me, should decide when the defence are able to tell me about their assessment of it. At this stage, Ms Crabtree, I will order its disclosure to the defence together with the expert's report and the digital image attached."

Penny gave Cecilia a long, cold stare before rushing out of court to check Barri-Bets. *Was it worth putting some more money on Royal?* she thought. But Veronica had already got wind of this disclosure application, and to her disappointment and that of Monty Bell, who was also consulting Barri-Bets, the betting had been suspended for Veronica to take stock.

Victor went back to Ektrina's flat, but she was no longer there, and had taken all her possessions. He couldn't imagine how, like Houdini, she had untied his careful knots and escaped. He didn't know how to contact her. He guessed that she was holed-up in a women's refuge somewhere. The staff would be filling her head with nonsense about men and advising her how to put Victor in the dock.

He hadn't meant to hurt her, just to scare her into silence as she knew too much about his illegal money-making activities. He tried to think back to what he had told her or what she may have overheard about his protection racket.

The service he provided was to ensure that businesses were not raided or were at least given notice of a raid if he couldn't prevent interference from local police or council officers without raising their suspicion. People who helped him had to be paid and this was more complicated now that he was in Homicide and had to share the spoils in a bigger pool of sharks.

Local authorities were increasingly tolerating and licensing the businesses which Victor would previously have threatened to shut down, and so he was losing his enforcement teeth. This was why the Public Prosecutor's Office had decided not to try and prosecute Ray Millan again, but to leave him alone, providing that he did not come to the police's attention for any other reason, such as sex trafficking or dealing in drugs. He found himself presiding over a rapidly diminishing empire. Maybe now was the time to quit.

Victor sat at home in a darkened room. It was not going according to plan. He had only one visitor during the day. Jack Couper came to reminisce about old times and tell him what he could expect during the inevitable close questioning in cross-examination by the defence team during Royal's murder trial.

On a Sunday evening in October, the phone rang. It was Couper. "Primed up for tomorrow? You're going to be the first witness on. Don't forget to wear your lucky socks and waterproof pants."

15

Hungarian Down

Ex-Porn Star Murdered by Sex Offender, the headline read. *Stella Godley 35, a former star of adult films, latterly working as a highly paid escort, was murdered by Philip Royal 49, a glamour model photographer who previously served a sentence of imprisonment for sexually assaulting a young woman, the prosecution claimed today in Riverside Crown Court. Godley died from asphyxiation; Royal having allegedly smothered her with a Hungarian goose down pillow as she lay naked on his bed when their sex game went wrong. The trial continues.*

Chi was on her way to meet Grant. As a potential defence witness, she had been told to stay away from Philip's trial, but when she saw the headline, she couldn't resist picking up the final edition of a free newspaper from a stand in the street. There was a picture on the front page of Stella on a beach wearing a bikini.

Chi read the sentence again, *Royal having smothered her with a Hungarian goose down pillow.* She had a shocking realisation of the meaning of what she heard Philip say to Stella in The Fastidious Fox on the night of the murder. He was threatening to kill her. He said that he'd finish her off with Hungarian down, she'd be screaming and there'd be a *mort*. So, Philip really had killed Stella.

"All stand," the usher in court one called out as HHJ Winter marched in and sat down, dwarfed by the high-backed judge's chair. She nodded to signify that she was ready, and the proceedings began. In the absence of the jury, she had already agreed to admit the polaroid photograph from Shadwell's bin as evidence.

As the jury were brought in and took their seats, Felicity stood next to the dock, asking Philip if he recognised any of them.

"I don't, but there are too many women, and they will be against me. Can we object to any of them?"

"Back in the day we could challenge up to three jurors without giving a reason. Nowadays, it's not allowed."

The room fell silent as Monty Bell QC opened the case for the prosecution. "Members of the jury, you are going to be shown pictures which may upset you, of a dead, naked lady named Stella Godley. She was handcuffed and smothered with a pillow made of the finest Hungarian goose down on Mr Royal's bed in his flat. Mr Royal is already a convicted sex offender.

"The defence may suggest that Ms Godley was a willing participant in a sex game, but Mr Royal cannot rely upon her consent to rough sex gone wrong. It has recently been made clear by statute, so that there can be no doubt, that consent to assault for sexual gratification is no defence. So, she cannot have consented to the infliction of violence by him which led to her death. Did he intend to kill her or cause her serious bodily injury? That's the high bar the prosecution must reach for a murder charge. Or did he intentionally do an unlawful and dangerous act from which she died? Then it would be an unlawful act manslaughter. And if you find him not guilty of murder, you may always return a verdict of guilty to manslaughter instead.

"You will hear evidence that he intentionally restrained her hands, sat heavily on her abdomen and rib cage so that she was immobile, and covered her nose and mouth with a Hungarian down pillow to prevent her from breathing, so making her helpless. How could they have a safe signal and how could he check her condition if she could not move her hands or make a noise and he could not see her face? He knew that suffocation could cause death or serious injury to her heart and the brain, because earlier that evening he had researched this on his laptop. If he had intended this to be mutually pleasurable and had not meant her to suffer, he would not have made it impossible for them to communicate with each other."

Monty's opening took all morning, and it was after lunch that he called his first witness, DCI Victor Shadwell. Victor's witness statement, describing the crime scene, how the body was examined, the circumstances of Philip's arrest, and his 'no comment' interview of Philip, was read to the court as his evidence. Monty asked him questions to add further detail to his account, and then told the jury that the defence had insisted on the DCI's attendance so that they could cross-examine him.

"Your witness, Mr Hind," Monty said, addressing the defence.

"Where is Mr Hind?" Judge Winter asked.

"Call of nature, Your Honour," Felicity replied, "he won't be long." She looked anxiously at the court room doors that she had seen him leave through minutes earlier.

"Call of nature? I thought that euphemism was dying out, not unlike your leading counsel," Winter responded. "Members of the jury, forget I said that. I don't want to be appealed for appearing hostile to a defence advocate. I don't think he can help it. I'm sure you can amply fill his shoes, Ms Crabtree. Now, can we get a move on."

"You were the officer who led the investigation into Ray Millan for trading in prostitution?"

"I was. But I thought that I was here to answer questions about Ms Godley's murder."

He's looking shifty already, Felicity thought.

"You are, just bear with me. The case against Millan collapsed because police officers involved in the investigation had sexual relationships with the women who were going to give evidence to support the prosecution case."

"What's the connection with this case?"

"I'm asking the questions, not you. Please answer."

I must show him that I'm in control of this exchange, not him, she figured.

"Someone paid the girls to trap the investigators."

"'The girls', is that what you call working women? Stella Godley, the deceased, she was one of Millan's 'girls'."

"The women call each other girls. If it's good enough for them. And, yes, she was."

"She was having a sexual relationship with you."

"That was in the past."

He's admitting a connection with her. He may come to regret that, she hoped.

"You were in an intimate relationship with Ms Godley at the time when she was murdered?"

"No, we were just friends."

"Despite being 'just friends' with her and having had sexual relations with her, which you claim was in the past, you took the lead in investigating her murder."

"Yes."

"Without disclosing your relationship with her to your colleagues or your superiors in Major Crimes."

"Yes."

"Why did you do that, when it was clearly contrary to your force's policy which requires an investigator to be and be seen to be independent and objective?"

"I wanted to make sure that her killer was brought to justice. I am sure the jury members will understand that."

Some jurors nodded sympathetically.

He's clever, the way that he looks confidently at the jury for validation.

"Even though your participation may cast doubts on the integrity of the investigation, as I believe it has, and so defeat your object?"

That should get rid of your smug expression.

"Mine, in hindsight was not a wise decision, but I felt very emotional at the time, and I believe that my motives were noble, wanting justice for Stella."

He's digging a hole for himself.

"An interesting word you use 'noble'. Did you borrow it from the phrase 'noble cause corruption'? A good end achieved by illegitimate means?"

"It's just a word."

I know how to give the jury something that they will remember, she calculated.

"In America it's called the 'Dirty Harry problem'. Are you a rogue officer? How many misconduct notices have you received in your career, Detective Chief Inspector?"

"Who is on trial here?"

"Just answer the question please."

"Eleven, but you know that don't you."

"Yes, but the jury don't. You are a law unto yourself, aren't you? You ignore laws, rules or conventional ways of doing things."

"I get results and put criminals behind bars."

He's looking at the jury again for confirmation.

Where is Hind? He's left me to do all the work, but he'll still claim his QC's fee.

"Shortly after the Millan case collapsed, you were moved, from the Vice team."

"Police officers working in Vice are often rotated as a matter of course, to stop inappropriate friendships developing with their adversaries."

"Wasn't that what you had with Ms Godley? An inappropriate friendship with an adversary?"

He can't escape this.

"Yes, I put my hands up to that. Heart ruled the head. I know that it's a possible misconduct issue. That's why I could not identify her at the crime scene. I soon put a stop to the relationship, but still cared about her, I couldn't help that."

He's looking at the jury again, playing them. Not sure that they look convinced.

"Another misconduct issue. You must hold the record in the force."

"Questions, not comments, Ms Crabtree," Winter said.

"You happened to be near the scene when the murder took place?"

"Yes."

"That's why you were able to claim that you should be assigned to the investigation, because you were not on duty that night, were you?"

"I was not."

"Convenient for you, that you happened to be nearby, and picking up police messages. Is that your usual practice or was it just on this occasion?"

I know why he was nearby earlier and listening to his team.

"Twenty-four-seven I am a police officer with an officer's powers. We are short staffed and as a senior officer, even when I'm not on duty I like to be aware of what's going on in my patch in case I'm needed. When I heard the address of the property, I knew Mr Royal was involved and I had reason to be concerned. As soon as I attended the crime scene, I put myself on duty."

"Were you in Mr. Royal's flat on the evening of the murder, before the crime was reported?"

He knew that this question was coming but I have no idea how he will attempt to answer it. A simple denial surely, the easiest and safest option, she reckoned.

"Yes, may I explain why?"

I'm entering unchartered territory here.

"We know that you were in his flat, because you smoked a Camel cigarette there and left the butt on a bedside table."

"I did, it was like leaving a warning for Mr Royal to see."

His answer doesn't make sense, does it? she asked herself.

"So, you sneaked in, like a burglar, but you also wanted him to know that you had been there?"

"I wanted to warn him, to show him that I was on to him and what I could do."

Will the jury believe that? Sounds so contrived: wanting to be caught out by Royal.

"What were you on to him about and what could you do? Sounds like you were threatening him."

"Ms Godley was convinced that Mr Royal had stolen her private notebook and she begged me to get it back for her."

"When did she approach you about her notebook?"

"The day before her death, she was sitting in The Fox, writing in her notebook, when Mr Royal asked her to tell him what it was. She unwisely confided in him that she recorded the payments made to her by her clients; with their names; a narrative about each of them including what they had done together; and their idiosyncrasies, likes and dislikes. She was planning to make money by writing a 'confession of an escort' type book. She left the notebook in her bag when she went to the bar to get another drink. When she returned, it was gone and so was Mr Royal. The next day, she challenged him about it, but he denied taking it."

"Liar, you've made all that up," Philip Royal shouted from the dock.

The jurors looked shocked at the outburst from someone who had not spoken until then.

"Silence, Mr Royal, or I'll have you removed," Winter told him.

"Why would Mr Royal want to steal her notebook?"

Has he really thought this through? she wondered.

"It's not for me to say. Royal was possibly concerned that she had written about him; or Royal was thinking that he could blackmail some of her clients with the information contained in it."

"You liar," Philip shouted.

The jurors looked startled.

"Last warning, I won't tell you again," Winter said sternly.

"Why were you prepared to risk damaging your career for a notebook?"

"I told you that I cared for her. The notebook had dates, details and names. If her clients found out that she had kept information about them, she could be in danger from them."

"In danger from whom?"

"Her boss and her clients. They are not nice people. I was trying to persuade her to give the work up. I didn't have grounds to apply for a search warrant, so I told her to get Mr Royal drunk, take his keys, give them to me and keep him out of the way for a couple of hours whilst I searched his flat."

He has an explanation for everything. We won't finish him today, so I'll have a chance to plan what to ask him.

"Did you find the notebook?"

"I called her and left a message to say no luck finding Peggy, that's what she called the notebook, it means 'pearl'. That's how highly she valued it. She called me back and asked me to return the keys to her, so I met up with her and gave them back. When I heard that police had been called to Royal's flat, I guessed that Ms Godley must have gone there alone to confront him, against my advice. That's the concern I had, the reason that I went there although off duty."

"If Ms Godley was so at odds with Royal, as you claim, isn't it highly unlikely that she would engage in a sex game with him?"

"He may have made it a condition of his returning the notebook to her."

This really is like a game of chess.

"The flat, including his studio, was gone over by a police specialist search team and her notebook was not found?"

"I was there when they searched. He'd left the flat before the search and had time to dispose of it; he may have been keeping it somewhere else."

"You are an experienced, senior detective and yet this is the first time that you have given an account of taking Royal's keys and entering his flat to look for Ms Godley's 'pearl'. You should have made a written statement in this case about it. Do you have a notebook entry about this visit?"

"No, because I didn't go there on police business. It was personal."

"You have just made all this up."

"It's the truth. I didn't expect that my visit would become part of a murder trial."

"Ms Godley's phone, with that message from you about the notebook, was never recovered, was it?"

"No."

"Where is your phone, which would show that you called her?"

"It's at home. I'm just carrying a work phone today."

"It can be here tomorrow?"

"Of course."

"And you took a photograph, a capture of the dead body, with Mr. Royal's polaroid camera."

The jurors shifted uneasily in their seats.

He must surely deny this.

"That was during my later visit, on duty. After the forensic guys had left, I wanted a keepsake of Stella. I shouldn't have done that."

The judge directed the jurors to look at a screen which had been set up in the court room.

"The photograph was found, cut up into tiny pieces, in your rubbish bin."

"I destroyed it, I couldn't bear to look at it."

Mustn't mock him in case some of the jurors are naive enough to swallow his account and empathise with him, she cautioned herself.

"If you concentrate on the picture on the screen, you will see a cigarette butt on the bedside table."

"Yes."

"That is the butt that you left behind, isn't it? It has your DNA."

"Yes. But this picture was taken after the forensic guys had removed my first butt. This is the remains of my second cigarette. I had a smoke again after they'd gone. I was upset. I sat on the bed and left it where I had left the first one. I wanted to spend final moments with Stella and look after her body. That's why I waited for the coroner's officers to take her away."

He's a pathological liar. He believes his own lies, that's why he sounds so convincing to the jury.

"Why did you destroy the photograph so carefully, cutting it up into little pieces?"

"I didn't want somebody to get hold of it and maybe digitize it and put it on the web."

As if he cared.

"You are making all this up, aren't you? To hide the truth that you took a picture of the crime that you had just committed."

"I know you are only doing your job: to defend your client you must accuse someone else of the crime. Today, it happens to be me."

Trying to sound so reasonable, even when he's accused of murder. I must ask him this next question, even though I know how he will answer. Still, it might do a Perry Mason on him. Perry Mason conducted 284 trials on television as a defence attorney and only lost one, and that conviction was reversed on appeal.

"Did you kill Ms Godley?"

"No, that's a ridiculous suggestion. We were good friends. I cared for her."

"She was selling herself for sex to any man who would pay her price for it. You were jealous of those men?"

"I wanted her to have a different job, only for reasons of her safety."

"It's 4.30pm, I'll rise now," Winter announced. "Members of the jury, 10am tomorrow please and no looking on the internet for anything about this case or any of the people involved. DCI Shadwell, you're in the process of giving your evidence. You will know that you must not discuss your evidence with anyone until we resume tomorrow morning."

HHJ Winter clambered down from the judge's chair and left the courtroom.

When Victor arrived home, he received a phone call from Jack Couper. "Something's up. DS Bonetti kept the bin bags of rubbish that Ms Fukuda took from you, and they have searched them again."

"Stole from me, you mean. Can't I charge her with theft?"

"There's a letter they found from Eagle Insurance Company, acknowledging payments you were making on two life policies. They contacted Eagle, who say that one is on your life and the other is on Ms Godley's life. Both of you are beneficiaries. Also, the defence have seen DS Bonetti's notebook in which she recorded that you said you had no cigarettes when you arrived at the scene and that whilst you were there, she brought you a packet of Marlboro, not Camels. They want her called so that they can cross-examine her on it."

"I can explain."

"I've taken you by surprise. Don't say anything to me about it now. Forewarned is forearmed my old mate. See you tomorrow."

16

Spirit Board

Grant was feeling confident. Felicity had forced Victor to set out his account in full. He was sure that she would make progress in exposing his lies after she'd had time to prepare further cross-examination.

Ian was concerned that Victor's answers to her had sounded contrived, and that Victor would need his best powers of invention to deal with the new evidence. Ian needed a bit of luck. Felicity could be run over by a lorry: he knew that she cycled to and from chambers along that road in the East End that cyclists call 'murder mile'.

Philip was feeling hopeful: s*o that's what happened: Victor killed Stella.* Philip had always realised that with his sex offence conviction he was an easy target for any police officer who wanted to fit him up.

Carly had watched Ian with interest during the trial. He had behaved nervously as he sat behind Felicity: stroking his hair, yawning, fidgeting, playing with his tie, shifting in his seat and looking around. He had avoided looking at Victor during the cross-examination, as if he was afraid of exchanging glances with him.

Carly went back to Union Street and ran a check on Stella. There was no record of her. She found Steve Stant on his own in the room they used for writing up their notebooks.

"Steve, now there's no record on the database of Stella. It's vanished. That might explain why the police lab couldn't match her with any of the exhibits, but Alfie got a hit for her with *Full Throttle*."

Carly called Alfie who was working late. It wasn't long before he called her back. "DNA on the magazine you sent matched Stella Godley's sample on the police national DNA database, as I told you at the time. After you contacted me today, I checked again, and her sample has since been deleted. I obtained a sample of DNA from the deceased that the police lab had retained, and it doesn't match Ms Godley's DNA in several significant respects. I have no hesitation in saying that the dead body is not Ms Godley."

Although it was now past midnight, Carly called Kate with the news. Kate insisted on going straight to the Paradise Club where Yuri worked as security. She wanted to ask him about Stella. She found him on the door, dressed in black.

"Don't worry, I'm not the police. Yuri isn't it, tell me what you know about Stella Godley."

He looked around nervously, for a way to escape the questioning.

"Why should I? I need to speak to Victor."

"A woman has been murdered. You identified her in the mortuary as Stella Godley, but in fact she was somebody else. Victor is in serious trouble, so will you be. You can expect a long prison sentence followed by deportation, if you don't tell me what you know. I don't believe that you killed her, and I can help you."

Yuri explained that his only involvement was in identifying Stella's body, despite having never met her. Victor had shown him a photograph and told him to go to the mortuary and name the body in the photograph as Stella Godley. There was also a postcard he had to write and send to her. He said that he didn't want any trouble. He was from Russia and had overstayed his welcome.

"I don't know any more about it, please don't tell police or Immigration Enforcement."

Yuri's supervisor shouted over to him, "stop chatting, Yuri, and get the fuck over here, we've got some trouble inside."

"I'll be back to see you again," Kate called after him. "I don't think that you're telling me the whole truth."

Kate phoned Carly with Yuri's information.

Carly sent a text message to Henry.

I found a bank card in your room. It's not in your name. Why have you got it? Can you ring me urgently please?

Chi and Grant were sitting at a dining table in The Grafenburg. "Something's up," Grant said. "You're very quiet, not your usual bubbly self."

"It's the Stella Godley trial. It started today. What are the chances of Philip Royal getting off, considering everything I've told you about DCI Shadwell?"

"Circumstantially, the evidence against Philip is overwhelming. But juries don't like to be fed answers. They are obstinate and perverse, want to assert their independence and show that they won't be told what to do. They like to discover the 'truth' themselves. There are these people who are anti fox hunting, called hunt saboteurs. If they want to disrupt a hunt, they drag a cloth covered in fox scent through the woods, away from the fox's den. The hounds follow it instead of the fox and the fox survives. The jury are like the hounds. The fox is Philip. Victor and the suspicions about him are the cloth with the fox smell. The defence will use Victor to lay a false trail. Tally ho, the jury are off chasing Victor, just a smell, instead of Philip the fox."

Chi looked surprised at Grant's knowledge of juries.

"A close mate is a criminal barrister," Grant added hastily. "That's what he tells me."

"What will Philip do, if he's set free, is he likely to attack another woman?"

"Statistically, the chances are that he will. Sex offenders are highly likely to re-offend, so I've read."

"I'm worried, I've got real doubts about Philip's innocence, and I've been helping to point the finger at Victor."

"Tell me more."

Chi showed Grant the newspaper.

"So, what's the problem?"

"I'm sure that I heard Philip, in The Fox on the night of the murder, threaten Stella that he would finish her off with a Hungarian down pillow and that she would scream and die."

Grant looked concerned. He didn't want Chi to spoil his plans. He started to panic.

"The final edition of the newspaper says that a woman named Tessa, who is a shop assistant in Oxford Street, has told them that she sold the Hungarian down pillow to him recently. She said that he took a lot of time to choose it, as if he was selecting it for a special purpose. I must tell DS Bonetti about what I heard."

"Is that wise? You can't be sure that's what he said. I know The Fox and it's always full of noisy drinkers, you could easily be mistaken. If it was comedy night, maybe he was entering into the spirit of things and having a joke with her."

"Grant, that's so lame. I couldn't live with myself if Philip walked free because I didn't speak up, and he went on to assault or even kill another poor woman."

Grant made a difficult decision. "I think it's time for me to be honest with you. I'm not really an investment banker. I'm a barrister's clerk for the chambers which is defending Philip. I've bet all your money on Philip walking free. If you speak to Bonetti, you risk losing your £50,000 stake and the chance of doubling it. Think about it."

Chi dropped her fork in surprise. "Kusoyaro (you little shit). You lied to me about who you are, and you have gambled all my savings. I thought that I could trust you. What else have you lied to me about?"

"I wanted to impress you, pathetic really. Please forgive me, but don't throw away your chance of winning all that money, enough to set yourself up in business. You could make a killing, if you'll excuse the phrase."

Grant did some quick sums in his head. £20,000 at 20/1 and £30,000 at 5/1 would net £550,000. Plus the stake, that's £500,000 for him after he had paid Chi. He could sell his ex-council flat in Bermondsey and buy a smart new one-bedroom pad in London Bridge, like Tim Huffington, the youngest barrister in his chambers.

"I'm not hungry," Chi told him angrily. She stormed out, leaving Grant to pay the bill.

Chi went straight home to clear her mind and decide what to do next. Kate was out and Chi made herself a large jug of coffee, to keep awake and think about how she should arrive at an answer. She decided on a 'pros' and 'cons' list: for speaking out and telling Bonetti that Philip had threatened Stella and against her doing that.

It didn't take her long to fill a sheet of paper. She did the 'pros' first. She wanted her friends, Kate in particular, to think that she was someone whom they could trust. Someone whom they could rely upon to be honest and open with them when it mattered. Think of the shame if Philip was acquitted because she had kept silent, and Kate later found out what Chi had known. She was under a duty, a moral obligation, to Kate to report what she had heard so that the law could take its rightful course. After all, Kate had rented the room to her, been so welcoming and given her regular work. People say that honesty is the best policy and she liked to think of herself as an honest person. Then there was her self-respect: she wanted to feel comfortable with herself and maintain her sense of worth.

Women should stick together and support each other against the Philips of this world. Stella deserved justice. Could she live with herself if Philip was set free and went on to attack, or even kill, another woman? Then there was the risk of karma. Chi was not a practising Buddhist, but her parents believed in karma and if she had asked their advice, they would have warned her about bad karma if she stayed silent and how she could be reincarnated as something unlovable.

Then there were the 'cons'. *Wait, this is getting difficult,* Chi thought. *And it's late. A good reason to release endorphins with that bar of dark chocolate in the fridge. That should do the trick: boost my brain and clear any fog so that I can finish this task.*

She sunk her teeth into the bittersweet pieces whilst sitting on the floor, her back propped up against the wall. She continued with the 'cons'. The first one was easy: £100,000. Just think what she could do with that. She would be set up for life and able to be proudly independent, with her own café business. If she gave evidence against Philip and he was convicted, he would be bound to be released at some time in the future and might hunt her down to seek revenge. She could donate some of the winnings to a women's aid charity, so enabling some good to come out of her doing a bad thing. Her friends would say 'go for it' if she asked them.

She looked at her list and knew that despite the chance of winning big money, her conscience would simply not allow her to stay silent. The decision was made.

The buzzer sounded. Chi looked at her watch. It was midnight. "Who's that?" Chi asked on the intercom.

"It's Nahra," the voice said. "I'm sorry it's so late. I'd like to see Kate. I'm a friend of Annie, the lady who came to see her. Annie's missing and her husband Ian says that she's on some sort of retreat in the wilds of Wales. But she didn't tell me that she was going, and she's not contacted me at all. It's not like her and I'm very worried."

"Press the door and come up."

Chi and Nahra sat down at the kitchen table. Chi poured her a glass of wine. "Ian's been having an affair with a woman, Stella Godley, and Stella's dead," Chi told her. "Murdered by someone called Philip Royal who is being defended by Ian. You know what that means: Ian is defending someone who murdered his lover. We suspect that Stella has also been in a relationship with the senior police officer investigating her death, as well as with Philip Royal. The entire world seems to have had sex with that bad bitch."

"Do you think that Annie's going missing has anything to do with the murder?"

"It's certainly strange that she hasn't been in touch with you, not even a text message. Have you asked Ian where she is?"

"Ian told me that she is in contact with him. He said that she calls him and then talks to the children, asking them how they are. He said that she was stressed out and needed a break. I asked him for the mobile number that she uses to call him, and he said she always calls from a different land line phone."

"Sounds weird. Now you're here, Nahra, can you give me advice?"

Chi told Nahra about her dilemma, whether to speak out against Philip or not. "I have decided to do the right thing, sort of. But I could win a lot of money. What do you say?"

Nahra thought for a moment. "I've got a novel solution, let's use a Ouija board to try and speak to Stella and find out what she thinks you should do. It's called a spirit board. Stella's spirit will talk to us if we're lucky."

"Good thinking, only, where do we get a Ouija board from at this time of night?"

"We can make one out of that bread board over there. Have you got a black marker pen?"

Within minutes, Nahra had written up the board with the letters of the alphabet, the numbers 0 to 9, a y*es* and *no*, *hello* and *goodbye* and the sun and moon symbols. Then she made a heart shaped pointer out of cardboard.

"Let's take it into my bedroom in case Kate comes back unexpectedly."

They both sat on Chi's bed. "Are you ready?" Chi asked. "I'll turn the main light off to give a bit of atmosphere."

"Turn that beast's head the other way first," Nahra said. "He's staring at me."

"The *onigawara,* is a friendly demon and wards off evil spirits," Chi replied, "but okay, if it's bothering you."

They placed their fingers on the pointer.

"Is anyone there?" Nahra asked. The pointer sped over to *yes* taking their fingers with it. It then hovered over *hello*.

"Who are you?" she asked, nervously.

S-T-E-L-L-A it spelt out.

"*Ehhhhh, uwa* (what, wow)," Chi said, echoing Nahra's shocked expression.

"How are you?" Chi asked the spirit.

I-A-M I-N P-E-A-C-E it spelt out.

Chi and Nahra looked at each other anxiously.

"Who killed you?" she asked.

The indicator passed *P*, hovered over *V*, and then returned to *P* and next stopped at *R*.

"PR, Philip Royal," Chi announced.

"Should I tell the jury that Philip threatened you on the night of the murder or keep quiet if it means that by doing so, I win £50,000?" she asked.

B-R-I-C-H, it spelt out.

"Be rich," Chi concluded, "she's telling me to go for the money."

"Are you sure that you're not manoeuvring the pointer, perhaps without realising?" Nahra asked. "Only it answers all your questions without hesitating."

"No, I've used the lightest touch on the pointer, like a feather."

Chi poured Nahra another glass of wine.

The pointer suddenly pulled their fingers over to *goodbye*. The table light they were using, flickered and suddenly went out, leaving them in darkness. Both women screamed. Nahra spilt her wine on the floor. The light came on again.

There was the sound of someone coming up the stairs. "It's Kate," Chi said. "I'll hide the bread board. Please don't mention a word to her about this."

Ian did not attend the second day of Philip's trial. He thought that he would find it too stressful. Meanwhile Philip was getting increasingly impatient with Ian's laid-back approach to his defence and Benjamin Hind was nowhere to be seen. If it weren't for Felicity Crabtree's diligence, Philip would have applied to transfer his defence from Ian to a different defence team.

Ian kept his turn as duty solicitor at Waterloo Youth Court. He was in the cells with his client, Ms Zaser Hamson, aged fifteen, who had been arrested for criminal damage, again. They were called up to court.

Zaser sat, slumped in her seat, taking refuge inside her over-size padded coat.

"You are charged with an offence of criminal damage, yesterday, at Kingsmead School. It is said that you broke the windscreen of a car belonging to Ms Newton, valued at £250. How do you plead to that charge?"

Zaser looked blankly at Ian. Ian nodded to her.

"Guilty, I suppose."

"Miss Johnson, you prosecute, give us the facts please," the chair of the bench of magistrates said.

"I'm sorry Your Worships, I haven't got a file. It's lost somewhere in the system."

"Mr Blake, you are defending Zaser, can you give us the facts?"

"I was called up from the cells Your Worships, before I could take any details from my client." Ian gave a cold stare towards Betty Williams, the usher and list caller as he spoke, accusing her of prematurely summoning them to the court room.

"Zaser, can you tell us what you did?"

"I jumped on the hood of her car."

"Bonnet, Your Worships," the court clerk explained.

"I put my boot through her windscreen."

"She is a teacher of yours. Why did you do it, Zaser?"

"She was really getting on my nerves. She took my phone away for no reason."

"Zaser is currently on a court order, Your Worships, being managed by me, for breaking windows at the school last month," Iris Thomas, the Youth Offending Team person said. "She has six convictions for criminal damage and three convictions for assaulting staff members at the school. It is a school for children whose behaviour is challenging."

"We will need a report, three weeks on bail."

"We have been informed, Your Worships, that she has been staying out at night and not going home," Miss Thomas continued. "We recommend a 7pm to 7am curfew as a condition of bail to ensure that she doesn't offend and attends court."

"She won't listen to me," Zaser's mother contributed.

"That's because you're a fuckshit," Zaser shouted, turning to stare at her mother.

"Mind your language young lady," the chair of the bench said to her.

Zaser shrugged her shoulders.

"She's been seen at night in the company of much older men," Miss Thomas added.

"You are a fucking liar," Zaser screamed at Miss Thomas. "You are always getting me into trouble. Why don't you just fuck off and leave me alone."

"Well, don't get upset, Zaser," the bench chair said. "Just be indoors at 7pm each night until you come back to court. Mr. Blake, anything further to say?"

"No, Your Worships, I'm just the duty solicitor."

"Fucking bastard," Zaser said as she walked out of court.

"I'm sorry for that, Your Worships," Ian said.

"She was actually addressing you, Mr Blake," the court clerk said, to laughter. "She's not happy with the curfew, thought you might oppose it."

Zaser had left with her mother before Ian could sign her up for legal aid.

Chi had decided not to tell Carly about Philip's threats to Stella in The Fastidious Fox. She turned on her phone. There was a message from Grant.

Victor wasn't at court this morning and he couldn't be found at home. The place has been emptied of his personal possessions and left in a mess, as if he was in a hurry to go somewhere. They've put out an all ports and airports warning so that if he tries to leave the country he'll be stopped.

17

Person Unknown

Grant phoned Chi to tell her what was happening at the trial. "The prosecution and defence barristers have gone with Detective Chief Superintendent Drake and DS Bonetti to see Judge Winter in her room. DS Bonetti has found out something that might mean the trial can't continue."

"What happens to our bet? Does it mean we've won?"

"I don't know. I'll call you again when I do. Don't get too excited."

"Shadwell's done a runner and the body's not Stella Godley," Felicity said breathlessly on the phone to Ian as he left the Youth Court. "At the moment, they don't know who it is. Winter won't allow Monty to amend the charge to 'murder of person unknown'. I objected as it would have changed the whole nature of the case when we are already partway through the trial. Philip's smiling as he thinks that he might be released. We're going back in front of Winter after lunch."

"Thanks for telling me."

"You don't sound surprised. Say something, Ian."

That afternoon, Monty Bell QC addressed Winter in court. "Your Honour, in view of certain information provided to the prosecution, we wish to withdraw the charge against Mr Royal. It was laid on a wholly mistaken assumption. We are not in a position yet to lay a new charge of murder."

"Mr Royal is no longer on trial for the murder of Ms Godley. The case is altered such that the charge against him has no legal basis," Winter announced. "There being no other charge currently before the court, there is no valid reason for Mr Royal's continued detention. You won't need to make a habeas corpus application, Ms Crabtree, because Mr Royal is free to go."

The jury were brought into the courtroom. Winter looked serious. "Members of the jury, it's my sorry duty to discharge you. The facts of the murder are not as the prosecution presented to you. The dead person is not Ms Godley and the investigating officer, whom you heard give evidence yesterday, has disappeared in suspicious circumstances. Thank you for your time. I hope that when you return tomorrow morning you will be found another case to try." The jury members trooped out of the courtroom.

Chi waited nervously for Grant's call. She was already imagining how to spend her winnings. She would open a smart looking little café serving matcha teas and lattes. She had it all worked out. To make it distinctive she would call the café Matcha Ado About Everything, and use matcha in croissants, cookies, brownies, baguettes, and cheesecakes. She would also make bliss balls: a base of cashews and coconut mixed with the matcha powder and a little honey.

The phone call came mid-afternoon. "Well?" Chi asked, "don't keep me in suspense."

"Brace yourself. Winter discharged the jury. No charge was left on which she could direct them to find Philip not guilty, so there's no verdict. I phoned CC and he read me the rules. Apparently Barri-Bets keeps your stake, and nothing is paid out. I'm sorry, I feel dreadful."

"You will feel more than that when you sell your flat to pay me back. You're such a loser. I never had an orgasm you know, I just pretended to. So, like you, I was faking it, and you never knew."

When Kate came home, Chi wasted no time in telling her about Nahra's visit.

"Nahra says that Annie has not contacted her and she's Annie's best friend and Annie tells her everything. Ian told Nahra that he's in contact with Annie: she calls him to ask how the children are and then speaks to them and tells them that mummy will be back soon and to be good."

"Why would Annie take off like that, leaving the children behind?"

Kate's phone pinged. They read the message: *I love you passionately, madly, and effortlessly, as you are part of my very soul.*

"Jacqui," Chi said, "how did I guess? I've never known someone with such romantic exhilaration. If Grant said that to me, I'd laugh. He can't woo me with dramatic passionate gestures. My friend Mai has an English boyfriend in Japan. He begins every email to her with *to the most beautiful woman in the world.* Yuck!"

"She's sexually priming me, I read about it in the *Sunday Splash Magazine*, subconsciously sending me signals so that I am excited about having sex with her when we meet in the evening."

"Does it work?"

"It's supposed to be subliminal, so I wouldn't know, would I?"

"Well, how do you feel when you see her?"

"Horny, but I don't know if that's just as a result of the texts."

"When you first met Jacqui, how did you know it was okay to flirt with her on the train?"

"She gave me *the look*: unflinching eye contact. It's like a secret sign."

"Like *The Look of Love*. Dusty Springfield sang that in *Casino Royale*. Great film."

"Anyway, you're a *Christmas cake*, past it now that you're over twenty-five. Soon you'll be a *New Year noodle*, a has-been at thirty-one."

"You read that article last week, 'Marriage in Japan', what rubbish. Anyway, I don't want a romantic partner, they're too bothersome."

"I've never met Grant. Why don't you bring him back here? I also read that Japanese women find even ugly foreign guys attractive. Is that why you've not introduced him to me?"

"*Nyao.*"

"What's that?"

"It's the sound of a Japanese cat, you know, miaow, miaow to you. Anyway, Grant's history, he's a cheating low life."

Kate phoned Carly and put her in the picture about Chi's conversation with Nahra. "I must speak to Ian Blake about his claiming that Annie contacts him and the kids," Carly said. "But I'll try to speak their children as well, to see if what he says checks out."

On a cold November afternoon, Bonetti waited outside Jack and Maisie's school. The children came out with their grandmother Pauline. Bonetti showed her warrant card to Pauline.

"Don't be alarmed, I just want a quick word with the children about their mother Annie." Pauline looked taken aback.

"Jack, Maisie," Bonetti said, "I'm Carly, a friend of your mummy's. Has she spoken to you on the phone since she went away?"

Both children replied in unison, "no."

Maisie burst into tears. "Is she all right, where is she?"

"Is she ever coming back?" Jack asked. "We miss her."

"I'm sure she will be back soon."

"Leave us alone now," Pauline snapped. "Come on children, we're going to get ice creams," and she shepherded them away towards her car.

Bonetti drove to Ian's house. He answered the door and invited her into the hall.

"Has Annie been in contact with you?" she asked.

"A few times, I never know when she's going to ring, or where from. She's at a retreat in the Welsh countryside somewhere and communications are poor. She chose somewhere remote on purpose. She's trying to cleanse her brain and reinvigorate. That's what she told me. She asked me not to try and contact her as it would disturb her enjoyment of relaxation and solitude and I respect that."

"Does she speak to the children?"

"Of course, she's not completely heartless, she knows that they worry. She and Jack talk for quite a long time but Maisie gets too upset to say much to her."

"Can I use your bathroom?" Bonetti didn't wait for an answer. She found the family bathroom upstairs. She remembered reading a column in a Sunday newspaper magazine where the writer shamelessly admitted that when he visited someone's house, he liked to look through all the objects in their bathroom, including the bathroom cabinet. What he found, he explained, told him a lot about the people he was visiting. *It's none of his business*, she thought. *His interest in other people's private things was odd and creepy.* Her interest in Ian and Annie's bathroom was purely professional.

Bonetti came downstairs shortly afterwards, holding Annie's toothbrush, lady shave, badger brush, make-up bag and a pair of earrings.

"These are Annie's, aren't they?"

"Yes, the fact that she has left them shows you that she intends to return."

Bonetti hadn't applied for a search warrant as she lacked sufficient information or evidence to suspect Ian of anything.

"Don't mind if I borrow them, do you?" It was more a statement than a question. Ian was taken aback and didn't answer straight away. She took that as his agreement.

"Do you have a picture of Annie for me?"

"I think you'd better leave. I don't know why you are here."

Bonetti decided to go before Ian asked for Annie's

toiletries back. When she was out of sight, she put the items into separate plastic exhibits bags.

That evening, Bonetti sent Annie's belongings to Alfie in the lab, marked 'very urgent'. She asked him to compare the DNA from Annie's toiletries with the DNA of the deceased. She searched for any social media accounts for Stella, Annie or Ian, but if they had existed, they were all now deleted. She phoned Kate.

"Why didn't I think of this before. You must have dozens of photographs of Stella with Ian."

"I've even a photo of him with Annie as well," Kate added.

"Can you ping them over to me?"

Bonetti looked at the pictures that Kate sent and recognised Annie, not Stella, by her hair as the deceased at the crime scene.

Alfie was in contact with her the next morning, and able to confirm Bonetti's identification.

Bonetti phoned Ian. "The dead body is Annie, but you know that already. The DNA from her possessions that I took from the house matches the body."

Ian remained silent.

"I need you at Union Street, two o'clock this afternoon. I won't arrest you, unless you fail to turn up, but it will be a formal taped interview. You should bring your solicitor with you."

Ian had a court appearance to make in the morning before he could go to Union Street. He was defending Dixie Clark, accused of beating her boyfriend Stuart in the back garden of the house that they shared.

Dixie and Stuart lived in a Victorian terrace house in a

suburban street. They kept chickens in a coop in the back garden. Without a proper poultry fence around the coop (too expensive), Dixie worried about a fox attack. She had read that foxes were skilled hunters, able to penetrate ordinary wire netting. Apparently, a llama would chase a fox away, but Dixie did not own a llama. Another problem was that the chickens woke as dawn broke and made loud chicken noises which disturbed the street's fast-asleep residents. Stuart's answer was to dig a hole in the ground inside the coop and put the chickens in there each night, with boards over the top of the hole, so that the chickens could not see daylight until he removed the boards at a reasonable hour. The chickens, understandably, did not like going into the hole, particularly in the hot weather and on the evening concerned Stuart, according to Dixie, was kicking at the chickens to get them to go in.

Dixie went into the garden and kicked Stuart instead, shouting abuse at him at the same time. Stuart fell into the hole and twisted his ankle. He called the police and Dixie was charged with assault. Her defence was that she was acting necessarily to protect property which belonged to them both (the chickens) from being damaged by Stuart. Ian, finding it difficult to concentrate, was relieved when Stuart failed to appear as a witness at court. "He's chickened out, as usual," called out one of Dixie's supporters in the public gallery. Everybody laughed, Dixie's case was dismissed for lack of evidence and Ian was able to leave the court before lunch.

Ian went up to the front desk at Union Street Police Station. He had chosen a spicy curry at a Thai restaurant nearby as his last meal of freedom and had drunk a few bottles of Thirsty Fox over lunch to toast the inevitable loss of his liberty. He was now feeling a bit lightheaded.

"It's Mr Blake, the solicitor," the officer on duty announced to an empty waiting room. "Not expecting you today sir. There's nobody in the cells just now."

"I'm here to see Detective Sergeant Bonetti. She's expecting me."

Ian took a seat and waited. DS Bevridge appeared from a back office and called out to him. "Mr Blake? you can't stay away, can you? How's business?"

"It would be better if you upped your arrest rate," Ian said. "I'm having to help you out."

"Not making citizen's arrests of shoplifters are you? That's the latest trend, the public trying to be helpful. But you can't nick them and then defend them. You know that don't you?" Bevridge laughed.

"Mr. Blake, where's your brief?" Bonetti asked as she made an appearance.

"I don't need one, I've been doing the job for almost twenty years. I'm not having someone tell me what to do."

"As you like, but you know the saying: 'a physician who treats himself has a fool for a patient.'"

18

Ghostbusters

Bonetti took Ian through to the interview room, then fetched Detective Chief Superintendent Drake. She switched on the tape machine and the three of them introduced themselves for the recording.

"Mr Blake declines legal representation," Bonetti added.

Drake shuffled some papers and examined them in a studious manner.

You want me to believe that you have a mass of evidence and information that I don't know about. Not very clever, Ian thought.

"Mr. Blake, when did you stop loving your wife?" Drake asked.

That's like asking 'have you stopped beating your wife?' You asked me a question which has the unjustified assumption that I have stopped loving her. You should know better, he thought.

Drake gave him a piercing look.

"Mr Blake, did your wife know about your intimate relationship with Stella Godley?"

You're doing it again. Your question assumes that I was having an affair with Ms Godley, and you're a senior detective. You could do with some interview training, Ian thought.

There was a long silence. The three of them looked at each other.

It's the long pause that you hope I'll feel the need to fill. Well, I bet I can stay silent longer than you can, he thought.

Drake couldn't resist breaking the silence. "We have a witness who overheard you planning your wife's death."

Not that old chestnut: 'we've got a witness.' One of the oldest tricks in the book. I know it's not true. But I don't really care what happens to me. This guilt is too much to bear. I'll tell them everything, get it off my chest, he reasoned.

"Stella seduced me. She arranged to have pictures of us both having sex in the living room of her flat and then threatened to publish them unless I paid her. Foolishly, I turned to DCI Shadwell for advice. He said he would stop her and recover my money by having someone called Yuri kill Stella. He would arrange it so that Philip Royal was framed for the murder. But the plan went wrong because, for some unknown reason, Annie met Yuri at Philip's flat instead of Stella. I tried to stop her."

"Tried to stop whom?" Drake asked.

"Well, Stella, at least I thought it was Stella. I called out, 'Stella, stop!' but she didn't hear me."

"Didn't try very hard did you," Bonetti commented. "There must have been more you could have done if you had really wanted to save her. Why didn't you go to where Stella was meeting Yuri to put a brake on it?"

"I didn't know the address. I didn't want to know those sorts of details."

"You could have followed her taxi."

"It would have implicated me, being at the scene if the killing took place. I tried to contact Shadwell instead. I sent him a message, *stop it now*."

"Did he reply?" Drake asked.

"Yes, but it was sometime later. His message said *stop what*? Look, I fully admit planning Stella's murder, but I never intended Annie to be the victim. And when it happened, I was at Stella's flat."

"Yes, we know all about the romantic dinner *a deux*. I'm formally arresting you for the murder of Annie Blake." Drake cautioned Ian. "There'll be a further interview later."

"I'll have to put you in a cell," Bonetti told him.

Ian was brought back into the interview room in the early evening. Bonetti switched the recording machine back on.

"We have obtained the log that Ms *Fookoodah* kept of her observations of you and Ms Godley over a period of weeks in December and January. You spent many hours together at her apartment and in public," Drake put to him.

"Yes, we were lovers."

"She didn't blackmail you."

"She did, I'm telling you the truth."

"Then, why didn't you report it?"

"I did, to DCI Shadwell, and he said not to report it officially as he'd deal with it himself."

"We've spoken to Ms Godley's neighbour, Cynthia Phelps. Did you tell her (he read from his notes), 'I wish Annie, my wife, wasn't around any longer so that Stella and I could be together properly?'"

"Yes, something like that, but I didn't mean that I wanted her dead. I said it, but I didn't mean anything by it."

"Miss Phelps told us that you borrowed a key to Miss Godley's apartment from her, around the time of the murder. Why did you go there? You must have assumed that you would be dining alone."

"I went to look for the blackmail pictures and my money."

"Did you find anything? If you did, it would help support your story."

"No, I didn't. She might have got wise to my suspecting her and kept them somewhere else."

"What was the point of preparing that dinner?"

"I also needed a good alibi, so kill two birds with one stone. Sorry, that's not an appropriate phrase in the circumstances."

"Or was it that you expected Stella to join you, because you had plotted to kill your wife instead?"

"I've already told you that I didn't plot to kill Annie."

"Your wife is dead. I would have expected you to look more distressed than you do."

Ian shrugged his shoulders.

"Suspect shrugs his shoulders," Drake said to the recording machine.

"I'm in shock."

"You must have recognised your wife's body when you saw the photographs from the crime scene. Why didn't you alert us then?"

"I was afraid of being charged with her murder."

"So, why have you made a confession now?"

"Because I hate myself."

"You went along with a plan to frame Mr. Royal, and you let him stand trial for the murder of a woman whom you knew was still alive."

"I'm not proud of myself."

"Where is the £350,000 pounds that you withdrew from the bank?"

"Ask Stella."

"We would if we could find her," Bonetti chipped in.

"We'll terminate the interview," Drake said. Bonetti switched the recording machine off.

"It's a turnaround, a 'switcheroo', they swopped Annie for Stella. What do we charge him with?" Bonetti asked Drake when Ian was out of earshot.

"If we can show that he intended to kill his wife, then it's the murder of Annie Blake. If the jury believe that he intended to kill Stella Godley, but Annie Blake died because of a mistake or accident, then it's still the murder of Annie Blake, because of the doctrine of transferred malice."

"And what about an additional charge: attempted murder of Stella Godley?"

"We'd have to prove that the crime of killing her came near to taking place."

"How about conspiracy to murder Stella Godley?"

"Yes, if that was the real intention of them both. But we should be able to prove the principal crime of the murder of Annie Blake, so little to be gained by going for a charge of conspiracy as well.

"And before you go, the judge wants to know why we didn't identify the body much earlier as not that of Stella Godley. The police lab should have been able to report that the DNA from the deceased didn't match Godley's sample on the database. This is really embarrassing."

"Sorry, boss, but Shadwell insisted that we send a limited number of exhibits to our lab, marked 'non urgent', to save money. I couldn't accept that his selection met our professional duty to investigate all leads, so, I sent two other exhibits to Forensic Answers marked 'urgent'. When they tested them, they found a match for Godley's biometric data on the system. Our lab did their tests later and it seems that Godley's entry on our database had been erased in the meantime."

"You went against your senior officer's instructions, Sergeant. I can't just ignore that insubordination. And who paid for the private lab's work?"

"Sorry, sir. Kate Sullivan, the PI, was also trying to find out what had happened to Ms Godley, and she had the funds to pay for it."

"How did Godley's data come to be removed? It looks like a suspicious intervention by someone."

"DCI Shadwell actioned it. He said on the application form that she was entitled to its removal because her conviction for fraud had been overturned and that she'd asked him to help her get a 'clean slate', but he'd not got 'round to it before."

"Shadwell? Well, what a surprise. Forget what I just said about insubordination. And when did he spring into action about deleting her record?"

"Not long after the murder, sir."

"What a mess. This place is like a madhouse. I'm fighting crime with one hand tied behind my back. Where did Sullivan's funds come from?"

"You don't want to know, sir."

Let me speak to the duty prosecutor about charging Blake."

"Thank you, sir."

Drake returned soon after and visited Ian in his cell. "The duty lawyer has agreed that you should be charged with Mrs Blake's murder. I'll take you to the Custody Officer's desk so that we can get this done and then you'll be returned to your cell. I'll oppose bail and you'll be in court tomorrow."

"Is there anyone you want me to call?" Bonetti asked Ian.

"*Ghostbusters*? Sorry, it all seems unreal. Yes, will you call Felicity Crabtree. I'll give you her number if you let me have my phone to look it up."

Bonetti phoned Stant and told him about Ian's confession. "Steve, before you go, I found a bank card in Henry's room belonging to a Hung Fo. When I asked Henry about it, he said that Hung was a girl whom he knew, who had asked him to hold on to it for her. Her parents had grounded her for smoking dope and wanted to punish her by taking her bank card away. I do want to show Henry that I trust him."

"Take him at his word and tell him to give it back. Don't ask any more questions about it. The less you know the better."

"Thanks, Steve, got the message."

By the time that Felicity met Ian, he had been charged with Annie's murder, appeared in court and was in custody in HMP Gormley.

"I'm sorry that I haven't been to see you before today," Felicity said as they sat together in the legal visits room. "I was away for the summer holidays. Ian, this is Anesta Fisher. She is a solicitor who will instruct me to represent you." Felicity introduced the woman who was with her.

"I'm fine with Anesta. I only hear good things about you," Ian said, addressing Anesta.

"I'm glad you have chosen me," Felicity said. "I'm able to take your case because in the light of your statement exonerating Philip Royal, which they will rely upon against you, the prosecution have decided not to re-try Philip. But I'll need a QC to lead me as it's a murder."

"What, for a guilty plea? I know that the sentence will be long, life with a minimum of fifteen years if we can show how I was provoked. But you can manage the mitigation in court on your own, can't you?"

Felicity looked at Anesta and back at Ian. "Not so fast, you were obviously not paying attention to Lord Osling's transferred malice lecture that we went to. Listen carefully to what I have to say, as it's important. You remember Lord Osling spoke about the case of Saunders and Archer in the 16th century. Saunders was convicted of his daughter Eleanor's murder because, (she read from her notes) 'if a man, by mistake, murders a person other than the person he intended to murder, he is guilty of the crime to the same degree as if he had achieved his object.'

"What Lord Osling said, was that the judges whilst recognising the concept of transferred malice, also considered the liability of Archer as an accessory, since he had encouraged the crime that led to Eleanor's death. *Qui facit per alium facit per se* (he who acts through another, acts himself). The fact that the victim was not the person whom Archer knew Saunders intended to kill, could have made no difference if Archer was liable, like Saunders, for an accidental departure from what had been foreseen.

"If you read Edmund Plowden's 16th century law report of the case," Felicity continued, "Archer could not have been an accessory to Eleanor's murder because it was not an accident that Eleanor died. Saunders could have stopped her from eating the apple. The poisoning of Eleanor was not an accidental departure from their plan. On Crowden's analysis, it was a 'distinct thing' from that which Archer had agreed to. The accessory must know what it is that the principal intends to do and if the principal intends to do something wholly different, which the accessory has not agreed to, the accessory will not be liable."

"My understanding of the law," Anesta said, "is if you paid Yuri and Victor, to murder Stella, and that was the common plan, but they murdered Annie by mistake or accident, then you are still liable for Annie's death. But if they intended to murder Annie instead of Stella, without you knowing it, then you are not liable for Annie's death as they had departed from the common purpose to which you were a party. They were not acting as your agents.

"There is a further line of defence," she continued, "if you unequivocally withdrew from the plan and tried to stop the murder."

"I know about Edmund Plowden, who wrote that law report," Ian said. "He was a Catholic at a time when they were persecuted. I read that the nursery rhyme 'Goosey, Goosey Gander' is about the agents of the Protestant state who hunted down Catholic priests and worshippers. A priest who was in danger would hide and a good place was in the chamber of a lady living in a grand house. If the Protestants found him and the priest refused to say Anglican prayers, the Protestants would bind his legs and execute him by throwing him down the stairs. Sorry, I'm rambling."

"Your confession was actually a very clever move," Felicity said.

"I spoke the truth because I feel that I'm as guilty as sin."

"On your account you are morally wrong but not guilty in law."

"If it's a trial, I still want you in the lead," Ian said to Felicity. "Anesta has a jury ticket, she can be your junior."

"Well," Anesta said, "we must be able to satisfy a jury that you did not want Annie dead and that her death was not simply a mistake or accident. We will have our work cut out. Victor and Stella are sunning themselves in Rio by now and Yuri is long gone, back to Mother Russia. Is there anything that you need?"

"Some humour?"

"Well, in the custody record DS Bonetti has recorded your answer when she asked you if you wanted to call someone."

"Oh, you mean *Ghostbusters*. I'd been drinking, last chance saloon sort of. I had the ghost of Annie running through my head, screaming. So, it sort of made sense."

Ian sat in the cage in the prison van as it negotiated its way through the traffic in Central London. He had left HMP Gormley early in the morning and was to be dropped off at the Family Court for South London in Waterloo. He was constantly having to brace himself for the unpredictable stops and starts of the vehicle.

How could it have come to this? In less than a year, his life and career had nose-dived: from being at the centre of a loving family, a celebrated partner in a successful solicitors' criminal practice, and appointed a judge, to being driven around in a locked box.

He remembered the excitement of his first days in practice. He had a client, John Stone, charged with counterfeiting. Mr Stone was printing near-perfect copies of British bank notes on a grand scale in a unit on an industrial estate in North London. He was taking a break in the sunshine for a cigarette outside when the tenant of the neighbouring unit joined him. "How's business, making money?" his neighbour asked innocently. "Yes," he replied, smiling to himself at the truth of his answer. Stone's unit was raided by police, following a tip-off, and he was sentenced to eight year's imprisonment.

Ian had turned to Victor because he had to do something about Stella. They were the two people who had reduced him to this sorry state. He had been like the fresh and pure Rodion Romanovich Raskolnikov in Fyodor Dostoyevsky's *Crime and Punishment*. Victor had corrupted him, and Stella was the unscrupulous, worthless vermin Alyona Ivanova, preying upon vulnerable men like him. He could live with himself, betraying Annie by having a crazy affair with Stella, but he could not have lived with the constant threat of others seeing the pictures and video of them having sex together. It came down to his need to survive. Stella's planned murder was permissible, he told himself. As was Alyona's to Rodion's thinking. Annie was the hapless Lizaveta who happened to stumble across this depraved scene.

The prison van came to a final stop and Ian was released briefly into the bright daylight of the yard behind the courthouse. Handcuffed, he was taken into the cells. Shortly after, he was escorted up to a dull looking courtroom. His parents, Pauline and Michael Blake, with their solicitor Miss Parks, sat facing him. Two overweight prison officers sat down in chairs behind him. One of them started a crossword. They all stood as the magistrates entered the room.

"Your Worships," Miss Parks said, "this is an application for an order that will allow Mr Blake's children to continue to live with their paternal grandparents, who sit next to me. It will enable the grandparents to make day-to-day decisions about the children without having to refer to their son who, as you can see, is currently in prison on remand. Sadly, their mother is dead and their father, Mr Ian Blake is charged with her murder."

Ian could see the magistrates visibly draw back from him as if they feared that he would attack or contaminate them.

"Maisie is aged ten years and Jack is aged eight years," Miss Parks continued. "I spoke to Mr Ian Blake outside. He is not represented. He is himself a solicitor and he does not oppose my application, which has the support of the Family Court Advice Service. The maternal grandparents are retired and live in France and do not feel able to assist with the children. The father's brother David is also unable to help."

The magistrates turned and scrutinised Ian as if he was an exotic and dangerous animal.

"I agree," Ian said.

Ian had seen a defendant escape from court before: vault over the side of the dock; exit through the judge's door; jog along the judge's corridor; run down the stairs; push past the startled looking staff in the admin section; and finally, out into the daylight through the staff exit. In the Family Court he wasn't even in a dock but sitting at a table. By the time that the overweight prison officers had realised what was happening and had clambered out of their seats, he'd be lost amongst the crowds in the busy street outside.

19

Midnight in Moscow

"Please, Kate," Anesta pleaded, "you know that you're the best and we need your help."

"Ian's a monster. He not only cheated on his wife and contributed to her death, but he would also have allowed Philip Royal to rot in prison. Not that I like Philip any better. Why should I help Ian?"

"How about, because you're a professional, it's your job and you need the money like everyone else?"

"You want me to take a statement from Yuri, to see if he knows who was present when Annie was murdered and whether her death was a mistake or accident, or intentional. It's not surprising that he didn't want to draw attention to himself by attending the funeral. Why would he even want to say hello to me let alone incriminate himself now that he's safely back home? This is heavy stuff."

"Ian believes that Victor carried out the murder himself. There is evidence that Victor was at the crime scene but nothing to place Yuri there. If it was Victor, he knew Stella and could not be mistaken about the fact that he was killing Annie instead. So, Annie being murdered by Victor could not have been a mistake or accident and that gives Ian a defence if we can also show that Ian didn't know that this was Victor's plan. It's a long shot, but with Victor and Stella missing and Philip suffering from amnesia about that night, we don't have any other choice."

"I did have a brief talk with Yuri, but when I went back the next day to talk to him properly, he'd quit his job and cleared out his room. I bet you don't even know where he is now."

"Lucky break: Ektrina is in contact with him. They became friends because they both speak Russian. He's been emailing her because he says that Victor owes him money and he believes that Ektrina can arrange for him to be paid. She says that Yuri's gone home."

"Where's that? Deepest Siberia I suppose."

"No, Perm, it's about 770 miles from Moscow. I'm told you don't like flying if there's an alternative. Well, you can make the second leg of the journey by train. It takes seventeen hours from Moscow on the Trans-Siberia Express. I'm sure that it's lovely with the winter snow."

"Perm, as in 'why don't you grow your hair and perm it instead of having that you've just whacked your hair off with the kitchen scissors short cut lesbian look?'"

"Who says that to you?"

"My mother used to, on a good day. Is it safe? They may think that I'm a British spy and poison me with Novichok."

"Salisbury was last year, and nothing's happened since. Just don't pick up any stray perfume bottles lying in bins."

"It'll be freezing cold. And what about Covid?"

"No extreme temperatures. Chi says that you're proud of your furry Russian hat, and that you wear it on the underground in December where everyone stares at it. You could take it."

"Now you're making fun of me."

"And Covid hasn't reached Russia yet, according to the WHO."

"Practicalities, I don't speak Russian."

"No problem, Ektrina will go with you. We need someone whom Yuri will feel confident about opening up to. The difficulty is that we can't pay him for talking to us. If we do and he becomes a witness, the prosecutor could persuade a jury that we have bribed him to say what we wanted."

"Why is Ektrina willing to do this?"

"Because we're paying her as your interpreter. She needs the money. She's on her own now as Fazil forgot to tell his wife and three children about her. When his wife found out, she made Fazil give Ektrina the sack."

"Might she be a witness herself? She said that Victor liked to put his hand over her nose and mouth during sex."

"I wouldn't call her. She'd be questioned about the bedroom scene where she asked him to tie her down and it would look to a jury as if you and Carly were trying to entrap him. She knows about Victor's protection racket, but the judge would never admit that as evidence in Ian's defence. They wouldn't consider it relevant. So, there's nothing to prevent her from helping."

"Who's paying?"

"Ian, he knows that it is important."

Kate phoned Mary. "I'm going to Russia."

"Oh, when? Why, a holiday? At this time of year?"

"This week, urgent business. Trying to get the truth in a witness statement out of someone who is reluctant to help us."

"Okay, getting the truth can be like pulling teeth. Last night a child I'm responsible for called 999. He's under a supervision order and dad, who can be violent, is not allowed to see him except at a contact centre. The child told police that his dad was fighting his mum. When the police arrived, mum refused to tell them what had happened and told them to get rid of *him* but wouldn't say who he was. The man, who was hiding in the conservatory, left without the police speaking to him. Now the mum says that the man was not the dad, she won't say who he was, and the child has obviously been told not to speak to us. She claims the boy calls every man who visits dad."

"He obviously was the dad," Kate said. "It's called an excited utterance by the boy. It came up in a case that I was working on for Ian. A spontaneous statement made under stress is reliable. He was telling the truth to the emergency operator."

"Why didn't you become a lawyer?" Mary asked. "Much more secure than your PI work."

"Why did you become a social worker?" Kate asked in reply. "Everyone hates you, including the public. How many threats to kill you have you had?"

Kate and Ektrina's train left Moscow's Karoskzal station at midnight. The station was designed to look like a romantic castle from the outside, but as a refuge for the city's outcasts, parts of it inside resembled a scene from a hellscape painted by Hieronymus Bosch. Waiting for the train was a nightmare experience. Kate and Ektrina went to the café/bar on the first floor inside the station as this was the only place with vacant seats. They saw that it had only men intent on getting very drunk, rather than bona-fide railway passengers. One man was so drunk that he could not manage to put his heavy leather jacket back on. His arms could not find the holes for the sleeves, and he wrestled with the jacket silently for minutes before giving up and walking off, grumpily carrying it slung over his shoulder.

The only way in and out of the café/bar was a steep flight of narrow, dark, concrete steps. The drunken man had staggered off through the exit door.

As they waited, Kate told Ektrina about Claire's problem. "This is my niece, whom I told you about," Kate said. "She foolishly sent her boyfriend, intimate pictures of herself when they were dating. They broke up and he showed them to his new girlfriend, Lily. Claire was worried sick that they would put them on social media or a porn site, until Carly warned them off."

"He sounds like bad boy," Ektrina said. "She is silly girl, for taking pictures like that for boyfriend. But girls are under pressure from boys to act sexy, like in porn films, to keep boys interested in them. It was not like that when I was her age. That boy may grow up to be man who uses women and does not care about their feelings, like Victor. I hope that Carly has taught them a lesson."

"She commits a crime by sending the pictures in the first place," Kate declared. "Claire could have ended up in court and on the Sex Offenders Register. A schoolchild was cautioned last year for texting a topless picture of herself to her boyfriend. Anyway, how do you change such contemptuous attitudes towards women?"

It was at least thirty minutes later that Kate and Ektrina left the café/bar, to catch their train. As Kate exited the door, about to walk down the concrete steps, she almost fell over the drunk man who was lying precariously across the top step, asleep. She and Ektrina stepped over him carefully, so as not to send him rolling down to his death. As they walked to their platform, a man fell out of a doorway and landed flat on his face on the ground, in front of them. He had his arms by his sides and fell like a statue, making no attempt to break his fall. Kate screamed in sheer panic, but Ektrina just laughed at the drunken man's foolishness.

The journey was partly overnight, on a train headed for Vladivostok. Kate and Ektrina shared a sleeper compartment where they were looked after by a matronly woman in railway uniform who patrolled the corridor of their carriage, looking after the passengers as if they were her children. She brought them extra pillows and blankets and poured them tea from a large samovar into glasses held in silver plated holders. The reassuringly regular sound of the train wheels on the railway lines, interrupted only by the occasional click, click, click, click as it went over a set of points, lulled Kate into sleep.

They arrived in Perm at five o' clock in the afternoon. Yuri was expecting them and was waiting at the new Perm II station. He looked pleased to see Ektrina but was more reserved with Kate. He drove them down the impressive Petrovskaya Street in the centre of the city and over an imposing bridge across the Kama River, to the city's outskirts. They stopped at a local restaurant for dinner and then drove on to a street nearby where Yuri pulled up in the yard of a typical old house. Inside, it smelt of vegetables. In the hallway, Yuri introduced them to an exceptionally large black and brown dog wearing a harness. Kate had to squeeze past him. She had never been quite so close to a dog of that size. The harness suggested that restraining him was not easy and needed special equipment.

"His name is Tunk," Yuri announced.

"That's Russian for tank," Ektrina explained.

"He weighs sixty-five kilos," Yuri said. "We can talk tomorrow as I have to go out now."

Tunk appeared to be extremely interested in Kate and followed her upstairs to the bedroom that Yuri had prepared for them. Kate felt uneasy. She had no idea where they were in Perm. She assumed that this was Yuri's family's house, but Yuri was the only person whom they met inside. She did not know where she would go to for help, if she needed it, or how to call the police. Disturbingly, her mobile phone kept losing its signal. Now, to cap it all, they were going to be left on their own with Tunk. With nothing else to do and reluctant to confront Tunk in the house, Kate and Ektrina prepared for bed.

There was a loud sniffing noise. She could see the end of Tunk's nose pushing its way through the gap underneath the bedroom door. The door began to move under the weight of the dog.

"Ektrina," Kate said urgently, "Tunk's trying to get into the room. What shall we do?"

Kate and Ektrina got out of bed and pushed a chest of drawers across the floor, placing it against the bedroom door. Kate felt safer now. She heard the dog flop down heavily on the other side. *He's going to stay there*, she thought with alarm. *What happens if I need to use the toilet?* She climbed into bed and asked Ektrina, "what sort of dog is Tunk?"

"A Caucasian shepherd, I don't want to scare you, but they have certain reputation: very stinky flatulence." As if by command, there was a loud noise as Tunk broke wind. A great smell entered the bedroom from under the door.

"My God," Kate declared, "he's trying to gas us now." She hoped that daylight would come soon.

In the morning, they could hear Tunk being locked outside. Now that it was safe to leave the room, Kate and Ektrina raced each other to the only toilet, Kate shouting, "I'm bursting", and tripping Ektrina up on the way to make sure that she got there first. Yuri called them downstairs for breakfast. On the table were the smallest hard-boiled eggs that Kate had ever seen. The hens she could hear clucking outside had laid them. Kate thought that the small size of the eggs was due to the hens being stressed out by having to share their yard with Tunk. There was also a bowl each of white glutinous cereal with a piece of buttered toast at the side of it. Kate looked at Ektrina for an explanation.

"It's *mannaya kasha*," Ektrina said, "semolina porridge to you, delicious, we have it at home." In front of Yuri was a little frozen glass with vodka.

Yuri picked up his glass and drank it down in one. "Bottoms up, I learnt that in London," he said, laughing.

After breakfast, Kate took out paper and pen and started a small recording device.

"Yuri, we've come a long way to talk to you. We really need your help. How do you know Victor?"

"I worked for Victor for three years, collecting money for him. I visited each premises monthly and was given sealed brown envelope. I wasn't allowed to open it. Sometimes they didn't have money for me, and I had to act tough. I know he's cop but this not strange. Here in Russia, police often control prostitutes. They even drive them in police cars to meet their clients. Victor owes me over £3000. He hasn't paid me since before Christmas."

"Victor's missing," Kate explained. "He didn't turn up for the second day of Ian's trial. We need your help to defend Ian, the dead woman's husband. He's been charged with her murder, but we believe him when he says that he didn't know that Victor intended to murder her. Ian was led to believe that Stella Godley, who was blackmailing him, was always the target. Please tell us what you know about the murder."

Yuri looked unsure about what to do. Ektrina took his hand and looked him in the face. "Yuri, we are depending on you," she said sweetly.

"Why should I help?" Yuri asked. "How will you make it worth my while? Will you pay me money that Victor owes me? I can't return to England as I do not have right papers and they would see how I overstayed on my last visit."

"Victor left his car behind because he left in a hurry," Kate explained. "His Audi convertible must be worth at least £30,000. He registered it in Ektrina's name so that if the police saw it somewhere suspicious and ran a check on the owner, it would not come back to him. Ektrina's already talked with a garage which will recover it from Heathrow Airport and buy it and she will pay you the money that Victor owes you."

Encouraged by the promise of money and Ektrina's warm hand on his, Yuri talked. "Victor told me he had job would earn me lot of money, £10,000. He said that I wouldn't get caught. He would take me to flat and I must wait there until woman arrived. She would be expecting to collect money. I must tell her that money is in bedroom, then kill her. He would return and clear up after me. He said I was 'clean skin', as I did not have police record in England, so it could not be traced back to me."

"Did he say who she was?" Kate asked.

"He said her name was Stella Godley. He showed me photograph of her."

"Take a look at this picture, Yuri." Kate showed Yuri a photograph of Annie. "Is this the woman whose picture he showed you?"

"That's her."

"Who did you think she was?"

"I didn't ask any questions; I didn't know why he wanted her killed; you mustn't have feelings for victim."

"Now take a look at this picture." Kate showed Yuri a picture of Stella. "Have you seen this woman?"

"No, never."

"Why didn't you kill her, the first woman that I showed you? What happened?"

"Victor told me job off. Then later he said she was dead, and I must go to mortuary to name body. He gave me same photograph he had shown me before. He told me to say I was her only friend, and her name is Stella

Godley. I did as he told me. He owes me £500 for that. He told me go to her funeral, but I was nervous and came home."

"Will you return to England and give evidence about that? It's very important."

"You'll be able to see and visit me in London," Ektrina added.

"I don't know, I'm afraid of arrest myself. They could say that I killed her or that I helped Victor to do so. How can you make sure that I am not in trouble with police if I go to London?"

"I will do my best to get you a written promise about that," Kate told him. "The police officers investigating this case will welcome your help in convicting Victor."

"Why would British let me return?"

"We can contact the embassy here and explain why you need a visa to travel to London."

Kate completed writing out Yuri's formal statement with a declaration that it was true, and then witnessed his signature.

"Yuri, have you any criminal convictions in Russia?" Kate asked.

Yuri paused for thought. "I served prison sentence, seven years for manslaughter when I was twenty. I was bouncer at club and punched man in face. He fell and hit head on concrete. I didn't mean to kill him. He had baseball bat."

"Yuri, would you have killed Annie?" Ektrina asked.

"We don't need to know that, Ektrina," Kate said anxiously, not wanting to hear his answer, "it's not relevant."

By lunchtime, Kate was able to send a message about Yuri to Anesta and Felicity: *mission accomplished.*

Kate and Ektrina decided to fly back to Moscow, to save time, but the only flight that they could book left them with the rest of the day and the night in Perm.

"There's no flight to Moscow until tomorrow, how are you going to spend day?" Ektrina asked Kate. She was taken aback by Ektrina's use of 'how are you' instead of 'how are we'.

"What are you going to do?" Kate asked in return.

"Yuri said he would take me for drive, show me around."

"Well, I'm not going to play gooseberry with you and Yuri and I'm not spending another night like last night. I didn't sleep a wink; I'm moving to a hotel. What about you?"

"Yuri said he will stay in house tonight and look after me," Ektrina said, blushing. "What is play gooseberry? Is it a game?"

"It means that I would feel like a spare part with you both. I'll see you at Bolshoye Savino airport tomorrow morning."

Kate took a taxi into central Perm and to save money, checked into a locally run hotel. She went to the business centre on the hotel's second floor, intending to use the internet to plan her day and evening in Perm. The so-called business centre was not business-like at all and not surprisingly was doing little business. The one computer screen was occupied by a young woman whose job was to help the guests make the best use of the centre. She had arranged her personal possessions around her on the computer desk so that they were all conveniently to hand. She did not take kindly to being interrupted by Kate asking to have internet access. She made it plain, through her facial expressions and exasperated sounds, that it would be a big disturbance for her if she had to gather up all her things and move.

Kate was insistent though and soon had the computer to herself. The computer's desktop screen was covered with shortcut icons for pop bands, fashion brands and social media. She quickly discovered the sightseeing attractions of Perm and easily filled the afternoon.

In the evening, Kate had planned to relax in her room and get an early night in readiness for the flight to Moscow and journey on to London the next day. But all the channels on the television in her room were in Russian. At nine o' clock, feeling hungry, she decided to order room service for dinner. She telephoned the number given in the directory, but there was no reply and when she phoned the hotel switchboard instead, the operator spoke only in Russian.

Kate went down to the reception desk. Two young women, one tall and one of medium height were seated there, talking to each other in an animated fashion. Kate waited for them to stop talking and speak to her. They continued with their conversation, ignoring her.

"Excuse me," Kate said, "I need room service."

"Kitchen she's closed," the tall woman Yelena replied, in English.

"Do you know where I can get something to eat?" Kate asked.

The women looked at each other and thought hard with furrowed brows.

The medium height woman, Katrina, suddenly pulled a smiling face, as if thinking a nice thought. "Sputnik, madly in love with this place," she said. "The last time we had waiter, polite with adequate sense of humour. Found us table next to socket, we had to turn on laptop, very politely and gently picked up order. Tea intuition, just guessing exactly what we needed. Our chat with pizza and two pots of tea cost 600 roubles. Mood improved by 200 per cent." The tall woman nodded in agreement. "We'll call you taxi," Katrina said.

Kate soon found herself inside a smoke-filled Sputnik at a large table eating pizza and drinking tea, surrounded by, and talking to a group of friendly students from Perm State University. They were keen to practice and show off their English language skills to her.

"Incredibly cosy and cute," Lena said, about a new shop which had just opened near the university. "Immediately found boyfriend gift for birthday."

"Wonderful warm socks with hedgehog, 500 roubles," Sasha added, "and there with squirrels and other cute animals. Bought myself set of panties for 1,500 roubles."

The discussion turned to which club they would go on to later that evening.

"K7 has large dance floor where you can realise all your movements, also last time lovely girl in bikini dancing on stage next to DJ," Sergei said. They all laughed.

"That's true," Sasha agreed, "inside is very fiery atmosphere, we had fun from heart."

"The music is incendiary, you can rip on all cylinders," Katia said enthusiastically.

"But both elevators not working," Sasha said. "Had to climb to top in heels, stiletto is little tipsy and problematic."

"*Privet,*" another student called out and joined them.

"That means 'hey man,'" Sasha interpreted for Kate. Nikolai, who just arrived, joined in the conversation enthusiastically. "K7, this is upside place! Music, lights, people, bar, dance floor. Having fun all night and sleep during day."

"Dance Box is popular among the young and more mature age," Lena contributed. "No fighting and getting drunk in your eyes, everyone is trying to entertain with style and share of culture. The music is not bad, waiters delight, price conventional, should go there, see people, make love."

"We do not go to Beach Bar in person," Sasha said, looking serious, "because too many drunken pushy men. Lone female would not be in club, never. Music is mediocre, men all cattle."

"Don't go Beach Bar," Katia addressed Kate. "At entrance sullen guys greet me, obviously not happy with their lives and their salaries. I got into super gusto smoke filled room, even eyes sliced, young people talking about life, not talking, shouting, drowning out music, seven circles of hell."

"Pleased with Blue Velvet but *feis* control take people out of queue without explaining their reasons," Nikolai said. "Woman working door is *suka* on power trip, she made point of kissing certain people welcoming them in then telling others they couldn't enter."

"*Suka* means bitch," Sasha said for Kate's benefit. Kate knew about *feis*, meaning 'face control' in the London scene. Clubs where your appearance stands for your level of wealth, beauty, power, social standing, and overall desirability. People often complained about the power of bouncers and the velvet rope. "What is she doing here? Someone call face control," was a common bitchy remark.

At nine o' clock the next morning, Kate went down to the restaurant on the hotel's first floor. It was empty apart from two hotel staff members who were seated at a table, eating.

"Where is breakfast?" Kate asked.

"Breakfast, she finished," one of the staff members declared.

Kate checked out of the hotel and took a taxi to the airport.

20

Flying Down to Rio

"Victor, where did that criminal bank clerk go in *The Lavender Hill Mob*?" Stella asked. "You remember, they melted gold bars down into miniature Eiffel Towers. He was chased by police with some of the gold in a suitcase."

"'Instead of changing at Charing Cross I came straight to Rio de Janeiro.' He lived a life of luxury there for one year, ran out of money and was arrested."

"There must be a reason why criminals love Brazil."

"They say that anyone can be bought there. And Brazil lacks an extradition treaty with the UK. I suppose that if it's good enough for Ronald Biggs, then it's good enough for us."

Victor's first plan had been for them to go to his apartment in Spain and lay low there. He would be able to access his funds in the Gibraltar Bank. But he was concerned that the Spanish police already had him and his address in Marbella on record: the result of a stupid fight in a club over spilt drinks.

Victor collected Stella from her Airbnb and they travelled to Heathrow Airport in the Audi convertible, which he abandoned in haste in one of the airport car parks.

They tried not to show any nervousness as they checked in and went through security and passport control, travelling with false identities and passports which Victor had paid a site on the dark web to provide. Unable to resist having the last laugh, he had chosen Lawrence Egal, or Mr L Egal as he sometimes wrote it, as his name. Stella decided to call herself Mrs Goldie Egal as she thought that would be easy to remember. Ian's money was converted into 500 euro notes and shared between a body bag around Victor's waist, and pockets sewn into Stella's underwear.

Stella complained about her new shape. "My arse is huge. It looks ridiculous."

"Count yourself lucky, sitting on a pile of cash. Brazilian's love big bums. They prefer them to big breasts. Wouldn't be surprised if a woman asks you where you had it done. And watch out for someone wanting to goose you. Your new shape looks much better than mine: a comic drinker's paunch."

The Braz Air International flight from London to Rio de Janeiro landed in bright sunshine the next morning. During the flight, Stella had tried to lighten the mood, singing "flying down to Rio by the sea-o" from the 1933 musical comedy. "I'm a good dancer," she told Victor. "I could be Ginger Rogers, but you are no Fred Astaire."

Arriving In Rio, they took a Yellow Taxi to the Nacional Hotel in Zona Sul, near the beach. Their first thought was about the money. It would be too risky to keep it in a hotel safety deposit box. There were reports of tourists whose money had been stolen from their boxes. Instead, Victor found a local bank which allowed cash to be stored in a rented box. They went together to the Banco Dinheiro and registered as joint key holders. They supplied copies of their passports and gave details of where they were staying and the purpose of their visit. *Looking for a business opportunity,* Victor wrote. They filled in a 'Financial Action Task Force of Latin America' form. Under the heading 'Transaction Details', Victor wrote, *proceeds of sale of launderette,* stating the amount and currency of cash deposited and the origin of the money.

They spent their first weeks like any tourists. Daytime was on the beach. Night-time saw them strolling along the Avenida Atlantica or sitting in the clubs and bars in Lapa sipping caipirinhas and listening to bossa nova and samba music. The weather was comfortably not too hot, the late twenties centigrade, as it was the Brazilian winter. They dined either in the many churrascarias, the all-you-can-eat barbecue houses or, to save money, in the *por kilo* restaurants where the diners were charged according to the weight of the meat they ate.

"As well-dressed Europeans, it's like you've got bullseyes on your backs when you are sightseeing," the hotel concierge had warned them. "Don't count your money openly like you're eating a banana."

Other people had told him about a crack epidemic amongst poor young people brought up on the streets, who could be ruthless criminals if you resisted their demands. Victor only used the cash machines in hotel lobbies and kept clear of the favelas.

It all seemed too good to be true. Christmas and New Year were colourful and busy and Covid was yet to reach Brazil. The problems started soon after, when Victor went out every night on his own to clubs where he paid for female attention, leaving Stella in their hotel room. He came back in the early hours, the worse for drink and smelling of other women's fragrances. Stella, feeling bored and trapped, wanted some excitement too. *What is good for the goose is good for the gander* she thought. She started going out alone and didn't have to wait long before she had a phone full of messages from wealthy and attentive men.

Early one morning, Victor woke Stella, waving her phone in her face. "Do you think I'm fucking stupid?" he shouted. "Who is Lucas? He wants to save you from me. What have you been telling him? What are you up to bitch? You could have blown our cover."

"Lucas is just jealous of you and got a bit carried away. He's harmless. Anyway, you're drunk and what the fuck do you think you are doing, going through my private stuff?"

"I want clarity," Victor raged, and he opened the bedroom window, pulling the curtains to one side. He motioned to throw the phone out. Stella put Victor's wrist in a goose neck, bending it back to wrestle the phone from him. Victor slammed her hard against the wall, ripping her nightdress. She screamed loudly and Victor placed his forearm across her neck to silence her. He held it there for at least thirty seconds, so that she couldn't breathe. Stella started to choke, and Victor released her. Stella fell to the floor, holding her neck. Victor had never attacked her before.

There was knocking at the bedroom door. "Don't answer it," Victor said. There was the sound of a key turning in the lock and the door was opened from the outside. The night manager Tiego stood there with the security man and a house cleaner.

"Guests have complained about a disturbance in your room," Tiego said. He looked across to where Stella was getting up from the floor. Tiego spoke softly to the security man who took out his phone and moved back into the corridor to make a call.

"I'm alright," Stella said, trying to get up and wiping the tears from her face. "I slipped in the bathroom."

"The bathroom is on the other side of the room. Your nightdress is ripped, and you have a large red mark across your throat. We've called for the police. They can sort out what happened. We will all wait here for them."

Stella felt shocked, humiliated, and angry. Despite the many and varied liaisons and sexual encounters she had experienced in the past, no man had ever assaulted her before. If she couldn't be in control, she'd walk away. She hated Victor at that moment.

Two officers from the local police station arrived at the Nacional Hotel and went to Victor's room. They spoke first to Tiego. Then one officer led Victor out of the room into the corridor. Tiego joined them to help with any language problems. The other officer talked to Stella in the bedroom, with a member of the hotel staff acting as interpreter. The officer showed Victor a shiny metal badge *Policia Civil do Estado do Rio De Janeiro*.

"I'm like a brother, also police," Victor said with Tiego's help, and shook the officer's hand.

The two Brazilian officers then conferred with each other, told Tiego that they would be taking no further action, and left.

Bonetti and Drake were back at 5 Century Buildings, in conference with Monty Bell QC and Cecilia Lassi. Jack Couper was there for the Public Prosecutor. This time, they were meeting to discuss how they could persuade a jury to convict Ian Blake.

"Looking at my notes of previous conferences," Bonetti said, "all that Mr. Couper has done is try to protect DCI Shadwell."

"Outrageous remark," Couper replied.

"Hear me out. At the first conference, Mr. Couper said that I was making (she read from her notes) 'groundless accusations against my senior officer who was away enjoying a well-earned rest.'

"We all know what DCI Shadwell did on his return from this well-earned rest, he beat up the new boyfriend of his partner Ektrina. She put us straight about his claims that the man fell down the stairs."

"Do we need to listen to this?" Couper asked.

"I've got a serious point to make," Bonetti continued. "Mr Couper mocked the account given by Ms *Fookoodah*; made a point about not being able to say her name because he found that amusing; and told me I was being emotional. After Shadwell was told to stay away from Union Street and we had a further conference, Mr. Couper said that we were (she looked at her notes again), 'jumping to hasty conclusions.'

"He accused me of 'wild speculation' and said that 'we should hide the evidence which the judge later ordered to be disclosed.' Mr Couper is not being objective in his approach to this case. His behaviour is unprofessional and obstructive."

"I shouldn't have to sit here and listen to this outrageous

attack on my character," Couper said, raising his voice and looking for support.

"You don't, I agree with DS Bonetti," Drake replied. "You appear to be conflicted: protecting Shadwell for some reason. I'll speak to your line manager and recommend that you are taken off this case." Couper looked at Monty and Cecilia, but they kept their heads down, studying the lever arch files holding their case papers.

"Well," Couper said, "if I'm not wanted, not that it's up to you," and marched out of the room.

"Now let's continue," Drake suggested.

"Before we do," Cecilia interrupted, "I need to arrange some biscuits." She opened the conference room door and called down the corridor. "Bradley, some of those Jammie Dodgers please."

"Ian Blake has confessed to paying Shadwell and through him Prokonova to kill Stella Godley," Drake continued. "Is he speaking the truth about Godley being his intended victim? Or was his plan all along that Shadwell and Prokonova would kill his wife, so leaving him free to pursue his relationship with Godley?"

Bradley entered and placed a plate of biscuits on the table. "Your bike, sir," he said addressing Monty. "You chained it to the railings again. The custodian is about to cut the lock off with an angle grinder and remove it."

"Apparently it's a security risk," Monty explained to the others. "Don't know why. What a bother. Here's the key to the lock, Bradley. Nip outside quickly will you and just bring it into the building."

"Blake could have just divorced his wife if he wanted to be with Stella," Cecilia suggested. "Not go the whole hog, take a huge risk and have her killed. And if they had planned to continue their relationship, she would not have been blackmailing him. Yet he withdrew the £350,000 prematurely and in cash from the firm's account. Why did he do that? Jammie Dodger anyone?" She passed the plate around.

"Blake and Godley would not have been able to be together if she was supposed to be a corpse," Drake observed, "unless he was going to disappear with her. But that's unlikely."

"Take the biscuit, we've got a cupboard full. Bradley goes to the cash and carry for us," Cecilia said, noticing Bonetti eye the last one on the plate.

"I thought for a moment you were complaining that I 'take the biscuit', you know, that I'm being stupid or rude," Bonetti said, smiling at Cecilia. "Of course, Blake may just have told the truth in his confession," she continued. "Victor and Stella stood to gain a lot of money from the insurance pay out if the underwriters accepted that Annie was Stella."

"But equally," Cecilia responded, "Victor stood to gain more from Stella's death if Stella really was dead and not around to share the prize money with him."

"Victor's gone, Stella's gone, Yuri's gone, and the money's gone. Ian's confessed to paying for Stella to be murdered but Annie died instead. Let's not overthink it," Monty advised. "He has admitted that the plan was for Stella to be sent to Royal's flat, where the killer was lying in wait. But that the plan 'went wrong', his words, because Annie went there instead. He doesn't say that the plan was changed. To prove our case, we only need to convince a jury that he intended to kill Stella, and something 'went wrong', like he said. An accident or mistake, so that Annie died in her place. Then, under the doctrine of transferred malice he's guilty."

"Your shoes, Monty, how do you get that shine?" Drake asked. "I can see my face in them."

"I have Bradley to thank for that. He won't let me be seen in public with messy shoes. He's got an extensive shoe cleaning kit. Does everyone's shoes in chambers if they ask him.

"Where was I? The defence will have to show that killing Annie was only Victor's plan which Ian knew nothing about. But how will they do that? Ian may give evidence and say that in the witness box. Why should the jury believe him? Having admitted to paying for Stella to be murdered, he has no credibility."

When Bonetti and Drake had gone, Monty turned to Cecilia. "What odds are Barri-Bets quoting on this one?"

"It's a difficult one for Veronica to call. On the one hand he has confessed to plotting to murder Stella. On the other, he says that he never intended for Annie to die. It's now 3/1 against his acquittal, so she thinks we are winning the game."

Ian had resisted the call inside his head to flee the Family Court. Instead, he returned to prison and later sat in the legal visits room at HMP Gormley where the mood was surprisingly upbeat.

"I am happy to report the success of Kate Sullivan and Ektrina Lavislova's visit to Perm to interview and take a statement from Yuri Prokonova," Anesta announced.

"Yuri told them that Victor had offered him £10,000 to kill Stella Godley."

"He told me he needed £30,000," Ian remarked. "He was cheating me right from the start."

"A couple of weeks before the murder," Anesta continued, "he showed Yuri a photograph of the woman he had to kill. She was Annie. He showed Yuri the same photograph when he instructed Yuri to name her as Stella in the mortuary."

"That proves that Annie was chosen as the target by Victor some time before the murder, and that it was his intention to kill her all along," Ian said excitedly.

"I think he's got it," Anesta said, mimicking the musical show character Professor Henry Higgins.

"Shortly before the murder was due to take place Victor cancelled Yuri," Anesta continued "telling him that the job was off."

"So, the bastard did it himself. Victor knew Stella, so it was no mistake or accident when he killed Annie."

"By Jiminy, he's got it," Anesta said.

"Anesta, you're being really annoying," Felicity remarked, laughing. "She's been rehearsing for an alternative version of *My Fair Lady* with her amateur dramatics group."

"Our case is simple," Felicity said. "Victor intended to kill Annie. The fact that he killed her was not a mistake or accident. What Victor did was a 'distinct thing' from that which you had agreed to. So, you cannot have been an accessory to Annie's murder."

"Bingo," Anesta said, "and now we must prove it. We have a sworn statement from Yuri but that's not enough.

He must give evidence in person. He's promised to do so if Ektrina pays him the money that Victor owes him, plus expenses of course. Ektrina has sold Victor's car so that she can send Yuri the money."

"Have you heard anything about the trial listing?" Ian asked.

"I'll speak to the list office tomorrow," Anesta promised.

"You will try your hardest for me, won't you?" Ian implored Felicity.

"Fearless Felicity Crabtree, night and day she works away," Anesta replied in a sing-song voice.

"Anesta, I'll be so pleased when you stop pretending to recite lines from that darned show of yours," Felicity said with an irritated voice.

"What are our chances?" Ian asked.

"With a little bit of you know what," Anesta sang to them.

"Anesta, stop it now."

"So, we could win?" Ian asked.

"That would be lovely," Anesta said in a sing-song voice.

Felicity looked at her out of the corner of her eye. "I'm watching you. Ian, ignore her, let's be serious, you look like you want to say something."

"In heaven, hell and Halifax horrendous wind systems are highly unlikely," Ian enunciated slowly.

"Bravo," called Anesta and they all laughed.

Felicity went back to chambers to continue working. Grant was still in the clerk's room. "How are the odds doing on Blake's murder?" Felicity asked.

"Still 3/1 against his acquittal. When Yuri Prokonova's

statement is disclosed, they could change dramatically and go the other way."

"I know that we're not supposed to discuss bets but are you going to put money on it?"

"Yuri is like a super sub striker who will come on at the last moment and win the match for us. I'm going to back him, but it must be done now before the odds go into reverse."

Yuri's statement was made available to the prosecution the next day. Veronica made an immediate change when she heard the news, and no new bets were taken.

Ektrina sent Yuri the money he was owed. Ian's trial was due to start in two weeks' time and Anesta sent urgent emails to Yuri asking him which flights he wanted her to book and telling him that she would arrange a hotel for him in London. She also offered to pay his daily expenses. He was only needed for one day of the trial, but they couldn't say precisely which day, so they asked him to come to London for three days. She had been in contact with the British Embassy staff in Moscow, who had agreed to give Yuri a tourist visa so that he could travel to London to give evidence.

She admitted to Yuri that she could not get the written promise of immunity from the prosecution that he had asked for. But she told him that when he gave his evidence, he should emphasise that he had no intention of going through with the killing. It would be clear to everyone that he did not understand the significance of what he did in the mortuary and had not intended to pervert the course of justice. If any questions were too probing, then Felicity would remind him of his right not to incriminate himself. As soon as he had finished giving evidence, they would have him on a flight back to Moscow. If the police changed their minds after his return home and considered him a suspect, he should be reassured that the Russian authorities would never extradite him.

Anesta had an unpleasant surprise when Yuri replied that he didn't want to come to London and was staying in Perm. He said that it was inconvenient for him to travel. He was terribly busy at work and couldn't take days off. On top of that, he had an elderly relative who was ill, needing his care; and there was no one who could look after Tunk if he was away.

Emails went backwards and forwards between Anesta and Yuri. Anesta told him that Ian's freedom probably depended upon his evidence. Yuri replied that Anesta had his written statement, and he didn't understand why they needed him in person in London.

Anesta met with Felicity to discuss the situation. "Like you, I'm satisfied that Yuri's evidence is admissible," Felicity said, "but if the prosecution object, which they are bound to do, we will have difficulty in persuading a court to accept his written statement, as it is hearsay. We would have to show that he is unavailable abroad and it is not practical for him to attend Ian's trial. In these days of cheap and frequent air travel it will be difficult to argue that he can't be here. But he could possibly give his evidence on a live video link from Russia instead. I'll contact the British Embassy again and see if they can arrange it with the Russian Justice Department. They do this in fraud trials."

Anesta received a positive response from the Embassy: the video link facility at the Criminal Court in Perm could be used and there would be no charge.

Anesta emailed Yuri at once with the good news. Yuri did not reply. She tried to contact Yuri, but his phone was always switched off. Ektrina tried phoning and emailing Yuri, but he didn't respond to her either.

It was February and Ian's trial was now imminent. Anesta engaged a Russian PI to track Yuri down. They soon reported back that Yuri's house was empty. The neighbours said he had gone away and didn't know when he would be back. Tunk had been placed in a local dogs' boarding kennels. The kennels said that they were paid for one month's board in advance to look after him. They complained that he was expensive to keep because of the amount that he ate, being an excessively big dog. He was hard to control when they took him out for exercise and was disturbing everyone by constantly barking, wailing, and breaking wind. Yuri's co-worker said that Yuri had taken leave because a member of his family, in another part of Russia, was ill. Covid had struck Russia.

Felicity met in conference with Anesta and Ian at HMP Gormley to tell Ian about Yuri's disappearance. "I'm afraid that it's a case of now he's got his money from us, there's no longer any incentive for him to give evidence against Victor," Anesta said. "Even Ektrina's not a strong enough magnet."

"There is another way that we can get Yuri's evidence in," Felicity told Ian. "We must prove that he can't be found. The judge would need to know where he was last seen, in what circumstances and what steps were made to trace him."

"I can get a statement from the Russian PI covering those points," Anesta said.

"What are the chances that the judge will agree to admit Yuri's statement?" Ian asked.

"I don't know," Felicity said. "It doesn't help that Yuri has made himself unavailable and that he has a conviction in Russia for manslaughter. Even if we can prove his disappearance to the judge's satisfaction, they can still exclude the evidence on the grounds of unfairness to the prosecution."

Ian felt his mood darken. "Let's hope that we get a defence minded judge," he said.

21

Missing Piece

Stella went to the Banco Dinheiro without consulting Victor. She didn't trust him anymore. She divided the cash and placed her share in a different box in the bank where she was the sole key holder. When she was about to leave, she saw two Federal Police officers enter the bank and walk into a back office. Stella turned to Ana Luiza, the bank worker who managed the safety deposit and was used to dealing with foreign clients. Stella asked her why the police officers were there.

"Brazil is a member of FATF," she said. "A new law now criminalises anybody who transfers money whilst hiding its source. We have all had money laundering training and must report any suspicious financial activity to the police. The police make regular visits to check our records. For example, Ernesto, our compliance officer, will have seen my entry of the cash that you and your husband deposited in the safety deposit box. Ernesto may have decided to report it.

"Don't worry," said Ana Luiza, noticing the changed expression on Stella's face, "it's just routine."

"Can the police order you to open a safety deposit box?"

"Only with a warrant from a judge."

"So, how do criminals hide their cash now if they can't put it in the bank anymore?"

"They go to a lawyer like my neighbour Gabriel Da Silva. He will take the cash without asking any questions and use it to buy the client a property such as a flat. When the flat is sold later, the money is clean. I don't approve, but he lets my children use his garden and swimming pool and what he does is not my business."

"Fair enough."

Stella could not sleep that night, worrying about whether her cash was at risk from the police. By the next morning, she had decided what to do. She returned to the bank and told Ana Luiza that she wanted to withdraw her and Victor's joint deposit.

"Is this something to do with our conversation yesterday?"

"In a way. You have made us think that we'd like to buy a flat."

"My brother has a lovely little flat in the Santa Cruz neighbourhood for a quick sale to a cash purchaser. Property prices are lower because it's on the outskirts of Rio, but there's potential for capital growth. It would suit you both very well and I can make sure that Gabriel doesn't cheat you if you choose to use him for the legal bit of the purchase. He will hold your money in his business account whilst the sale goes through, which can take a long time with all the bureaucracy in Brazil. And afterwards, he can even arrange to rent it out for you."

"One problem: Victor, my husband, doesn't actually know that I will take the money out of the safety deposit boxes, and I haven't consulted him about what I intend to do with it."

"Is that related to the bruise on your neck?"

"Can you help me? I want to finish with him. I earned all that money really."

"I can arrange for the bank to send a Notice to Victor informing him that the Federal Police are investigating your safety deposit box and have applied to a judge for permission to open it. It will say that meanwhile, the box stays locked, and the contents must not be touched. That way he will not be able to know that you have already removed half of the money to a second box or have any warning when you empty both boxes. Just let me know when you are ready to transfer the money to Gabriel."

"But who would send such a Notice from the bank?"

"Ernesto will, if I tell him that it's a favour to Gabriel and that you will pay him as well. Ernesto buys expensive things to please his girlfriend and he's always short of money. And he needs to keep pleasing Gabriel. Ernesto and his girlfriend like to use Gabriel's pool."

Two days later Victor opened an envelope posted under the door of their hotel room. "What the fuck, I don't believe it. We're going to lose our money." He held the bank Notice up to the light, as if that would show whether it was a fraud or not. "I don't understand how they know we are staying here. I can't contact the Federal Police to find out if this is just a wind up or they might start digging and find out who we really are. Do you think those bastards at the bank are trying to steal our money? I need a drink."

During the next few days, they kept out of each other's way as much as possible. Stella went for long walks along the beach whilst Victor sat moodily in the hotel bar.

About one week later, there was a loud banging on the bedroom door. Victor opened it and two men in plain clothes stepped in. One was tall, wearing glasses and spoke in English. The other, short, and stocky, spoke only Portuguese.

"Federal Police," the tall man said. "You are Detective Chief Inspector Victor Shadwell, and your accomplice is Miss Stella Godley."

Victor stood there speechless.

How do they know that? He thought.

"The two Civil Police officers have identified you both from your photographs on the Interpol pages of *Criminals Evading Justice*. A senior police detective from Europe wanted for murder is unusual and immediately attracted their interest. We are taking you both into detention."

"I must have impregnated countless women in Rio whilst we've been here. Surely, I can find just one who is pregnant? Then I can claim that I have a right to family life here in Brazil and should not be deported and separated from my child." Victor and Stella were sitting in a locked room in the hotel basement, waiting to be told what would happen next.

"Or, I could be pregnant," Stella said. "I have many ardent admirers. At least I know their names and contact details. Unlike your ships in the night."

Before he could reply, the officers returned. "I'm surprised you have the time to bother with the likes of us," Victor said. "I thought that you were all busy supporting the *Unidade de Policia Pacificadora*, pacifying the favelas and patrolling the *bocas* in the favelas where they sell their drugs."

"I see that you have done your research," the tall officer said, "and thought that we would all be too busy cleaning up the favelas to take notice of you and the lady. Sorry to disappoint you."

"I've got money," Victor said desperately. "I can make you both rich."

"Sorry, to disappoint you," the tall man replied. "We are not like the local police who work in the streets."

Victor and Stella were marched unceremoniously out of the Nacional Hotel. Tiego stood by the door and saluted Victor in a mocking way as they were led past him in handcuffs. The Federal Police officers took them to the local police station first. The Civil Police officers who had spoken to them a few days before, came into the room in which they were being held, just to look at their prize catches. They were hoping for a reward.

After spending one night in the cells, they were both taken to a suburb of Rio. They were driven in a police van to a large prison complex. Victor was taken to a male penal unit, whilst Stella was detained in the women's prison.

"You are lucky that the police-operated jails in Rio have been closed, by order of the State," the tall Federal officer told Victor. "Not long ago, you would have been held in a former horse stable. Now we can only hold people in official prisons."

Victor's cell was a room that he shared with seven others. One of them, Rodrigo, spoke English and interpreted for Victor to the rest of the group. They were all *faixina* prisoners, trustees awaiting trial who paid for their privileges. They each had their own mattress on the floor, for sitting and sleeping, video games to play and a TV to watch. There were fans to keep them cool in the Brazilian summer as temperatures in the cell would otherwise reach 130 degrees Fahrenheit.

"We're a mixed bunch in here," Rodrigo told him. "Robbers, murderers, drug traffickers, sex offenders." The prison governor had allowed Victor to keep secret the fact that he was a police officer. "I don't want you to be killed in my prison," he had said.

At night there were rhythmic banging noises from the room above. "Conjugal visits," Rodrigo explained. "If you don't have a wife or girlfriend to visit, we pay the guards to bring in nice young women from the local brothel instead. If you have money, I can arrange that kind of *cat call* for you and a different kind as well. There are stray cats which, to order, are fitted with furry jackets with pockets holding mobile phones and drugs. They climb in at night-time when we put food out for them. We empty the pockets and send them back."

Ian thought about the offer of young women. *There may be enough time for one of them to give me a child,* he thought.

Stella was detained in a long dormitory room with beds with white iron bedheads. There were mattresses on the beds, sheets, and pillows. Many of her fellow prisoners had been abandoned by their children's fathers and were trying to support a family on their own. Some women had young babies with them, who would cry in unison during the night. The women helped each other out and shared what food they had, eating together in a picnic circle on the floor. Stella was out of luck: she was not pregnant.

The women swopped stories as they sat together. Each of them had a sorry tale to tell. Boyfriends had used them to hide or carry drugs or guns or function as bait for their robbery victims.

One woman had killed a cop when he tried to rape her. Her car was stolen outside a friend's house during a party. She went to the police station to report it and an officer said that he knew where it might be. She became suspicious of him when he drove her straight to her car, parked in an otherwise empty yard off a quiet street. He then drove on and stopped by a cash machine, demanding money from her in return for finding it. When she angrily refused, he drove back to her car and parked next to it. He said he'd take something else in payment instead, pulled his gun out of its holster and ordered her into the back of her car where he tried to join her. She grabbed at the gun, and it went off as she wrestled with him, the bullet hitting him in the stomach. He died in hospital.

It was February 2020 and Covid had arrived in Sao Paulo, Brazil. It soon spread to other cities and Rio was a hotspot. Stella believed that their isolation in prison could save them from the chaos engulfing the country. It would be another two months before the first case in a prison was detected.

John Street from the British Consulate in Rio visited each of them with a Brazilian lawyer. "You may or may not have heard of the International Fugitive Round-Up and Arrest South America Operation – INFRA-SA,"

Street told Victor. "As you know, Britain is a member of Interpol, and Interpol's Fugitive Investigative Support Unit is co-ordinating this operation. The targets of operation INFRA-SA are criminals wanted by a member country and believed to be in South America. The police in Britain had an idea that you may have travelled to Rio, and they contacted INFRA-SA with your details. Your pictures were also loaded on to the Interpol website. The Brazilian State wants rid of you as soon as possible, and you and Ms Godley will be deported. You will be handed over to the British Police on your arrival at Heathrow."

It was March, and HHJ Jonathan Swift swept into court number two Riverside Crown Court, leaving the judge's door to swing in the breeze behind him. "This murder trial is listed to last for one week. I've looked at the papers," Swift said. "It seems that Mr Blake has confessed to being party to a plan to have one lady killed, Ms Godley, but another lady died instead, Mrs Blake, his wife. He has pleaded not guilty. So that I am clear, what's the issue to be decided?"

"Your Honour," Felicity began, "we intend to show that he played no part in Mrs Blake's death, because he did not know that those whom he was conspiring with had only ever intended to kill Mrs Blake, and not Ms Godley. Mrs Blake's death was a deliberate choice and act by people other than him, and not a mistake or accident."

"So, you will claim that he can't have been an accomplice," Swift said. "I went to that lecture as well. That explains why you had me read the *R v Saunders and Archer* law report."

"Also, he tried to withdraw from what he mistakenly thought was planned," Felicity continued.

"I know what you are referring to and you may have a problem there if that is to be a second string to your defence. You will have to argue that he is not responsible for the death of his wife, because he tried to prevent the death of Ms Godley when she was never going to be killed."

"We will show that had Shadwell 'stopped it' as Mr Blake had instructed him, there would not have been any killing at all, as 'it' referred to the entire plan that they had made, although Shadwell was intending to kill a different woman."

"Well, let's get started. You can argue these points again later, after we have heard the evidence. Bring in the jury please."

Ian's trial began and there was still no sign of Yuri. First DC Stant and then DS Bonetti gave evidence about the crime scene and the jurors looked at the photographs of the body. It appeared to be headless in a ghostly way, because of the position of the pillow on her face. Dr Snowden's crime scene assessment and post-mortem report were read to the jury, who were also shown pictures of the injuries to her eyes. DCS Drake gave evidence about the overall conduct of the murder investigation and DS Bonetti and DCS Drake told the jury about Ian's confession.

Felicity questioned DC Stant.

"You found a cigarette butt at the crime scene, which forensic examination confirmed had been smoked by DCI Shadwell."

"I did."

"And that find was before the DCI had arrived at the crime scene."

"It was."

"Please look at the polaroid photograph on the large screen which the jurors can also see. Does this picture match the crime scene when you arrived?"

"Not completely."

"Please explain."

"After I arrived at the scene, I placed make-shift evidence markers on the bedside table. That was before the DCI was present. The markers were later removed by the forensics team, together with the cigarette butt and the magazine that they related to. Those markers do not appear in the picture, neither does the magazine."

"Was this picture most likely taken before your arrival at the scene?"

"Yes."

"Where was the picture found?"

"In a rubbish bin belonging to DCI Shadwell."

"Who contacted Yuri Prokanova to identify the body?"

"DCI Shadwell, since Prokanova was named in a card addressed to Miss Godley and referred to as her 'dear friend'."

"Mr Prokonova identified Annie Blake in the mortuary as Stella Godley?"

"Yes."

"Were you tasked to find anyone else who could identify the body?"

"No. I did suggest her neighbour, Miss Phelps, but DCI Shadwell said that she was elderly and would probably have a heart attack if she saw the deceased."

"When officers went to Miss Godley's apartment, after the body was found, what did they see?"

"The dining table was laid with two place mats and cutlery. There was an opened bottle of red wine and two glasses which were half-full of red wine."

"Did it look as if someone was expecting Miss Godley to come home?"

"Yes, that was the look."

"In your opinion, would this have helped his defence, had he not confessed to his part in the plan?"

"Not really a question is it, Ms Crabtree? More of a comment. Please move on," Swift said.

Felicity then questioned Drake.

"Mrs Blake was disguised to look like Ms Godley, with her clothes and possessions."

"I can't say for certain what the intention was."

"DCI Shadwell had very recently taken out very substantial life insurance policies on his and Ms Godley's lives and would benefit financially from Ms Godley's death."

"Yes, but the insurance company would have investigated any suspicious circumstances before making a payment."

"We can assume that DCI Shadwell discussed his taking out the policies with Ms Godley and that they were connected financially in some way."

"I believe that you need the other person's consent before you can insure their life, and they must sign the application and agree to any medical checks. If you are not married to each other, you must also be able to show a provable monetary loss if they died. For example, that you are liable for their debts or that they owe you a considerable sum of money which would not be repaid if they die."

"This is so that you can satisfy the company that you don't want that person to die; that you don't have the wrong incentive for buying the policy?"

"Yes."

"When DCI Shadwell went to the crime scene, you would expect him, having had dealings with Ms Godley, to have realised that the deceased was not her."

"I would, yes."

"Unless of course, he wanted to carry out the pretence that Mrs Blake was Ms Godley."

"That's possible, although he may have had other reasons."

"If Mr Prokonova had been at Mr. Royal's flat, you would expect to have found traces of him."

"Unless a very good clean up job had been done."

"DCI Shadwell and Ms Godley are currently in separate prisons in Rio de Janeiro, Brazil, having left the UK on the same flight and stayed together in a hotel there."

"That's what I have been told."

"Isn't the most likely explanation that DCI Shadwell killed Mrs Blake and switched identities with the help of Miss Godley."

"That's for the jury to decide."

Miss Cynthia Phelps entered the witness box and described her conversation with Ian once, when he had waited for Stella in her flat. "He said that he wished that his wife was not around," she said, looking knowingly at the jury.

Felicity questioned her.

"If somebody says, 'I wish I were rich,' do you think that they are talking about something over which they have no control or something that they are going to make happen?"

"Well, I suppose if they wished it, then that means that they couldn't make it happen themselves, that's why they had to wish it."

Miss Phelps then related her conversation with Ian on the night of the murder. "He ordered food from a restaurant for her. He said that he was expecting her back for a special dinner."

"So, he gave you the impression that he assumed Miss Godley was alive and would be joining him for dinner?"

"Yes. Why go to all that trouble and expense otherwise?"

"You don't know if he was telling the truth when he told you that he was expecting Miss Godley to return."

"Well, it wasn't a cheap dinner. My dog Charlie shared it with me, and he gulped it down."

Monty closed the prosecution case.

Before Felicity opened the defence case, she told HHJ Swift that she had an application to make. The jury were sent out.

"I hope that you are not wasting the court's time. What is it you want to ask me, Ms Crabtree?"

Felicity told him about Yuri's statement and that he could not be found. She said that he was believed to be with his mother who was likely a victim of Covid, and that travel within and from Russia was restricted. She asked Swift to admit the statement, despite Yuri not being at court.

"It's the missing piece in our case. His evidence is central to our defence as it will show that Victor Shadwell only ever intended to kill Annie Blake," she said.

Monty objected, telling the judge that the defence knew Yuri's address and had recently been in contact with him to take the statement. If Yuri could not be found and was not in contact with them, it was because he had something to hide. There was no evidence before the court that he was ill, or that he could not attend a hearing by video link from Perm, or travel to the UK. Aeroflot was still regularly flying passengers to London. He was of bad character, having lived illegally in London and had a conviction for manslaughter in Russia.

"He sounds like an utter rogue," Swift declared. "No, I won't admit it. It would be unfair on Mr Bell who would be unable to question him and expose any lies. I will exclude that piece of defence evidence. Now, can we have the jury back and get a move on please."

Felicity called Ian to the witness box. The recording of his confession had been played to the jury as part of the prosecution case and Ian confirmed that it was the truth.

Monty had questions for Ian.

"You paid DCI Shadwell to murder a woman."

"Yes."

"To pay a man to murder a woman is an evil act."

"Yes."

"You are telling the jury that you are an evil man."

"Objection, Your Honour," Felicity called out. "This is a court of law, not morals."

Ian replied before Swift could intervene. "I suppose, yes I am evil."

"Not a popular description of our justice system, Ms Crabtree, 'a court of law not morals', but a correct one," Swift said for the benefit of the jury. "Unless of course the immoral act is also prohibited by law. However, Mr Blake's character is in issue, so carry on, Mr Bell."

"As a result of you paying DCI Shadwell to murder a woman, another woman died."

"I don't know that."

"If you had not paid DCI Shadwell £30,000 to have Miss Godley killed, your wife would still be alive."

"Your Honour," Felicity called out again, "he can't know that. It's a hypothetical question. It's conjecture, not fact."

Ian answered Monty without waiting for Swift to deal with the objection. "I suppose you're right. Shadwell would have had no reason to become involved in my situation."

"So, in effect, you murdered your wife."

"Your Honour," Felicity called out again, in frustration. "Whether my client murdered his wife or not is a matter of law, for you to advise the jury on and for the jury to decide."

"I suppose I did," Ian said, paying no attention to her and answering the question.

"Mr Blake, you have a very competent barrister representing you and that is for a reason. Do listen to what she has to say, before you reply to a question which she objects to. The jury will ignore your answer to the last two questions. Now, we will resume tomorrow."

The next morning, Monty Bell concluded his detailed analysis of the case. "There can be no doubt in your minds that Mr Blake paid DCI Shadwell to kill Ms

Godley. He has admitted that. And that they both had motives for killing her. Mr Blake because he believed that she was blackmailing him. DCI Shadwell because he had taken out a life insurance policy on her which would financially benefit him. There can also be no doubt in your minds that an unfortunate outcome was that Mrs Blake was killed.

"Mr Blake is guilty of murder if you are sure that Mrs Blake was killed mistakenly or by accident instead of the intended target. It is particularly important to remember Mr Blake's words when he first made his statement to the police: The plan 'went wrong' because, 'for some unknown reason Annie went to Philip's flat instead of Stella.' That is a description of a mistake or an accident, and his malicious intent towards Ms Godley is transferred in law to Mrs Blake. He is also, of course, guilty of Mrs Blake's murder if you are sure that her death was part of his plan all along and he was expecting Miss Godley to return home for a special dinner with him. A dinner to celebrate some event perhaps, such as that he was now free to be with her."

Felicity later finished her summing up for the defence. "DCI Shadwell knew that the dead woman in Mr Royal's flat was not Miss Godley and yet at the crime scene he went along with the pretence that she was. He corrupted the investigation and perverted the course of justice by lying about and covering up the identity of the deceased. Members of the jury, it is the defence case that DCI Shadwell pretended to Mr Blake that he would kill Ms Godley. But all along he had no intention of doing so, as she is his partner, in love, in business and in crime. He and Ms Godley are in a relationship together, two guilty people who fled to Brazil, so that they could escape justice, live the high life, paid for with Mr Blake's money no doubt, and sun themselves on Rio's famous beaches.

"DCI Shadwell signed Mr Blake up to a non-existent plan to kill Ms Godley. His real plan was to kill Mrs Blake. Mr Blake was never a party to that real plan. The 'special dinner' that you've heard so much about was an excuse for him to gain access to Miss Godley's apartment, to look for the blackmail money and pictures. And to give himself an alibi, and help his defence, if he was accused of killing Miss Godley. Mrs Blake's murder was not an accident or a mistake but a plan which Mr Blake had never agreed to or contemplated and so he cannot be held liable for it. Unless you are sure that this is not what happened, you must acquit him. Mr. Blake may have had an evil idea to begin with, but it was in no way connected to his wife's death."

Swift then summed up, drawing on the final speeches by Monty and Felicity, and the jury retired. They returned the same day. Their verdict on Ian Blake was unanimous: guilty of murder.

22

Exposed

"It's disgusting," Chi said, "barristers and judges in London betting on their own cases, tens of thousands of pounds are involved."

"What, you're not serious?" Nahra asked in astonishment.

"I lost all my savings, £50,000. My ex, Grant, told me that he was an investment banker and could double my money. It turns out that he's just an arsehole clerk working with the defence team, and he bet my money on Philip getting off. When the case was stopped because they had the wrong body, he lost it all."

Nahra Ravinasi was a journalist with the *Sunday Splash*. She sat there in stunned silence.

"This could be a huge story," Nahra said, after she had properly taken in what Chi told her. "Barristers betting that defendants whom they are prosecuting will be acquitted. Judges betting on the verdicts that their juries will return. If you can get Grant to tell you everything that he knows, we will pay you handsomely. I could arrange for you to be wired-up, so that he can't deny it later."

"How much would I get?"

"If the story is as good as it sounds, I might be able to persuade my editor, Robina, to go to £30,000. The bigger the scandal, the more money you get."

When Grant lost Chi's £50,000 stake, he had vowed that he would pay her back. He re-mortgaged his flat and took out a short-term loan. He should have used the £50,000 that was paid into his account to repay Chi. Instead, he did what gamblers do when they have lost: he went on gambling. Swept away in a mood of false optimism, following Kate and Ektrina's return from Russia, he placed the lot on Ian's acquittal. The odds at that time were 3/1 against that eventuality, as Veronica was yet to see Yuri's statement. He lost it all when Ian was convicted.

Stung by her rejection of him, Grant wanted to win Chi back and thought that if he said that he had lost his own money in trying to raise enough to repay her she would feel sorry for him and agree to meet him. When he tried to phone her, she wouldn't answer his calls. He sent her a message.

Bet too much money I had borrowed on Ian Blake getting not guilty, trying to get your money back. Unlucky again and am now in considerable debt. Not asking for your sympathy but miss you and would love to meet up and talk about old times XX.

Chi and Grant met in the G Spot. They sat as usual on the sofa in the dark and quiet corner. Only this time they were not holding hands. Chi was professionally wired-up by the *Sunday Splash* with a tiny microphone attached to her bra. Nahra had briefed her well and Chi had memorised the questions that they wanted Grant to answer.

"I've calmed down now about the money loss," she told him. "I don't mind your gambling habit and find your risk-taking exciting. I know you did your best to double my money and I'm confident you will manage to pay me back somehow. I can wait."

"I promise you'll get it back, if it's the last thing I do."

She let him kiss her, so that he did not suspect anything. "I want to know all about Barri-Bets, it's such fun."

Anxious to keep her interest, Grant told her everything. He even named, with a bit of encouragement from Chi, who had to let him kiss her again and had even used her tongue, some of the barristers and judges who had placed bets.

That's £15,000 per kiss, so far, Chi thought with her reward from the newspaper in mind, *definitely worth it.*

"I trust you will never tell anyone about this," Grant said.

Like I trusted you, Chi thought.

"If any of this gets out there will be a huge scandal, the likes of which we've never seen before. Some members already think the betting has gone too far and want to wind up Barri-Bets," Grant continued.

"Of course, I won't tell anyone. Don't the barristers and judges worry that gambling on a trial could change its outcome, so that there is an injustice?"

"It's not like fixing a football match where players can usually guarantee a particular result. These are Crown Court trials where juries make the decisions. The prosecution and defence were playing games long before Barri-Bets came on the scene: delaying disclosure, hiding evidence when it suited them, and pushing the rules to the limit to win a trial. And set in their ways as barristers are, I don't believe that Barri-Bets made any real difference.

"Neither the barristers nor the judge can tell the jury what to do and if they try, then the jurors are likely to go the opposite way, just to assert their independence. Juries are unpredictable, they never give the reasons for their decisions. Most of the time we haven't a clue why they decide one way or the other. Anyway, even if the barristers tried to influence the result, they are not as clever as they make out and usually win a case by luck rather than judgement."

"I thought that barristers and judges were well paid. Why do they need to risk being caught? Are they just foolish and greedy?"

"The Government cuts are to blame. Charles Hay, the Minister of Justice has reduced the profits of barristers by one third in the last four years and frozen the pay of the judges. He has also changed the judges' pension scheme for the worse. London's an expensive place to live; they all feel the pinch financially and want to try and supplement their incomes in a way that they don't think is harmful. Yes, there are losers as well as winners, but this way they have a bit of a laugh making their calculations based on the trial material; stand to win money; and if they lose, they can still holiday for next-to-nothing at one of the Barri-Bets five-star R and R spots. It's win-win really."

"But they could lose everything if they were found out: their reputations and their careers."

"It started out as just an innocent little game. But it has become a way of life. They play card games for money in the robing rooms at court and take drugs. Then they get into financial difficulties and take more risks. They snort cocaine, smoke cannabis, or take ecstasy and some even do this whilst sitting at their desks in their chambers. They blame this drug taking on pressure of work. Barristers are chancers and hugely competitive. It's in their blood and they want to win, that's why they become barristers."

"Is Lord Osling in on this?" Chi asked delicately.

Grant started to feel a little nervous at the mention of the great man's name.

"You sound like a journalist now."

He leant in to kiss her again, as if to reassure himself that she was just the Chi he used to date. He used his tongue enthusiastically this time. She let him kiss her again, engaging in a bit of tongue sword play, so that she could keep him on her side.

Around £10,000 per kiss now, she thought. *Mustn't cheapen myself too much.*

"Well?" she asked.

"No, he's so honest, the secret's been kept from him."

"You're just a clerk, I don't mean 'just' as a put-down, I'm sure it's a very important job."

"You bet," Grant replied, laughing at his unintended pun.

"How is it that you can bet as well? Can you also use the R and R spots?"

"I can take you on holiday to one. How about Bali next Summer? The clerk is the engine room of the oil tanker which is the barristers' set of chambers. Although I might look up train times for them and book a hotel if they are working out of London, take them cups of tea and biscuits and call them sir and ma'am, they know who the boss really is. I can give them decent work that earns them large fees or low-level work that they must do for little reward. They wouldn't dare to exclude us clerks from Barri-Bets. My chambers' members even ask me for advice about what they should put their money on. I draw the line at cleaning their shoes though, unlike my mate Bradley."

"Why has nobody found out about the gambling before?"

"The syndicate has its own protection. It's an unwritten rule that any barrister who leaks information about Barri-Bets can kiss goodbye to their career. John Peebles, a barrister in New Club, got very drunk one night at Christmas time and told a stranger in a bar about his Barri-Bets gambling habits. Luckily, the person he was talking to wasn't sure whether to believe him and asked another barrister, who denied its existence. I mean, who would believe that this is happening without real proof? His clerks Kevin and Ginnie stopped handing him briefs to prosecute or defend meaty trials in the Crown Court. Instead of a GBH with intent at the Old Bailey, they would give him a careless driving in Burton-On-The-Marsh magistrates' court, where his travel costs are more than his brief fee. In the end he re-skilled as a train driver. I've said far too much. Can we go back to mine?"

"Love to, but I'm just too tired, I was out on a surveillance job for Kate last night and didn't get any sleep. I'll contact you, soon."

Grant could not hide his disappointment. "Quick kiss?" he asked, "before you go."

"Sorry," said Chi, as she pulled away from him. "I'm putting my needs first these days." She gathered her things and left the G Spot.

In the offices of the *Sunday Splash*, Nahra could not believe what she was hearing. "This is a gift," she said, stopping the recording. "Thank you, thank you. I want you to meet up with Grant again. Don't wear a wire this time, so you can take your clothes off, if that's what it takes."

Chi winced. "I'm not a prostitute," she complained.

"Think of yourself instead as a courageous spy, sleeping with the enemy. You must try and find out who Veronica is. She will hold all the records that can prove this is true and reveal the full scale of it. If you can get his laptop and his phone, then that would be great. We can't be sure where he stores everything to do with Barri-Bets. He might have something on paper that backs up what he's telling you. That would help me to convince my editor Robina that he's not just a fantasist. Let's finish the job."

"Don't want me to do much do you? It's worth £40,000 then. Your earlier offer was too little."

"I'll see what I can do."

Chi contacted Grant. "I really enjoyed that evening with you. Can we meet again?"

She remembered that he kept a box file under his bed. She had noticed it one morning when she was looking for her socks on his bedroom floor and pulled it out, thinking it was there by accident. When Grant saw her with it, he suddenly became very flustered.

"That's confidential," he said, taking it from her.

She saw the name written on the box file: *Burn After Reading*. She knew that Grant was a fan of the Cohen Brothers. He had an annoying habit of copying the CIA Director in the film by saying 'it's a clusterfuck' if anything was badly messed up. *He must have jokingly written that name because the file contains sensitive information,* she thought. *Could this be the proof that I'm looking for? It's a strange coincidence that in that film Brad Pitt is discovered hiding in a wardrobe, the same pickle that Carly said had happened to her in a Heathrow Hotel, and Kate and Carly had hidden in a wardrobe in Ektrina's bedroom.*

Chi met Grant at the G Spot. They had not been there long before she suggested they go back to his flat. He was delighted and hurriedly paid the bar bill. As they walked, Chi's first thoughts were how to resist Grant's advances once they reached there. Then she thought about the film. *I'm not sure that I would want John Malkovich, the film's retired CIA analyst, to get into my pants, although bald can be sexy. Brad Pitt or George Clooney is a different matter. But Brad's character Chad is a bit of a dope and immature and leaves the wardrobe a dead man. And George's character Harry has affairs with Katie, Monica and Linda whilst married to Sandy. What a womaniser.*

They sat on the floor in the living room, drinking from a bottle of wine that Chi had bought on the way back. She kept topping up Grant's glass. Chi insisted they play a game on Grant's laptop so that she could see how he logged in. Grant was not really concentrating as he was hoping to do something more intimate with her. When they finished that bottle, she brought out another bottle of red wine that she found in his kitchen. "Hey, look what you've been hiding," she said, and poured him some more.

"Give me your phone," she said. "Mine's out of battery and I want to look something up. What's the password to unlock it?" Grant told her whilst busying himself clearing objects from the sofa so that he could persuade her to lie on there with him. But Chi insisted that she was more comfortable on the floor. She took only little sips from her glass, so that she would remain sober whilst he became quite drunk.

In a change of plan, Grant handed her glass of wine to her, saying "drink it up," and then took her hand, pulled her up from the floor, closed the laptop and led her towards the bedroom. She carried the glass, rather than finish the wine, and put it down on the bedside table. Chi was still thinking about Brad Pitt and George Clooney. Grant misunderstood the reason for her smile, thinking it was an invitation to him. She lay down on the bed, with her T shirt and jeans on. Grant leant over and tried to kiss her, but Chi protested that his breath smelt, "go and clean your teeth first," she said.

Grant apologised and stumbled off down the hallway towards the bathroom. Chi had already hidden the toothpaste and she could hear him muttering with frustration as he searched for it. She looked under the bed. There was the box file, *Burn After Reading*. Chi pulled it out. Despite its title, she was confident that the information would not be drivel, as in the film, or self-destruct as soon she had analysed the contents.

Just as she went to open it, she heard Grant coming back in. She pushed it back under the bed.

"Can't find the bloody toothpaste, so I used mouthwash instead."

Kuso (shit) *I hadn't noticed that* Chi thought.

"Now for that kiss," Grant said. Chi closed her eyes and obliged.

Grant was on the bed and down to his underpants with amazing speed for someone who was drunk. He started to undress her. She had to think quickly. Her T shirt and jeans were off, and Grant's hands were now trying to remove her underwear. She had chosen the only bra of hers that was difficult to unfasten, and he worked the clasp furiously. She crossed her legs at the knees to make removing her knickers more difficult. Grant's hands were now buzzing around her impatiently like a bee around a flower. His patience snapped at the unyielding bra strap and without warning his hand dived beneath her knickers. But Chi was more than a match for him and shouted, "ouch, stop it Grant, your nails are scratching me, go and file them, now. You're not touching me again until you do."

Grant got up and went off towards the bathroom again. She couldn't help noticing his pained expression. Chi jumped off the bed and turned on the main light. This time she was able to pull the box file out from under the bed, take a quick look at the pages of betting records and take pictures with her phone of what Nahra wanted. She quickly pushed the box file back under the bed.

Chi could hear Grant returning. He was determined that nothing would stop him this time. As he arrived back in the bedroom, Chi could see the expectant erection bulging in his underpants.

"Turn the main light out," she said. Grant did so, leaving only a small bedside light which cast shadows on the wall. With her back to him, she picked up her glass of red wine and poured it all over Grant's white sheet.

"Oh my God, I'm so sorry, all over your clean sheet, I'd better soak it straight away."

Before Grant could protest, Chi jumped up, yanked the sheet off the bed and rushed out of the room with it. She took the sheet into the bathroom and soaked it with cold water in the bath. Grant followed her, and she noticed that his erection had all but disappeared by now.

"Keep holding it under the water," she instructed, passing him the sheet. He meekly did what he was told.

Chi returned to the bedroom and quickly got dressed. "I'm sorry about your sheet, Grant," she called out. "Put it in your machine, cold wash with stain remover should do it." She picked up his laptop and put it in her bag. She spotted his phone on the floor and took it with her as well.

As she went to leave, Chi confronted Grant in the hallway. "Grant, I can lie to you, but I can't lie with you." She was pleased with herself when she had composed this short speech the night before. She prepared it so that she could reproduce it in the story she would give the *Sunday Splash*.

"I want to go home. I've not had much to drink so I can drive myself," she called out from the flat door.

Chi swept out of Grant's flat, leaving him standing there, looking dazed, hurt, confused and speechless. Chi was pleased with her humiliation of him. She remembered what Kate had told Annie: "Don't get mad, get even."

"This is dynamite," Nahra said the next morning as she looked through the pages from Grant's box file. Chi was back in the *Sunday Splash* offices. "I'll have the laptop and phone analysed by one of our experts. Lucky that you know the passwords to open them." Nahra showed the pages to Robina, who pored over them open mouthed.

Chi had a phone call later. "Good work, Ms *Fookooudah*," Robina said. "I've shown these pictures to Commander Hill at Police Headquarters. Looks like Grant kept copious records of the bets placed by everyone he clerked for. There is also masses of information regarding Barri-Bets, and the elusive Veronica, on his laptop and phone. This has persuaded Commander Hill to open an investigation and the police have already found the Barri-Bets app. Hill has promised the *Sunday Splash* an exclusive if we hold the story until they've seized the evidence they need.

"They are obtaining search warrants for the chambers and homes of the barristers and judges they know to be involved so far. Lord Osling has been asked to grant all the warrants, as he's the only judge whom they can trust not to tip off the others. The police will need to look at many computer files and documents belonging to the legal profession, to find evidence of betting, and some of them will have legal privilege. They will have to employ a team of independent barristers from the Northern Circuit as special counsel to decide what the police can read. Charles Hay, the Minister of Justice will brief both the prime minister and the leader of the opposition later today. This newspaper is indebted to you."

"So, we do honey-traps after all," Kate said, when Chi told her about how she had obtained the information from Grant. "I hadn't seen you as a *femme fatale*."

"Oh, thanks very much," Chi said, looking offended. "Have you forgotten that time when were in The Playroom together?"

Kate's phone pinged. They looked at the screen. *Kiss me with the fire from a thousand suns.*

"Must be Jacqui," Chi said. "That sounds painful."

Kate smiled and pretended to mop her brow. "Getting back to business, this story could be good publicity for us, once the newspaper publishes it."

The story broke in the *Sunday Splash* one week later. The first that Grant knew about it was on the previous Friday, when a team of specialist police search officers got him out of bed at five am. To his surprise, they knew what they were looking for and went straight to his bedroom where an officer called out "got it" as he pulled *Burn After Reading* out from under the bed.

"How did you know…?" Grant's voice tailed off.

"Put it down to experience, sir," the officer replied, "and good intelligence."

He was taken to a Central London police station, where he was interviewed. He was surprised to find that the police not only had his laptop and phone but had been able to access them and analyse the data on them. He had suspected that Chi may have taken them, to sell to get some of her money back from him, but he hadn't suspected that she would inform on him. She was not answering his phone calls or messages.

In return for being co-operative, and telling the police everything he knew, the police had not objected to bail, and he had been released from custody. On the Sunday morning, Grant saw the headline on the front page of the *Sunday Splash: Criminal Courts in Crisis.* He bought a copy and sat in a local cafe to read it.

This is a Sunday Splash world exclusive by Nahra Ravinasi, Chief Crime Reporter. Police swooped on the homes of many barristers and judges early on Friday morning, the Sunday Splash can reveal, following an undercover investigation by this newspaper. We agreed to maintain silence, despite the unprecedented nature of this police enquiry, to allow evidence to be collected from those believed to be involved.

The police are examining evidence which allegedly shows that m'learned friends, m'luds and m'ladies have been betting thousands of pounds at a time on the outcome of criminal trials, including cases in which they are professionally involved. Barry Benson MP, Chair of the House Justice Committee, told the Sunday Splash yesterday "these pillars of the criminal justice system are themselves under investigation. The temple of justice, which they have sworn to support, is at grave risk of collapse. There are likely to be many innocent victims of their shocking behaviour."

An urgent debate has been called in both Houses of Parliament for tomorrow afternoon. Shadow Justice Minister Dan Preston said yesterday, "this shocking situation is the result of years of this Government's emphasis on self-enrichment and the leader's corruption of people's moral values. Nobody believes in truth, justice, or fairness anymore. This country's establishment is rotten to the core and has let the country down badly. It is time for a change."

Pictured below, Her Honour Judge Penny Winter, the Senior Judge at Riverside Crown Court, entering a police station with her solicitor. Pictured left, His Honour Judge Jonathan Swift, who also sits at Riverside, looks out of his bedroom window, wearing a dressing gown, as police officers wait for him to open his front door to them. The Sunday Splash reporter at the scene later witnessed a young woman, her head covered with a raincoat, hurriedly leave the property of newly divorced Judge Swift, in a waiting taxi. She has been named as Claire Luck, a barrister in the judge's chambers. The officers later removed files of papers from his house.

Charles Hay, the Minister of Justice, told the Sunday Splash that the government will introduce emergency legislation to quash the convictions en masse of defendants in all criminal trials in which those arrested were involved and bets were placed. "It would take too many months to review cases individually and search for evidence of miscarriages. The public will rightly perceive that these trials were not conducted honestly, openly, and independently and that the convictions are unsafe," he said.

This includes the conviction this month of Ian Blake, a solicitor, for the murder of his wife, Annie Blake. The Sunday Splash, when reporting that trial, also wrote about the disappearance of Detective Chief Inspector Shadwell, the officer tasked with investigating Mrs Blake's murder. We can report that DCI Shadwell was arrested at Heathrow Airport yesterday, when he arrived back in Britain, having been deported from Brazil. A female passenger named Stella Godley, believed to be his accomplice, was also arrested.

Patrick Connor, the Sunday Splash legal correspondent writes, the public will want to know what charges, if any, can be brought against these errant lawyers and judges.

It will prove difficult for evidence of an overt interference with a criminal trial, amounting to perverting the course of justice, to be found.

Instead, the offence of misconduct in a public office, which has existed since the 12th *century, will be easier to prove against them. It is committed if the office holder wilfully misconducts themself to such a degree as to amount to an abuse of the public's trust. The term public office holder is broad and prosecuting barristers are within its scope as lawyers who prosecute are essentially an arm of the state and must act in the manner of a minister of justice. A judge is clearly an office holder and takes a judicial oath to do right, meaning to act in a moral, ethical, and honourable manner. In addition, the judge must be seen to act openly and independently, above suspicion of any bias.*

Grant then read and re-read the front page. At least there was not a photograph of him. An evening with Chi would be a good distraction from his problems. He quickly rang her, hoping for sympathy, but she didn't answer.

Grant read the front-page guide to the continuation of the story on the inside pages.

How the Sunday Splash uncovered the rogue lawyers and judges, page 2. What this means for the justice system, page 3. Guilty criminals will be returned to the streets, page 4. Head of International Lawyers Association calls for wider investigation into the UK justice system, page 5. MPs respond angrily, page 6.

Then he read page 2. The headline sounded familiar: *How I lied to him to get the truth but refused his demand that I lie with him in his bed*. He read how Chi boasted about getting back together with him just to obtain the evidence for the story. It was melodramatic in places: *He was clawing at me all over, but I pushed away his greedy hands as soon as I knew I had the proof I needed.* It was late March and London went into Covid lockdown. He didn't bother trying to contact her again.

23

Bad Cop

It was during Easter that Victor and Stella were the first passengers to board the Braz-Air flight from Rio to London, accompanied by two security men. They were handed face masks to wear, to protect them and the other passengers from Covid.

"Where are all the Brazilian babies you were going to father? Or have the 'babes' disowned you?" Stella asked mockingly through her mask.

"They took my phone, so I couldn't chase up the women I met in Rio's clubs. Anyway, it's too late now even if a dalliance with one of the hot young things they brought into the prison has borne fruit."

"I bet you promised them the earth, poor suckers: have my child and I will support you for life."

"We've got to move the money somehow," Victor said, changing the subject and lowering his voice.

"I've taken care of that already, it's safe."

Victor pulled his mask down. "What are you talking about? Where is it? What have you done with it?"

"I can't tell you. If I did, it wouldn't be safe anymore, from you. I seduced him; I got Annie to help us; I organised the pictures and choreographed and acted them out with him; I arranged the phone calls to him; I got him to pay up; I got her to Philip's flat; and I finished her off. So, by my reckoning, I deserve all the money."

"You disloyal bitch. You've not heard the last of this."

Uniformed police officers walked down the aisle of the aeroplane after it had landed, and Victor and Stella were handed over to them. The officers told them that they were under arrest for the suspected murder of Annie Blake. There was a snap sound as handcuffs were applied. Blankets were placed discreetly over their wrists to hide the 'cuffs from public view.

They were taken first to a police station at the airport and then by car to Union Street Police Station where Detective Chief Superintendent Drake was waiting for them with DS Bonetti.

"I never thought that we would see this day, sir," Bonetti said to Drake.

"I'm not enjoying this," Drake replied, "seeing such a senior officer in handcuffs. I could possibly excuse his dad, starting out a young copper in the late 1960s and early 1970s. It was a bit 'wild west' then, routine to break the rules. They claimed that it was *noble cause corruption*, lying to make sure that a criminal did not escape prison through lack of evidence or the tricks of a clever defence lawyer. They were just left to get on with it and even received plaudits. Then Sir Robert Mark arrived to clean up the force. Victor started as a uniformed beat officer in a different age, and to begin with he was just your average well-meaning copper. But he later joined CID and became cynical and greedy, and we suspected him of having links with organised crime and prostitution. It was suggested that we bug his house, office, and even his car, but he obviously had friends higher up and it never happened."

The officer who checked Victor and Stella into custody made doubly sure that all the proper procedures were followed, and that Victor received the same treatment as any other detainee.

"Are you allergic to anything?" the Custody Officer asked Victor, going down his checklist. "Only oysters," Victor replied. "Not much risk of them being on the menu here, sir," the Custody Officer replied politely.

As they sat in their separate cells, waiting to be interviewed, Victor thought about what lay ahead. *If I tell the police that Stella completed the killing of Annie, I will still be admitting to murder as her accomplice. Nobody will believe me if I say that I changed my mind about killing her moments before her death. Silence is the wisest choice. Answering questions requires lying and liars get found out eventually. I will say nothing and let them try to prove it against me.*

Drake and Bonetti chose to interview Stella first. They considered her the weak link, who could give them information they could use to get Victor to talk. Stella believed that she had half a chance of turning the tables on Victor and had arranged for a solicitor, Jim Hilton of Hiltons, with small but stylish offices in Mayfair, to be waiting to advise her when she arrived at Union Street. When she told him what she proposed to say, he was in immediate agreement as he loved brokering a deal.

"Jim Hilton wants a chat," Bonetti said to Drake, "before we interview his client."

"No harm in that, I suppose, just let him do all the talking."

Bonetti and Drake took Hilton into a small empty office. "You want to get Shadwell and Miss Godley will deliver him to you, on a silver platter," Hilton said. "Providing she is assured that her co-operation will be suitably rewarded by a promise that she will not be prosecuted."

"We can get Shadwell, as you put it, without her help," Drake said. "Why should she get off scot-free?"

"You might be able to get him in theory, but in practice, can you rely upon a jury to get him for you?" asked Hilton. "Shadwell's good at telling tall tales and juries hate to convict police officers. The 'thin blue line' between them and anarchy and all that. Do you really want to take the chance that he might prove you wrong? A rogue officer like him, let off by a jury, is unemployable in the police service but how would you get shot of him. Suspend him and he could spend years on full pay. Get him to retire for medical reasons, 'the golden backache', and he will draw a pension for the rest of his lifetime. You may even have to pay him compensation for his pain and suffering: a senior officer of the law wrongly accused of a serious crime. Do you really want to watch him make a fool of you?"

Hilton outlined to Drake and Bonetti what Stella was willing to say in a prepared statement, read to the tape in interview. He said that she would back it up in the witness box if Shadwell insisted on maintaining a not guilty plea.

Drake went off to speak on the phone to someone senior in the Public Prosecutor's Office. He returned, gave the promise Hilton wanted, with some *ifs* and *buts*, and they went into the interview room where Stella was waiting with Bonetti.

"Ian seduced me," Stella read to the tape. "It happened at Ray's party. He wouldn't leave me alone after that. His wife Annie had me tailed and found out about us. She confronted me, but we became friends and I felt sorry for her. She wanted to divorce Ian and keep the children, but she said that he wouldn't agree to a divorce and would try to hold on to the children, just to spite her, and wouldn't give her any money. Everything they owned was in his name. She asked me to arrange to meet him again so that she could take pictures and a video of him and me together having sex, as leverage in a divorce to get him to agree to let her stay in the house, make a generous financial settlement and allow her custody of the children.

"I didn't know that instead she would hide it from him: the fact that she knew about him and me; pretend to be somebody else when she contacted him; and use the pictures and video to blackmail him for a large cash payout. When I found this out, I told Victor what Annie was doing and asked him for advice. I didn't know that Victor would go to see Annie and tell her that he'd arrest her for blackmail unless she shared the money with him. She had no option but to agree and Victor advised Ian to pay the blackmailer £350,000 from his firm's account.

"Victor told Annie she could collect her share of the money from Yuri, and he gave her what he said was Yuri's address. Victor told Ian that I was the blackmailer and persuaded Ian to pay him to arrange for Yuri to kill me. Victor told me that he planned to kill Annie instead of me, without Ian's knowledge of course, keep her share of the money, and pretend that the body was me. He'd taken out a big life policy on me and we could share the proceeds. At the same time, I was implicated in the murder of a gang member and Victor said I was in danger. I refused to help Victor at first, but he said that if I didn't, he would disclose my identity to the gang, and my life would not be safe from them.

"So, I got Philip drunk and gave Victor the key to Philip's flat. We went to the flat together and I left some of my things there, personal things, and clothes of mine. He'd told me what I had to do. Victor must have taken Annie's clothes and possessions away later because I left before Annie arrived. I regret everything and now I just want to see him behind bars."

Stella started to cry and Bonetti pulled a sceptical face at her tears.

"Can we terminate the interview please?" Hilton asked. Drake switched the recording machine off and Bonetti took Stella back to her cell.

"It's a bit far-fetched, her account," Drake said, when Bonetti returned.

"Well, she came all the way from Brazil to give it," Bonetti replied snappily. "If what she said is true, she'd have a defence of duress to any charge. No point in turning her against us by putting her on trial as well."

"Duress is never a defence to murder," Drake reminded her. "But the most that we could prove against her is perverting the course of justice in helping Shadwell to frame Royal and mask the identity of the body. Just providing him with the flat key is not enough to make her a party to the murder. And the would-be fraud on the insurance company was his doing."

"You realise," Bonetti said, "that if we rely upon her to prosecute Victor, they won't be able to re-try Ian because she supports his account that Victor intended to kill Annie and Ian wasn't in on the plan."

"I can live with that," Drake replied.

Hours later, Stella was released without charge.

"Now for Shadwell," Drake said.

Victor called Ben Bolt, who was surprised by a request to represent his old adversary.

Drake read out Stella's prepared statement. Victor laughed and said, "pure fiction." Drake put a series of questions to Victor, but he simply replied, "no comment", to each of them. Later, Victor was charged with Annie's murder and the next day the court remanded him in custody.

The gates of HMP Gormley swung open and Ian Blake blinked in the bright sunlight. His conviction had been set aside as unsafe by an emergency Act of Parliament, following the discovery that the trial lawyers and the judge had all bet on the trial's outcome. The prison gates closed to hold a bowed Victor Shadwell.

Kate received a message from Bonetti. *This is a bittersweet moment. On the one hand, Victor is in prison. On the other, I feel that I don't know my own son. I went into Henry's bedroom this morning, when he was out, to tidy up as he'd left it in a terrible mess, and it was smelly from lack of fresh air. I didn't care that he'd banned me from going in there. Under his bed was his blue puffer jacket and a phone fell out of the pocket. It wasn't his usual phone but one with a pay-as-you-go sim card inside. His password was easy to guess: his birth date. I looked at the messages. I was horrified to find he was in a group chat with other boys, boasting to them about what he'd done with girls, which I don't believe, saying disgusting, horrible things about them. They were also rating girls, giving them marks out of ten for parts of their bodies. Why is a girl who has sex called 'slutty' and 'dirty' whilst a boy who does the same thing is admired and congratulated? I know Henry may have been showing off, but why is he so disrespectful about women?*

Kate went to Jacqui's flat to relax. At home, having breakfast the next morning, she told Chi about her visit to Jacqui's the night before.

"I asked her, 'How's your day been?' She replied, 'I can't hear you, you have too many clothes on.'"

Chi put her fingers in her mouth in a gagging gesture. "Why do you tell me these things?"

"I enjoy seeing your reaction," Kate replied, laughing.

Victor instructed Ben Bolt to choose a woman as the lead barrister in his defence. "I want Hilda Sprack, she won't spare Stella's blushes. Providing she doesn't make the jury feel pity for Stella when she twists the knife in cross-examination."

Bolt waited with Victor for Hilda Sprack QC to arrive. "Cheer up, boys," Hilda said as a greeting. "Now, Mr Shadwell, let's get down to business."

His brief to her was short: "I will plead not guilty. I didn't kill Mrs Blake, Stella did. But I won't give evidence."

Hilda Sprack was used to running a defence case on such limited instructions. *At least I won't have to pretend to him that I believe some ridiculous story,* she thought. *I hate the way in which clients lie to me and then ask, 'but do you believe me?' They are never satisfied with my reply 'it doesn't matter whether I believe you or not, it's what the jury thinks that matters.'*

"You can put it to her, that she is the murderer," Victor continued. "That is my positive defence. What Stella told the police is not true. When she killed Annie, Stella even quoted that Rudyard Kipling poem to me, about the female of the species being deadlier than the male."

And I'm not prevented from running the defence that someone else is the real criminal, because Victor hasn't admitted the crime, Sprack thought.

"But I will dish the dirt to you about how she earns her living," Victor continued, "to give you ammunition when you cross-examine her and show the jury that she's a fake and a liar."

"I will need a junior," Sprack told Bolt. "A good-looking young woman will help to distract the judge and the men on the jury. A rival for Miss Godley, so that they will have someone else to coo over. Claire Luck is a bit of a stunner. See if she's available. She can also play good cop, to my bad cop. Well, you're the bad cop," she said, turning to Victor, laughing, "but you know what I mean."

24

Planted

"Tony, long time no see," Victor said. "Thanks for coming."

He indicated for DC Tony Trant to sit opposite him at a table in the visits room at HMP Gormley. Trant ignored Victor's outstretched hand. It was late June, and the lockdown was over.

"Don't know what I might catch," Trant replied.

"Do you like my bright yellow braces? Makes me easy to spot if I make a break for it."

"Cut the crap, Victor, and put your mask back on. What do you want?"

"I need some help, the sort that only you can give me."

"Go on, I will enjoy saying no chance."

"My trial starts in just over two weeks' time, and I need to have somebody on the jury who I know will have my back and put my case convincingly to the other jurors."

"What is your case? I don't doubt that you killed her. It comes as no surprise to me."

"The case against me relies upon dubious circumstantial evidence and the word of a porn star Stella Godley, who should be in the dock instead of me."

"I thought she was your girlfriend."

"You don't know anything, as usual."

"Charming, as ever."

"Listen, I need one of my peers in the jury room to put the other eleven straight about things. Your sister-in-law Tracey works in the jury bailiff's office. I want her to tell you the names of the jury pool for the day my trial starts. Then you check those people out and find someone who can be leant on or paid to help me out. Then that person's card is marked, and they are selected to be on my jury."

"Not asking much, are you? That could get me, and Tracey locked up. Why should we do it? I don't even like you, never did."

"How about this for a reason: when we raided Ray Millan's house, he told you the combination number of the safe in his office so that you could empty it before anyone else in the search team found it. I wondered at the time where you'd disappeared to. Then I saw that you had gone straight to where the safe was and were able to open it. You removed Ray's money, like he told you to, but not before you had also taken all the coke stashed in there, only he let you deal it and keep the proceeds."

"What a load of crap. Prison life must have done something to your brain. I'm not staying to hear any more of this."

Trant went to stand up.

"I've got the CCTV recording on a disk," Victor continued. "He didn't tell you that he had a hidden camera trained on his safe with an audio device which records everything said in that room. Not very trusting, is he? Anyway, a little bird, well not so little really, told me about the hidden camera. I viewed the recording after the search. I watched you remove the nose candy and put it in a sports bag. You announced what it was to an empty room because you were so chuffed about it. You estimated the weight and even calculated its street value. You took the money out and counted it. The money and the drugs were never booked in as having been found during the search. Your bosses don't like you. They'd love to have an excuse to get rid of you. I'll give them the recording unless you help me. No hard feelings, Tony."

Trant sat back down. "How do I know that you're not lying?"

"You know I'm telling the truth, because there is no other way that I could have found that out. If you need more convincing, you even said, 'Larry's going to love this little lot.' Larry Strong, I presume, who has all the kids who should be in school or at home riding around on those E-bikes delivering his shit. Then you took a phone call from your lovely wife Amber and told her that you had something special to give her that evening. Looking at your beer belly, I assume that you can only have meant the cocaine. Making up to her for your ill-advised session with one of Ray's girls no doubt."

"I'll see what I can do."

"Do that."

Tony organised a Sunday lunch with his brother Mickey and Mickey's wife Tracey. When he had the chance, he took Tracey to one side and told her about Victor's trial. It was one of three listed to start on the same day at Riverside Crown Court.

"Victor Shadwell's a bent copper with some heavy underworld contacts. We think he's going to try to nobble the jury. We need to make sure that the jurors who are selected to hear his case are clean and incorruptible. I need to check them out. It's called *Operation Whistle*, after, you know 'clean as a whistle.'"

Tony persuaded Tracey to send him the names, addresses and dates of birth of all the people who were in the jury pool. He checked them against the police intelligence database. He found that one of them, Toby Treanor, was known to police.

Several years before, following a tip off, a cannabis factory was discovered in a small warehouse building. The owner of the warehouse told the police he had rented it out through agents and knew nothing about the tenants or their cannabis plants. The tenants had given false details to the rental agency and could not be found.

Police checked recordings from a camera on an adjacent building. The only person whom they could identify and trace was Toby. He was seen entering an office attached to the warehouse. They arrested him and found that his fingerprints matched those on an empty soft drink can in the office.

He told the police he had been invited to the office by one of the tenants, having met him in a local pub. The tenant offered to sell Toby a sofa which was in the office and Toby went along to look at it. As they discussed the sale, the tenant passed the can of soft drink to Toby. Toby didn't buy the sofa. He insisted that he knew nothing about the cannabis plants, which were not visible from the office. The police strongly suspected otherwise and sent a file to the Public Prosecutor, who advised against a charge. Trant thought Treanor may have potential, because of the arrest and other intelligence on file about Treanor's association with a known drugs dealer.

Toby Treanor was an urban gardener. He did not have an allotment. Instead, he grew his plants on the top floor of his council house in Bermondsey. He regularly went upstairs to view and inspect the crop, the plants all standing to attention in their individual pots of coco coir, arranged in long lines under brilliant fluorescent lights and cooled by oscillating fans. He enjoyed the tropical feel of the upstairs rooms, heated to between eighty- and eighty-five-degrees Fahrenheit. The electricity to power this operation was expensive, so Toby had conducted bypass surgery on the meter.

Contrary to the typical human genetic selection, where males are preferred and females rejected, Toby had removed the males, leaving only female plants with their tell-tale white hairs. They smelt sweet, in the glossy, white-walled rooms with black blinds covering the windows. The plants were fooled by the lighting into thinking that it was autumn, to persuade them to grow buds which Toby would harvest later. Toby inspected the lines of plants, giving them their daily food of water mixed with nutrients. He was interrupted by an unexpected loud knocking at the front door. He closed the doors to the upstairs rooms and went down to find out who wanted to speak to him.

Trant needed a ruse to get inside the property and start a conversation, so that he could size Treanor up. Was he someone who would take a bribe or could Trant find another kind of hook to use?

"DC Tony Trant, I'm in the neighbourhood advising on crime protection." He showed Toby his warrant card. Trant was carrying a clip board, to help him look the part. "Who am I talking to?"

"Toby Treanor," came the reluctant reply.

"We're all TTs aren't we, my name and yours," Trant said disarmingly. "Can I come in and check how secure your window fastenings and back door locks are?" Without waiting for an answer, he stepped past Toby into the hallway.

"Hang on, it's not convenient at the moment, I'm in the middle of, err, cooking."

"Don't worry, I won't take long, we can chat in the kitchen whilst you just continue with your cooking. Kitchen through here, is it?" Trant walked towards the back of the house.

Trant stood in the kitchen. It was obvious that the only cooking that ever took place there was in the microwave. He breathed in deeply. "Don't smell any cooking, Toby, but I am familiar with that sweet aroma, and you may need some crime protection, from me, to stop me nicking you."

Trant marched upstairs, followed by Toby who was protesting loudly. He opened the door of the first upstairs room. The cannabis plants stood there, guiltily, unable to hide.

"Toby, Toby, what is this?" Trant investigated the other rooms. "One hundred and fifty plants, at a quick count, all blooming, quite a little market garden here. We'd better sit down together and talk about this."

He got back in contact with Tracey and gave her Toby's name. "I've checked him out and he's dependable. Make sure that he is selected for Shadwell's trial. *Whistle* is a highly secret police operation, and you are to tell nobody about it."

A few days later, Tony visited Toby with a recording of Sidney Lumet's 1957 film *Twelve Angry Men*. "Your jury service soon. There's a serious risk to you and your little plant chums if the jury members fail to find the defendant Victor Shadwell not guilty. Watch this film and learn from Henry Fonda about consensus building and how one man can swing a jury from guilty to not guilty. You also need to get yourself elected foreman so that you can keep things organised and under your control."

It was July and the start of Victor's trial. William Somerset QC, the prosecuting barrister, outlined the Crown's case. The statements of witnesses who did not have to attend were read to the court. Then, he called Stella as his only live witness. She was clearly going to be the star turn at the trial, dressed demurely all in black with a high neckline. HH Judge Crispin Rambling looked at her admiringly. His comforting smile put her at her ease. She knew how to charm men like him. From her point of view, Rambling looked and sounded disarmingly like some of her regular clients. She smiled sweetly back at him. Rambling was enjoying this.

Victor watched the women jurors look at her, sizing her up. He knew how mean and disapproving women could be to each other. The male jurors didn't know whether to look at Stella or Claire Luck, Sprack's junior, who was concentrating on tucking in some stray whisps of hair which had escaped her wig.

Stella gave her evidence according to the prepared statement she had made to Drake and Bonetti in the police interview. She couldn't bring herself to look at Victor, who gave her hard stares. Victor turned to the jury from time-to-time with 'I can't believe these lies' looks and sighs of exasperation.

Sprack rose to cross-examine her. "You are the picture of innocence today."

"I'm sorry, what do you mean?"

"You are an actress, Miss Godley, aren't you?"

"I have been, and proud of it."

"*Nympho Nurse, Naughty Nun, Naked Nanny, Lusty Librarian.* I don't know why they are so keen on alliteration for the titles of these adult films. Lack of imagination? Anyway, to get to the point, you starred in all those films, didn't you?"

"Yes, and as I said, I'm not ashamed of it."

"You're acting now, aren't you, Miss Godley?" Sprack turned to smile knowingly at the jury.

"No, acting is what I do when I am at work. This is real life not film life. I've told the court what really happened."

"You're a fake, aren't you, Miss Godley?"

"What do you mean?"

"You fake things. You fool people, for a living. For example, how many orgasms have you faked in your films or with your clients?"

"I don't see what her acting career has to do with this trial," Somerset addressed Rambling.

Stella looked amused and replied to Sprack, looking at the jury, before Rambling had a chance to give his ruling.

"You all remember that famous restaurant scene in *When Harry Met Sally*. If you met Meg Ryan in the street in Hollywood, you wouldn't call her a fake person just because she had pretended to have an orgasm in the restaurant. She was just acting. Even ordinary women fake it, because they want the sex to stop or to big up their partner. As a woman, you should know that. Doesn't make them into fake people."

One woman juror laughed.

"I'll move on Your Honour. Miss Godley, you're for sale, aren't you?"

"What do you mean?"

"For the right price, you sell yourself, don't you?"

"Your Honour," Somerset protested, "this witness is not on trial. What she does in her private life is nobody's business."

"Do I have to answer that last question?" Stella asked.

"Selling yourself for sex is not necessarily a criminal offence," Rambling commented, "and I'm not sure where Ms Sprack is taking us, but I will let her continue for the moment and yes you do, but I'm watching you, Ms Sprack and your questions very carefully."

"Men pay me a lot of money to keep them company."

"'Keep them company', is that what you call it? Even now you are lying, aren't you? For the right amount of money, you will do more, won't you?"

"Your Honour," Somerset intervened again. "Ms Sprack is being gratuitously offensive towards my witness, what have these questions to do with the case?"

"Ms Sprack," Rambling asked irritably, "is this line of questioning really relevant?"

"Yes, Your Honour," Sprack replied, "as it goes to her credibility. I aim to show the jury that this witness is not an ordinary, average, honest, decent, trustworthy woman whose evidence they can rely upon. Instead, she will play-act, lie, and sell herself to the highest bidder."

"I want questions, not comment, Ms Sprack."

"I will move on. Why did you travel to Brazil with Mr. Shadwell if he was threatening you?"

"I was present when two gang members fell out and one shot the other. The FHM gang want either to pin the blame on me or harm me to make sure that I don't shop the killer. It is dangerous for me in London and you questioning me about this when the press are present and may report it only makes it worse."

"You could have stayed in England but gone far from London. Scarborough for example."

"The sea is cold; the water can be polluted; there's nothing to do. Do you want me to go on? What does Brazil have that Scarborough doesn't? Is that a serious question?"

Some members of the jury laughed.

"You know the reason. There is no extradition treaty with Brazil. That's the reason you went there; not to escape from a gang."

"Questions, not comments, Ms Sprack. I won't tell you again," Rambling said.

"Tell us more about this shooting. Why were you present with the gang members?"

Stella conferred briefly with Somerset. "I will not answer that question as I may incriminate myself."

"What's your price for giving evidence against

DCI Shadwell? Is it that you will not be prosecuted for murdering Mrs Blake."

"Your Honour," Somerset objected, "that question makes the unfair assumption that she would have been prosecuted if she had declined to help the prosecution. When the reason she was not prosecuted could be there was not a realistic chance of her conviction."

"The jury have a right to know if you may have a motive for giving evidence for the prosecution, other than a simple desire to see justice done," Rambling said. "Ask the question again, properly this time, Miss Sprack."

"Were you told, Miss Godley, that if you gave evidence against DCI Shadwell, you would not be charged with any offence, yes, or no?"

Stella looked at Somerset for help. He looked back at her, unable to intervene.

"Yes."

There was an audible intake of breath from the jury.

"And with the help of your solicitor, no doubt, you have concocted a fanciful story."

"What I have said is the truth."

"A very convenient truth."

"Questions, not comments, that's the third warning, Ms Sprack," Rambling said irritably.

"You killed Mrs Blake."

"That's not true."

"You boasted about it to Mr Shadwell, saying that he wasn't capable of doing it."

"He obviously was capable."

"*The Female of the Species*. You know that poem don't you because you quoted it to him."

"The poem is about a female who is a mother needing to be single-minded and dangerous to protect her children" Stella replied. "Not a childless woman like me, accused of killing a defenceless woman for money."

"No further questions. My client, Mr Shadwell will not be giving evidence, as is his right. There are no defence witnesses."

"That just leaves your closing speeches and for me to sum up," Rambling said. "It's getting late, so members of the jury I'm going to let you go home and I will see you back here tomorrow morning. Until then, don't talk to anyone about this case or carry out any of your own research about it."

That evening at home, Toby looked accusingly at his neat rows of plants. They had got him into this trouble. They appeared to smirk back at him.

The next morning, Rambling addressed the jury. "You must consider whether you can be sure, so that you have no reasonable doubt in your minds, that Ms Godley is a truthful and dependable witness. Miss Sprack has gone to great lengths to paint Ms Godley as a woman whose evidence cannot be relied upon. But if you are sure that Ms Godley is telling you the truth, then Mr. Shadwell, must be guilty of murder as he has chosen not to question the factual content of her account. He has chosen not to put forward a positive defence, other than to make a claim in cross-examination, not supported by any other evidence, that Ms Godley is the actual killer of Mrs Blake.

"If you have doubts about Ms Godley's evidence, then you must ask yourselves instead whether the circumstantial evidence that you have heard is enough for you to be sure that Mr Shadwell murdered Mrs Blake. Mr Somerset has presented evidence that Mr Shadwell left a cigarette butt at the scene; took a polaroid photograph of the deceased and, having cut it up, disposed of it, in his rubbish bin; took the photograph and left the cigarette butt before he had officially arrived on the scene; appointed himself as the lead investigating officer despite his relationship with Ms Godley; allowed his colleagues to believe that the body was Ms Godley; dressed the crime scene so that Mrs Blake was made to appear as Ms Godley; took out a life policy on Ms Godley that would substantially benefit him; and fled to Brazil with her. There may be good reasons for all those actions, but you will never know what those reasons are, as Mr Shadwell has chosen not to give answers to either the police officers who interviewed him or you, members of the jury, as he remained silent in interview and did not go into the witness box to give evidence and expose himself to cross-examination.

"If you consider that there is evidence enough for you to convict him, then you may in addition draw your own conclusions from his refusal to answer questions in the police interview and his failure to give his own account to you now. Do try at first to reach a unanimous decision."

Victor returned to a cell below the court, where Ben Bolt joined him to de-brief before the jury's verdict.

"I'm curious, experienced guy like you, Victor. Why didn't you shred the polaroid and the Eagle insurance letter, rather than just binning them?"

"I didn't cut the picture up. That was Gloria, a jealous cow whom I was seeing. I was in the shower when she went through my drawers and found the picture. She thought it was Ektrina, whom she knew about but had never met. She cut the picture to little pieces and binned it. I didn't even know she'd done that and couldn't find it when I looked for it. And I was going to shred the Eagle letter, but the machine was jammed because I'd been feeding too many sheets of paper at a time into it the night before, just in case my house was searched."

"Okay, but you really screwed up leaving that Camel butt, and you a detective."

"I was distracted at the time. I meant to remove it, then Stella put the magazine on top."

"When it comes down to it, life is just a series of chance random events."

"Tell me about it," Victor said wistfully.

25

Twelve Ordinary Citizens

The jury retired to the jury room where they sat down along both sides of a long table, looking at each other, waiting for someone to take the lead. Toby was the first to speak.

"You've each got a number in front of you, 1 to 12. I'm hopeless at remembering names. I wonder if we can stick to the numbers for the moment. I'm number 8."

"Well," number 3 said, "we're not here to get to know each other. I don't mind being called by my number." The others nodded in agreement.

"We have to elect a foreman," Toby explained. "Having raised that, it's only fair that I offer to do it." The others were silent.

"You're doing all the talking so far," number 3 replied, "you'll do."

"If everyone agrees," Toby added.

There was silence. "So, I'm the foreman. Can I suggest that we do a quick stock-take now, so that we know what the starting point is? If you believe that Mr Shadwell is guilty, put your hand up." Everyone except Toby put up their hand.

"I put my hand up for not guilty," Toby declared.

"You're on your own then," number 3 said dismissively.

"I don't care if I'm on my own or not, it's my right to say that I believe he's not guilty."

"It's your right? What, your human right to be awkward? I've got a ticket for a football match tonight and it's my right to go."

"Well, what do you want?" Toby asked reasonably. "That I just say guilty to agree with everyone else? I'm entitled to my opinion. We'll take as long as it takes. Let's approach it the way that the judge suggested and consider first whether we believe Ms Godley or not."

"I'll go with that," number 2 said. The others mumbled their agreement.

"I should tell you," Toby reported, "that the police were able to find out that the dead body was not Ms Godley's because they already had her details on their database. They took her DNA when she was arrested for taking a punter's money after agreeing to have sex with him, and then ran off with it. So, she's a fraudster and a thief."

"But how do you know that sort of thing when we don't?" number 3 asked.

"I have police friends," Toby explained, "and they tell me things that by rights you should all know as well. The defence wanted to tell you about it, but the judge refused because her conviction was overturned on a technicality. What you also don't know is that she was present during the gang murder because those dangerous young men were supplying her with cocaine."

"So, she's a drug addict as well," number 7 said, looking meaningfully at the others. "Why was that hidden from us?"

"The judge and the lawyers try to strictly control what you base your findings on. But they are more concerned about following their rules and procedures than getting to the truth. You only see the part of the picture that they allow you to see," Toby explained. "Let's go 'round the table."

Number 1: "She's an opportunist. She's giving evidence to save her own skin. I don't trust her."

Number 2: "She's one of those types who uses sex to get what she wants. Did you see the way that the judge looked at her? I thought that he was going to ask her for her phone number."

Number 3: "That's not such a bad idea, getting her phone number. Her and Luck's. But Godley's a prostitute or was. Prostitutes are not to be trusted, don't ask me how I know."

Number 4: "I don't think she's as bad as you all make out. But I'll go along with what everyone else decides."

Number 5: "Speaking as a woman, I felt sorry for her. That defence barrister really ripped into her. Men use sex workers as much or more than sex workers use men. But I don't know if she is telling the truth or not."

Number 6: "I felt sorry for her as well when she was being interrogated, and not just because I'm also a woman. But she's done a deal with the police and the prosecution, and for that reason I don't trust her."

Number 7: "His barrister says that she boasted to Shadwell about how she killed Mrs Blake. She says that's not true. I don't know who to believe."

Number 9: "A strange thing for him to make up, the poem I mean. She's involved more than she'll admit."

Number 10: "To be honest, I just want to get home to my kids."

Number 11: "I'll toe the line with the rest of you."

Number 12: "She's the kind of woman who breaks up families. She's not a nice person and I don't think that she knows what honesty means."

"She creates fantasies for men," Toby said, rounding off the discussion, "and probably can't tell the difference between that and reality. If you cannot be sure that Ms Godley is a reliable witness who is always telling the truth, put your hand up. I don't think we should cherry pick: that she's dependable and trustworthy on some things, but not on others."

Twelve hands went up.

"So, we can discount Miss Godley's evidence. Next, is the circumstantial evidence enough to convict him?" Toby asked.

"Everything says he did it," called out number 3. "I'm not an idiot. I couldn't change my mind if you talked until next Christmas."

"I think he's guilty," number 5 agreed. "And the judge clearly thinks that we should find him guilty."

"This is judgement by his peers, twelve ordinary citizens, not the judge," Toby explained. "We decide whether he has committed a crime or not. Listen to my arguments first, then make up your minds."

"Well, why did he take the keys to Royal's flat on the night of the murder and go there? How does he get out of that?" number 5 asked.

"My police friends tell me that when Mr Shadwell gave evidence in a previous trial," Toby reported, "he explained how Ms Godley accused Mr Royal of stealing a notebook where she kept a record of her escort work, including the clients' names and her remarks about them. She asked Mr Shadwell to get it back for her. That's why he went to Royal's flat, to look for the notebook."

"That's what these high-class escorts do," number 7 said. "I've read about it. They keep a diary, then go on a creative writing course and bring out a book: *Confessions of an Escort*. Ticking time bomb that notebook if it got into the wrong hands. Not surprised she wanted it back."

"Why were we not told about all of this?" number 3 demanded.

"And the judge said we must only take into account the evidence that we have heard in court," number 5 added.

"Mr Shadwell was advised by his lawyers not to go into the witness box and give his explanation. You wouldn't go against the advice of the people defending you, would you?" Toby replied. "So, there is evidence and there are other facts that you don't get to hear. You can't ignore the other facts once you know about them, that wouldn't be just."

"Okay, but what about that photograph of the body?" number 5 asked. "What was it doing in his rubbish?"

"My police friends tell me that he wanted to try out Royal's polaroid camera. So, as he was waiting for the private ambulance, he thoughtlessly took a picture of the dead woman. Police officers are desensitised to dead bodies. He realised that it was a crass thing to do and destroyed it so that nobody could misuse it."

"Why didn't Mr Shadwell tell us this, instead of you?" number 5 continued.

"It's his legal right not to give evidence. You can't convict him just for that," Toby said.

"Supposing this, supposing that, supposing your police friends are wrong," complained number 3.

"That's right," Toby replied, "it's called 'I don't know.'"

"What's the matter with you guys?" Number 3 asked angrily. "You're letting him get away. What about the insurance policy? That makes him guilty, doesn't it? He killed one lady and pretended she was another so that he could claim on the policy."

"The policy was not unusual," Toby said, "for a couple in a relationship who expected to be financially dependent on each other. Ms Godley is a high earner. Mr Shadwell will have known that the insurance company would smell a rat if Ms Godley was murdered so soon after the policy was taken out and refuse to pay out to him."

"Then why did he pretend at the crime scene that the body was Ms Godley?" number 3 demanded.

"My police friends tell me that he was in a relationship with Ms Godley. He was taken by surprise at the crime scene when he recognised it was not her, despite his colleagues announcing that it was. Everyone else insisted that the body was Ms Godley. He didn't want it to go on record that he knew Ms Godley. He would have been charged with gross misconduct if his bosses had discovered their connection. They would know that she worked for a major criminal whom he had disastrously failed to bring to justice and suspect him of having interfered with that investigation."

"I still think he's guilty," number 3 declared. "Nobody's proved otherwise. He could have said that he only knew her by sight or had seen a picture of her, and it wasn't her."

"He doesn't have to prove anything. The burden of proof is on the prosecution. That's the law," Toby calmly explained. "And he was taken by surprise at the crime scene; in a state of shock, he made a snap decision; safest course was not to know her."

"I don't know about the rest of you," number 5 said, "but I'm getting a bit tired of all this bickering, back and forth, it's getting us nowhere. So, I guess I'm going to change to not guilty."

"What?" number 3 exclaimed in surprise.

"You heard me; I've had enough."

"What do you mean, 'I've had enough'? That's no answer."

"You're not going to intimidate me."

"I don't really know what the truth is," Toby said. "But I know that if we have a reasonable doubt, we must say *not guilty*. Can we do another hands up to see where we are with a decision? Put your hand up if you still can't decide whether he's guilty and want to continue talking about it."

No hand was raised.

"We've made our decisions then. Put your hand up if you are sure that Mr Shadwell is guilty."

Only number 3 raised his hand.

"And if we tell the judge that we are not unanimous, he will only send us out again to try and reach agreement. Then, after more time deliberating, if you still don't change your mind, he's likely to accept a majority verdict of not guilty anyway."

"Well, if she's telling lies, she or someone else must have killed the poor woman," number 3 argued. "Why would she kill Mrs Blake? What motive could she have? And what would Mr Royal be doing with Mrs Blake? She was a schoolteacher. It doesn't make sense."

"We don't have to find the answers," Toby said. "That's the job of the investigators."

"If it wasn't Mr Shadwell, there's only Philip Royal and Ms Godley left. Why aren't they on trial? Answer that," number 3 challenged him.

"Easy: that's not our concern. We are here to focus only on Mr Shadwell," Toby replied.

"Alright, you win, I've had enough. It's all just mischief and trickery," number 3 said. "Not guilty it is. Now can we go home?"

"That decides it then. I will tell the jury bailiff that we have a unanimous verdict. Thank you everyone, I'm sorry that I still don't know your names."

"How are we going to explain our decision to the judge?" number 5 asked.

"We don't have to explain anything, we don't give reasons for our decision, we just announce it. Easy isn't it."

The jurors marched back into the courtroom.

"Members of the jury, who is your foreman?" the court clerk asked.

"I am," Toby announced.

"Have you reached a verdict on which you all agree?"

"We have."

"Do you find Mr. Victor Shadwell guilty or not guilty of the murder of Annie Blake?"

"Not guilty."

Bonetti put her head in her hands, *how could the jury be so wrong*? she thought.

There was a message from Stant on her phone. *I'm sorry, Carly, I'm at Union Street police station and Henry's here as well. A French woman was robbed of her mobile phone at the Golden Wharf Galleria today. She was pushed, fell, and injured herself. Henry was stopped nearby because he matched the description of the suspect, and she went on to identify him. Her phone was found in a bin next to where he was detained. I'm so sorry.*

"Tell him to say nothing," Carly replied. "Ben Bolt's here at court. I'll ask him to get down there and I'm on my way."

That night, Toby watered his precious plants at home. There was a knock at the front door.

Toby ushered DC Tony Trant into the front room. "How did I do?" Toby asked. "Did I deliver? Are we good?"

"You did very well. If you ever have some cannabis to spare, give me a bell and I can get rid of it for you."

26

Circus Parade

The gates of HMP Gormley opened to release the jubilant Victor. He knew he would face a gross misconduct hearing but had decided it would be better to resign before he was dismissed. But first, a long hot shower in his own bathroom with his special shower gel, followed by a bottle of wine and Italian food.

The thoughts that darkened his mood were about Stella. *She humiliated me by killing Annie when I froze. She sacrificed me in court to save her own skin. And she has hidden our money. There is urgent work to do, dealing with her. But first, I have had to find her. She will follow the money stashed away in Rio.*

Sitting idly in his cell, he had read about a Brazilian wandering spider belonging to the genus Phoneutria, meaning murderer in Greek; one of the most venomous spiders on earth. His fanciful plan was to track the spider down in Brazil and set it on her whilst she was asleep. *Just deserts*, he thought, *murdered by a murderer*.

Victor took in the brilliant sunshine outside the prison, breathing in the air of freedom, an overnight bag at his feet. He noticed two police cars parked nearby. As he went to walk past them, a familiar colleague stepped out, blocking his way.

"Guv, this is touching, coming to meet me at the moment of my liberation," Victor said with pretend *bonhomie*.

"Unfinished business," Detective Chief Superintendent Drake replied, holding the back door of the nearest police car open for him. "I will not cuff you. 'Bryan Western', name ring any bells? His body was washed up at low tide, a mile down the Thames from London Bridge. You won't mind answering a few questions. When you were locked up, your ex-Janice thought she was safe. Now you are out, she doesn't feel safe anymore and has been talking to us. Should get you back inside."

The Public Prosecutor's Office had relied upon Stella's evidence at Victor's trial, that Ian didn't know about Victor's plan to kill Annie. So, they closed Ian's file. But his offer of a judicial appointment was withdrawn, and the Solicitors' Control Board struck him off the roll of solicitors for bringing the profession into disrepute. His parents, Pauline and Michael Blake, did not trust him to look after his children and he was left with only himself for company.

Sitting in The Fastidious Fox, downing his sixth bottle of Thirsty Fox, his phone rang. "Ian, I hear that you are on your uppers. I feel responsible somehow." It was Ray. "I'm diversifying, taking over two clubs from someone who owes me a lot of money: Striptease at Scylla and Obsession. I'm looking for a manager to help me run them. It's good money. Do you want the job?"

"You're offering the job to me? The man whom everybody says is selfish, amoral and a bad person who doesn't deserve to be alive," Ian replied miserably.

"Well, my old sport, you know what Bob Marley said: 'if the cap fits'. I've got a couple of others after the job but sounds like you'd be a shoo-in."

Let down by everyone, including himself, his reputation in tatters, he had nothing to lose by accepting Ray's offer. Annie would be shocked if she could see him in his new role as an adult entertainment impresario.

Henry pleaded not guilty in the Youth Court to the mobile phone theft. The victim had gone home to France, refusing to return to London to give evidence at a trial. She had also declined to take part in a live link from Paris, an alternative way of admitting her evidence. She had been re-imbursed for her lost phone by the travel insurance company and now just wanted to put the unpleasant experience behind her and pretend that it hadn't happened. The prosecution lacked both an admission of guilt by Henry and cogent circumstantial evidence. The defence wrote a strongly worded letter to the Public Prosecutor who was easily persuaded to drop the case.

Chi was featured in the *Sunday Splash* magazine supplement *Women Love Sundays,* in a story 'I Hunted Down One of the Barri-Bets Gamblers.'

She cashed in on her newfound notoriety by appearing in daytime TV chat shows, including the popular *Dishing the Dirt* and by posing in a bikini in a series of shots for *WoW Magazine*, wearing a deerstalker hat and holding a magnifying glass. The editor received an avalanche of fan messages such as *Come and check me over; Hunt me down;* and *She can stake me out anytime.*

She joined Carly, Mary, and Jacqui, who had all left their respective employments and teamed up with Kate and Ektrina to become a formidable all-female private investigation team called Amazons Investigate. Chi's media earnings helped to launch their new enterprise.

The Amazons held a team meeting. "I've done an agenda," Kate said, "but not had time to send it around, sorry everyone. Item 1 is about Janice, Shadwell's ex. That's for me. I've met with her, and she trusts me. Drake is paying me to gather information from her about Victor and what he had to do with Western's disappearance, to help him put Victor back behind bars. Like all police forces, there's not enough money for me to do everything I'd like. Ektrina is trying to secure extra funding from them.

"Item 2 is investigating Victor's network of corrupt associates," Kate continued, "over to you, Carly."

"As you'd expect it's all very hush-hush," Carly reported. "Drake has a squad which is working off-site to keep it secure. I'm acting as a consultant and liaising with Kate. Yes, the money's tight."

"Item 3," Kate continued: "new offices, Jacqui and Ektrina that's you."

"We've been looking for our new offices," Jacqui said. "I've sent you all a brochure of the premises we think are best."

"They look a bit small for our needs," Kate commented. "And they're not cheap either."

"It's the address," Jacqui explained. "Where did the most famous private detective live?"

"Baker Street," they chorused.

"He didn't really live there," Mary interjected. "He's a fictional character."

"Yes, I know that, but if we tell a potential client, especially a client from overseas, that our offices are in Baker Street, they will assume that we are the crème de la crème of private detectives, like Sherlock Holmes. And overseas clients pay well."

"Item 4," Kate said: "our new client Lion Investment Bank. Tell us about it, Mary."

"This is a really interesting job," Mary explained. "I'm trying to find out who, in the bank, is sending nasty hate messages to one of their female executives. It must be someone close to her, who knows her daily movements at work. So, they have embedded me on the executive's floor, using the subterfuge that I am preparing a recruitment campaign for the company. This allows me to walk around and talk to everyone. What's fascinating is that I suspect that she's sending the messages to herself. Either self-loathing or a narcissist who craves the attention."

"Item 5, we're almost done: any other business. Ektrina, you're the office manager. Is there anything you want to say?"

"Yes, Chi, you are claiming for a lot of sweet bakery treats and drinks on expenses."

"This is so unfair," Chi protested. "You lot get all the good jobs and what am I doing again? More surveillance. And then you complain when I risk my health and gym body sitting around in cafes and bars watching a target."

"You risk your gym body by downing all those calories," Kate said. "But I guess that it's your choice and

I know how a sugar rush cheers you up when the work is tedious. We'll let you off."

The prison gates closed many times behind the judges and prosecuting barristers who had used Barri-Bets. Lord Osling sentenced them himself and in a blaze of publicity led by the relentless *Sunday Splash*, he was particularly harsh on those who had bet on trials in which they were professionally involved. Following pleas of guilty, Judges Winter and Swift were each sent to prison for thirty months and the barristers Bell, Lassi and Nicholls eighteen months each. Grant, Ryan and Bradley argued unsuccessfully that they were just cogs in the chambers' machine and were each sent to prison for sixteen months. Carruthers was singled out as the boss of Barri-Bets and was sentenced to three years. Veronica was made redundant.

"*Fiat justitia ruat caelum* (let justice be done though the heavens fall)," Lord Osling declared in his sentencing speech to a packed public gallery in the court room, by way of explanation for sending so many judges and lawyers to prison.

The defence barrister Crabtree successfully argued that she was not acting in the role of a public officer and escaped a criminal charge. She was disbarred by her professional body for not behaving honestly, independently and with integrity. Hind had never worked out how to use Barri-Bets.

The R and R resorts, and any monies held or paid out by Barri-Bets, were seized by the London Office of Takeback, known as LOOT, the agency responsible for recovering criminal assets.

The biggest scandal in judicial history demanded that Lord Osling and his personal assistant Sally work long hours at his office in the High Court. The strain of this late-night work and the shame he felt because of the disreputable behaviour of barristers and judges on his watch, made him stressed and destroyed his marriage. Lady Osling left for Scotland to live with her brother and his family. Lord Osling sought comfort closer to home with his understanding assistant Sally. Their age gap of thirty-six years was embarrassing for his friends, uncomfortable for his children and disappointing for Lady Osling. "What on earth can they have in common?" she asked her golf partners incredulously.

"I met up with him shortly after he'd retired," his former train companion Charles told the other regular commuters on their journey to Victoria station. "I told him straight, Gilbert, don't let your heart rule your head. He looked very sprightly and replied, 'don't be judgmental, Judge.'"

To protect Stella from the FHM and from Victor on his release from prison, she was squirrelled away by the police in a safe house in some god forsaken town in the North of England, where there was nothing to do. Not used to being alone with only daytime TV for company, she missed the bright lights and buzz of her former life in London; her many attentive male clients; and the rich pickings that they had brought her.

On hearing the welcome news that Victor was back in custody, she thought, *I can't live the rest of my life like this, hidden away and anonymous, as if I don't exist.* She urgently needed to liquidate their ill-gotten gains and going to Rio, where she already had a contacts list of admiring males, was the obvious choice. *Perhaps even build a new life somewhere overseas*, she thought, as she bought a one-way ticket. *Wish I had really kept a notebook with details of my trysts. I've so many shocking stories I can tell about those men who paid me handsomely, the so-called pillars of the establishment. I'll see what I can remember.*

This book is printed on paper from sustainable sources managed under the Forest Stewardship Council (FSC) scheme.

It has been printed in the UK to reduce transportation miles and their impact upon the environment.

For every new title that Troubador publishes, we plant a tree to offset CO_2, partnering with the More Trees scheme.

MORE TREES
LET'S PLANT A BILLION TREES

For more about how Troubador offsets its environmental impact, see www.troubador.co.uk/sustainability-and-community